CW00496259

Nancy Cornish PI

Back on the Case

Amanda James

Copyright © 2023 Amanda James

All rights reserved.

The right of Amanda James to be identified as the author of
The Work has been asserted by her in accordance
Copyright, Designs and Patents Act 1988.

No part of this book may be reproduced in any form, or by
any electronic or mechanical means, including information
storage and retrieval systems, without written permission
from the author, except for the use of brief quotations in a
book review.

Cover design and formatting by Let's Get Booked
www.letsgetbooked.com

Dedication - For Emma, with love.
You made everything better.

Chapter One

I often used to say that holidays were for other people. For one thing, there always seemed too much to do at home, especially when I worked full-time in the Whistling Kettle Café. And for another thing, why did people feel the need to cram their life into a few suitcases and inch along packed roads to busy airports, or staycations, grimly determined to enjoy themselves like so many lemmings? I used to say all that stress and faff was definitely not for me. I had enough to keep me happy and occupied right here in Padstow Cornwall, thank you very much. This was especially true after setting up my Nancy Cornish PI (Psychic Investigator) business in the summerhouse at the bottom of my garden. The last few years have been utterly brilliant, rewarding, and yes, liberating even. Why? Because I've been able to 'come out' as psychic and use my gift to help members of my community in a myriad of ways.

So, it was a huge shock, given that my views on holidays were well known by my husband Charlie, that he took it upon himself to "surprise" me with one of them. Not just any old holiday, no that would have been too easy – but a holiday of a lifetime, no less. A whole month touring the west coast of America, because that was the one place

I'd told him I'd like to go, if I ever had chance. But that was in the early days of our relationship and I'd almost forgotten all about it. I smile at the brightly painted fridge magnet nestled in the palm of my hand. A red ceramic Golden Gate Bridge spanning a blue San Francisco Bay, with a yellow sun splodged in the corner, almost as an afterthought. It's garish and tacky and touristy, but I love it. I can hardly believe I bought it on Fisherman's Wharf, San Francisco only two weeks ago, because it already feels like months. I put it on the fridge door, and mentally thank Charlie all over again for making me realise holidays are for me after all. Especially holidays of a lifetime. But now I'm back at home, Seal Cottage in Cornwall, and for that I'm thankful.

I'm about to make a cuppa and venture down to the summerhouse to get 'back on the case', or at least look like I'm doing something, when Gran pixilates through the kitchen door. She's not made a connection for must be nearly a year, when she passed on a message to warn Mum about Guy, her then predator of a boyfriend. I'm so thrilled to see her! She's appeared as a thirty something today, dressed in a multi-coloured kaftan, with flowers woven through her long red curls so like my own. She grins, points at the fridge magnet and sings, 'If you're going to San Francisco, be sure to wear some flowers in your hair.'

'Hello Gran. I remember you singing that when I was little – made me want to go there.'

'Now you have.'

'I have, and it was fantastic. I've missed you, Gran.'

She smiles and does a pirouette, but when she turns

back to face me, she's the age she was when she died. Her curls are shorter and streaked with grey, but her blue eyes are as just as lively and full of mischief as they were in her thirties. Has she come with a message, or is she just visiting?

'There's a woman, pregnant and hurt badly,' she says, staring out of my kitchen window at the hilltop view and the sun glinting off the Camel Estuary.

That answers my question then, it's a message, and my stomach sinks when I think of the poor woman in question. 'Who is it, Gran?'

A shrug. To the cloudless blue sky she says, 'No name. You helped her once. Books.'

I'm about to ask her more, but Gran gives me a brief wave and does the 'off switch' as I call it when spirits disappear, because it reminds me of an electric light being flicked off. Great. Now what? No time to sit about drinking coffee here this morning, because I need to get help for this pregnant woman. Hurt badly, Gran said. Hopefully not so badly that… Shaking that image from my mind, I grab my phone and hurry down my garden path to my work space, as I always concentrate better there. My 'office' is a Scandinavian pine summerhouse with double doors, and, in the summer, two beautiful blue agapanthus plants stand sentinel at either side. Across the top of the doors carved by a local craftsman, is a sign that reads *Nancy Cornish PI*. I give a brief nod to the sign and push open the door.

Inside, I switch on the radiator as the chill of mid-October nips at my arms, fill the kettle in the offshoot, and plump up the red scatter cushions on the green-leather

7

sofas. 'Now,' I mutter to myself, as I take my coffee and journal to the sofa, 'let's see what we can come up with.'

About to get stuck in, I see a flash of ginger fur at the double doors, complete with enormous green eyes and a bushy tail. My cat, Scrappy, has obviously decided he's joining me, and stands on his hind legs with his front paws on the glass, yowling pitifully. 'Come on then, monkey,' I say, as I let him in and he winds a furry figure-eight around my ankles, nearly tripping me up as I walk back to the sofa. 'Now, sit there and keep quiet, or you're out, okay?' Scrappy says nothing, just settles on the cushions with a little sigh and a contented purr.

I flick through my case study notes that I've made over almost three years, hoping for a clue. Though my gift and basic logic is already drawing me towards two particular people. Gran had said 'books.' The two people I've helped who had something to do with books, were Lucinda last year, when I helped her find her precious inscribed copy of *Rebecca* by Daphne du Maurier, and the year before, Alison, who's an author and I helped find her missing cat Rufus. Rufus turned out to be kidnapped, or rather 'catnapped', by her "very best friend". Images of both women zip into my mind's eye. Lucinda, thirty-something, five feet tall, close cropped black hair, and with her honey-coloured eyes, so large behind tortoiseshell glasses, she's reminiscent of a bush baby, and Alison, a slim fifty-something brunette with a nervous smile and shy brown eyes. Age dictates that only one of them is likely to be pregnant. I run a finger down the contact list of my phone and dial Lucinda at work.

8

It's picked up on the second ring. 'West of the Moon Bookshop, Lucinda Hendra speaking, how may I help?'

Phew! Lucinda's booming oversized voice reassures me that she's not lying hurt somewhere. 'It's me, Nancy. How are you?'

'Nancy, how lovely to hear from you!' Then her tone becomes softer, and assumes a breathy quality. 'Actually...I've been wanting to get in touch for a few weeks...I have a bit of news, but until this last while, it's been top secret.'

I don't really have time for a long conversation as I need to find the poor woman who's hurt, but the secret might be relevant to finding her. 'Sounds exciting.'

'It is. William and I are expecting a baby!'

I nearly choke on my coffee. Could Gran have got her message in a muddle? Could Lucinda be hurt sometime in the future, but not now? Bloody hell. I can't tell Lucinda what Gran said, because if the message wasn't meant for her, then I'll scare the poor woman to death. I have to say something though, and the logical thing to say is, 'Congratulations!'

'Thank you. It wasn't planned, but we are both so happy. You'll have to pop over for a cuppa soon...I was only saying to William—'

'Sorry to cut you off mid flow, lovely, but someone's knocking on the office door. I'll ring you back very soon, okay?' I cross my fingers behind my back and hope I'm not struck down for lying.

'Oh, yes, of course. Bye, Nancy.'

The disappointment in her voice was almost palpable

and I curse under my breath. Lucinda was dying to tell me all about her news. Poor lamb doesn't have many friends, as she built a suit of armour around herself. I heave a sigh as I remember that her mum died in childbirth, she never knew her father, so she was always a loner. Then she became even more lonely after her grandma, who looked after, her died a few years ago. But luckily, the lost book with help from me and the spirit of her grandma, brought her William, and love.

Okay, no time for reminiscing. I scroll down my contacts again and find the next number. 'Hi, Alison it's Nancy, how are you?'

'Oh, lovely to hear from you. Everything okay?'

The surprise in her voice makes me aware that we don't really keep in touch that often. Trouble is, I'm not sure what I'm about to say next will make her feel reassured. 'Yeah, all okay with me. The thing is, I had a connection from my gran earlier.' I quickly explain what the message was. 'So I suppose what I'm asking is, do you know anyone who is pregnant? A long shot, but I can't think of anyone else I know who's associated with books.'

The silence on the end of the line is starting to freak me out, then she clears her throat and says, 'Well, I've been sworn to secrecy, but my next-door neighbour's daughter, Tilly, is nearly nine-months pregnant. She's only seventeen, and her dad, Chris, is a bit controlling, so she daren't tell him about the baby, because the expectation is that Tilly will go to university and become a teacher like him.'

This sounds promising, and a bit of relief creeps in too,

because it could mean that Gran's message wasn't muddled, and Lucinda won't be hurt sometime in the future. It was just a coincidence. 'Okay, and what about her mum?'

'Mum died a few years ago of cancer, so there's only Tilly and Chris. The worst of it is that the father of her baby is twenty-five and married. Tilly got swept up in the romance of being with a sophisticated older man, so never questioned it when he said he was single and on business here for six months. Recently, she found she meant nothing to him and his work was done in Cornwall, so he was going back to his life *and* wife in Middlesbrough. Poor love is in a right pickle, because she didn't realise she was pregnant until she was late on. Her periods had always been patchy, apparently.' There's a sniff on the line and Alison blows her nose. 'I couldn't bear it if Tilly is the one in your Gran's message. Hasn't she suffered enough?'

'Yes, she certainly seems to have, poor thing. Let's hope that if she is hurt somewhere, we can help her. However, there is one thing I don't get. How on earth does she keep her pregnancy from her dad, if she's nearly nine months gone?'

'Tilly just told him she's put weight on. Lucky for her, the weather got a bit nippy, and so she disguised her bump with loose clothing and baggy jumpers.'

Intuition tells me that Tilly is the woman in Gran's message, but I need to be sure. I also need to find her and quick. 'Alison, you said she's sworn you to secrecy. So you're quite close?'

'Yeah. She sometimes comes round of an evening and

we watch TV together and chat about our day. Chris is often busy with school stuff and when he's not, he's in a chess club. Tilly's lonely and misses her mum, so I do what I can.'

'Good. So can you give her a ring if you have her number?'

'Okay, yeah. I'll ring you back.' Minutes later she's on the end of the line again. 'Nothing. I tried twice; it just goes to voicemail.'

It's as I feared. If she's hurt badly, she might be unconscious, but I don't share that thought with Alison. I need her to be calm. 'Okay. Is there anything of hers she might have left at your place? Because I need to get a connection from it, and hope it will give me clue as to where she is.'

'Err…' I can almost hear the cogs ticking over. 'God, I don't know. I don't think so. Hang on…maybe…' There's the sound of a door creaking open and footsteps tapping across a tiled floor. From what I remember of her house, she's left the living room and gone through to the kitchen. 'Yes!' A shout of triumph makes me yank the phone away from my ear for a second. 'She brought her own mug over the other night, because she'd already made herself hot chocolate when I called and asked if she wanted to come over to mine…' Triumph is suddenly ousted by doubt. 'Trouble is, I've washed it. Will it matter?'

I try allay her worries. 'No, because it belongs to her and she'll have used it loads.' I do hope I'm right, and it's not a favourite of Chris's instead.

'Yes, it's one of her cherished possessions because her

mum bought it for her. It's quite old, and has Peppa Pig on the front.'

Result! It's more likely to have an emotional imprint because of that. 'Okay, I'm coming over. Hopefully be about twenty-minutes.'

***

On the drive over to Wadebridge, my mind's in turmoil as I picture some awful scenarios of Tilly in trouble. Where is she? What state is she in? And will the baby be okay? I open the window a crack and shoo those thoughts out of my head and away into the fresh salt air. No point in imagining the worst, I need calm. A few deep breaths help, and now at a loose end, my mind drifts to the time I gave birth to my darling, Sebastian nearly eighteen-years ago. The familiar twinge of grief troubles my heart, and I wonder what he'd look like now. What ambitions would he have? He'd have taken his GCSEs and gone on to further study. What would he do for a living? Would he stay close, or venture far away? A knot of emotion swells in my throat. He's far away now, that's for sure. I shoo away that thought too, and remind myself that I'm luckier than many parents who have lost a child. At least the spirit of my boy visits from time to time. I smile as I recall that he helped me with two cases recently. Will he help with this one?

'Hi, Nancy come through.' Alison's on the doorstep with an armful of fluffy black and white cat.

'Hi Alison.' I tickle Rufus under the chin. 'Not been catnapped recently then?' I ask him. He narrows his big green eyes at me in disdain.

Alison shudders as she leads the way into her homely kitchen. 'Don't remind me of that awful time. If it hadn't have been for you...' She turns at the sink and blinks rapidly as if banishing unhappy memories from her caramel brown eyes. 'God knows...'

'And the spirit of your Jack helped, too.' I nod at a photo of her lovely husband on the Welsh dresser.

She picks it up and brightens as she looks into his calm blue eyes and traces a finger over his blond wavy hair. 'Ah yes, my Jack. Still looking after me, even when he's gone.'

Another knot of emotion tries to form, but I swallow it down before it can. 'Okay, let's make a start. I nod at a mug on the wooden kitchen table top. It has a light green background, with the pink face of Peppa Pig smiling widely up at the world. 'This is it, I presume,' I say, unnecessarily. But then I'm a bit nervous. If this doesn't work, what do I do next?

'Yes. Funnily enough,' Alison says, dryly. Then she sits opposite me at the table, she twiddles a strand of her straight shoulder length hair, her eyes expectantly flicking to the mug and then to my face. 'Go on then, do your psychometry tricks.'

Mild irritation flits through me like a bird fighting for a place on the nut feeder. 'Psychometry isn't a trick, Alison. I'm not some kind a magician. Psychometry is—'

'The practice of getting readings, or connections as you call them, from objects that belong, or used to belong to a person. The person's energy is retained in the object. This practice is often used by Mediums and psychics, but has been slated by science as being hokum, because there's no proof whatsoever that it's a thing, blah, blah. Yeah, I know. You told me about it once, and I looked it up before you came, so I was more familiar with it. Sorry if I annoyed you, but you know what we writers are like with words and their meanings.' Alison gives me a little smile, rests her elbows on table and her chin on interlaced fingers. She stares at me, then the mug, as if she expects it to do something.

The hokum comment rankled, and I feel the need to clear up her misunderstanding. 'I'm not claiming that what I do is scientific. And yes, it can and does go wrong, or come to nothing. My friend Penny is a Medium who holds evenings at the spiritualist church. She likens the psychic phenomenon and use of psychometry to radio wave messages. When things go wrong, the 'radio waves' sometimes get mixed and misdirected. Perhaps the message in the object is for someone else, and gets transmitted to the wrong person instead. But as you know, it can work very well too.' I pick up the mug. 'It's thought the energy of the owner of the possession can stay with it. Makes sense to me. Whatever the reason, I need to try and channel my senses, or radio waves…get them to help me work out where this young girl is, before it's too late.'

Alison looks disappointed. 'Right…so you don't always see spirits at all?'

Oh, for goodness' sake. 'Not always. I usually see the spirit messengers, as you know. But often I just see a series of images, like old photos snapped down in quick succession. I call it the playing card effect. Or sometimes it's more like a scene from a film – it rolls, but there's no

15

sound. These scenes or images are often – yet not always - accompanied by heat or a tingling feeling in my fingers. Now, could you please leave me to it?'

I'm aware that I'm being snippy, but I can't afford to be polite when a girl's life might be at stake. Wordlessly, Alison gets up and leaves the room. I cup both hands around the mug and gradually, the cool porcelain becomes warmer under my fingers. Closing my eyes, I focus on Tilly's name and the image Gran's message put in my head. After a few seconds, I feel heat spread across my palms and my fingertips get the familiar pins and needles tingle, then it shoots to the rest of the fingers on my right hand and up my wrist. Here we go…it's the playing card-effect.

SNAP.

An image of a little dark-haired girl about eight-years-old, crying at her mother's grave.

SNAP.

The same girl, but older. She's looking adoringly up at a young man in a business suit. He has snake eyes and a fake smile.

SNAP.

The girl lying in woodland, leaves surrounding her, a deathly white face, eyes closed. Blood on her temple.

Then…nothing.

The dealer's put the pack away.

Damn it! There's not much at all to go on there. I'm about to call Alison back to check on the description of Tilly and if there's woodland nearby, when a tall, slim woman, dressed in dark jeans and a red t-shirt materialises

16

through the wall. She has a tumble of chocolate curls, a sad smile, and her huge green eyes hold mine in a steady gaze. I know immediately who it is, because she looks so much like her daughter, except she has blue eyes. 'Please find her,' she says, in a trembling voice.

'Tilly?'

'Yes.'

'I saw her in a wood, and by your grave when she was little. But that's all. Something tells me it's nearby.'

'Jackdaw Wood.' Tilly's mum nods and points through the kitchen window over the rolling green fields.

I put down the mug and rush to the window, but can't see even a hint of woodland. 'Is the wood in that direction, then?' I ask, but when I look back, I'm talking to myself. Tilly's mum has gone.

Chapter Two

'Alison!' I run to the kitchen door, but it's flung open before I can get to it.

'Yeah? Have you made a connection – found Tilly?' Alison's in the doorway her brown eyes round, her hand clutching the floral scarf at her neck.

I quickly tell her the scant details of the connection and then mention Tilly's mum. 'So is there somewhere round here called Jackdaw Wood?'

'You saw Gabby?' I watch a deep furrow trouble Alison's brow and she leans a trembling hand against the wall as if she needs extra support. 'No…no, I can't think of anywhere.'

'Any woodland at all? Think carefully.' The image of Tilly lying in the leaves, deathly pale sends my heart racing.

'Um…no.'

Intuition tells me the grave snapshot was significant. 'How about where Gabby is buried?'

Alison's brows shoot up and hope fills her eyes. 'Yeah. Yeah, there's a little coppice I suppose you'd call it – not a wood though. Gabby's buried in a small graveyard by the church on the hill, overlooking the sea.'

'Nearby? Tilly will have walked, I presume?'

'Yes. It's about fifteen-minutes' walk from here down the back lanes. We can go in my car. We'll have to go round via the main road, but we'll still be quicker.'

***

Ten minutes later, we pull up outside an ancient church perched on a green hill with a panoramic view of the ocean, though the weather's turned and a stiff breeze is blowing off the water. A fair way down the slope is a tiny copse of perhaps five gnarled wind-battered trees, gathered together in a circle as if they're having a group hug. 'Okay.' I turn to Alison who's sitting beside me. 'Grab the blanket, and water and let's see if this is Gabby's Jackdaw Wood.'

The salt-wind whips around the collection of gravestones, jutting from the mossy grass like wonky teeth, and we hurry past them, all the while praying Tilly's here, and that we're not too late. Immediately upon entering the dark-green shadows in depths of the circle, we see a prone figure in the undergrowth, a crown of leaves at her head and a rock at her shoulder. A rock stained with red. 'Tilly!' Alison rushes to her and kneels by her side.

'Don't move her!' I kneel at the other side, and take Tilly's cold limp wrist in my hand to check for a pulse. There is one, and it's quite strong, thank God. I call 999 and cover her with the blanket.

'Oh Tilly,' Alison manages, as she wipes tears from her eyes and places her hand on Tilly's forehead. 'Wake up, love.'

We watch her face. Her impossibly young face, pale

under a scattering of freckles. Autumn leaves on snow. Her breathing becomes stronger as her chest gently rises and falls under the blanket. Moments later, there's an almost imperceptible twitch at one corner of her mouth and her long dark lashes flutter open and close a few times, like the wings of an uncertain fledgling. Then they open and focus on Alison, then flit to me. A puzzle forms in her eyes and she says, 'Alison? Why are you...?' Her shaking fingertips tentatively touch the gash on her temple and she winces.

Alison gently takes her hand. 'What happened, lovely? Did you fall?'

'Think so. My ankle turned over and I stumbled, but that's the last I remember.'

'Well, you're okay now. We've called an ambulance so you'll be checked out properly.'

Tilly moans and closes her eyes. 'I don't need an ambulance.'

'It's best to be sure,' I say.

'Who are you, anyway?' Tilly asks me.

Alison deftly changes the subject. 'Nancy's a friend of mine. Why were you up here?'

'Been to see mum's grave and thought I'd go and hug a tree in Jackdaw Wood. Me and Mum always used to hug these trees when I was little.' A tear escapes from under her lashes and trickles down her cheek.

'I never knew it was called that,' Alison says, wiping the tear away with a tissue.

'It's not. I named it that when we saw a Jackdaw up in the trees years ago...' Tilly's eyes suddenly fly open and she clutches the round of her stomach. 'Oww! Bloody hell

20

that hurt.'

I glance at Alison and see from the panic in her eyes that we're both thinking the same thing. 'Do you think it's the baby?' Alison asks in a whisper.

'Oww. Nooo. It can't be coming yet; I've still got two weeks.' Tilly props herself up on her elbows, her face contorting with pain.

Two weeks is nothing...Bloody hell! My mind goes into overdrive. 'Okay, we need to be calm. The ambulance will be here soon, let's hope the baby hangs on until then.' I glance at Alison who's opening and closing her mouth like a landed fish – panic rendering her mute. 'Alison, take Tilly's hand. It will all be okay, trust me.'

Tilly looks at me and moans. 'Nooo. No. God, I can't bear this pain...I feel like I need to go to the toilet, too.'

That's all we need. I will myself to keep calm and say, 'Tilly, take some deep breaths, in through your nose and out through your mouth. What you're feeling might be the urge to push. We need to get your jeans off, okay?'

Tilly starts to cry and shakes her head. 'No. I don't want this baby. I don't want it!'

Alison rouses from her stupor to give some encouraging words and helps me to get Tilly's elasticated jeans and underwear off. Then we both hold her hands, as she gives an almighty yell and bears down. Can this baby really be coming right here and now? The crowning head five minutes later gives me the answer. Thank God we have a clean blanket for her to give birth on.

'You're doing so well, Tilly. I can see the baby's head. Just try to keep calm and do your breathing like we said,' I tell her, though feel anything but calm myself. My blood pressure must be higher than the tops of the trees right now.

'Aaaaghh!' Tilly shakes her head from side to side and yells, 'I can't do it. I CAN'T!'

Alison looks at me aghast and tears well in her eyes. 'God, Nancy. What shall we do?'

'It will all be okay. The ambulance should be here soon.' *Please God.* 'I know it hurts, Tilly, but you have to try and go with the pain and keep calm.'

'Calm? How the hell can I keep calm? I'm in a fucking wood giving birth to a baby nobody wants, and my dad doesn't even know about...' Her words are swallowed by another yell of pain as she pushes again.

Alison and I grimace as our hands are almost crushed by the strength of Tilly's grip... and then the head's out. Panic gives way to practicality as I remember the countless episodes of Call the Midwife I've seen, as I kneel in front of Tilly and cup the baby's head in my hands. 'Okay, Tilly, I want you to pant like this,' I demonstrate with a few puffs of air. 'Now give us another push.' Tilly screws up her face and does as I ask. Moments later, the baby's shoulders are born. 'Fantastic! Okay, let's have a little more panting.' I have no idea if panting helps at this point, but it's what they say on the show. My heart lifts with hope as I position my fingers gently around the baby's shoulders. I think we're almost there. 'Calm yourself, my lovely and give one big push. Baby's nearly here.'

Tilly gives an almighty yell, and one last push has her baby daughter slipping into my hands, just as the ambulance's siren wails up the hill.

***

Two hours later, after I return from the hospital and I walk through my front door, the enormity of what happened in Jackdaw Wood comes crashing over me, like a wave on rocks, and I collapse like a sack of spuds on the sofa in my front room. I take a minute to catch my breath, look around the familiar surroundings, and listen to the sound of Seal Cottage. The hiss of flames as they lick the resin from a log in the burner, it's heart glowing red – a nice contrast against the whitewashed stone chimney. The much-loved leather brown armchairs sit at either side of the chimney on the Moroccan style rug, and I stretch my legs out along the fabric red three-seater, and look up at the huge seascape on the wall. The creak of old beams makes me smile as the wind shows them who's boss outside, and the heartbeat-tick of Gran's old clock on the shelf next to the window is a calm reminder of the past. My breathing becomes regular, normal.

Wow. What an afternoon, and what a good job Gran passed on the message. The doctor said that Tilly had concussion and needed lots of rest to get over the shock of the fall and giving birth. Not to say everything else that comes with becoming a new mum too. He also said without the help of myself and Alison, it could all have ended very differently. The church wasn't occupied at that time, and the area wasn't really near many houses. There might have been people visiting the graves, but Tilly couldn't have got to them. She would have had to give birth alone, injured and scared witless.

Heaving myself up, I go into the kitchen, flick the kettle

23

on and look out of the window. Our hilltop perch gives me a grand view over the rooftops of Padstow, to where the distant rush of the Camel Estuary flickers like a minnow in the golden autumn sunshine. The strong wind whips a few crows into an ungainly dance, as they try to alight on a telegraph wire, while a huddle of threatening clouds is broken apart and dispersed towards the far horizon. Maybe I'll get my pencils out later and do some sketching, it's been far too long. I make a square of my two forefingers and thumbs and hold them up to capture a bold outline of buildings, trees and water. Maybe the sketch will morph into something else, like it did the time I drew a random sketch of a man who turned out to be missing. Luckily, we found the man - Rory, an old school friend of Mum's and they are much more than that nowadays. My heart lifts when I think that Mum, after being so broken after Dad died, and then tricked by the despicable Guy, might have found real happiness at last.

Back before the fire with a mug of coffee, I think again about Tilly and her new baby. I left Alison with her and she was trying to persuade her to ring Chris and tell him he was a grandfather. Tilly wasn't having that. Nor did she want to talk about the baby, it seemed. All she wanted to do was turn her face to the wall and close her eyes. Perhaps she thought that if she slept, the whole problem would go away. Yes, of course she needs rest as the doctor said, but I have a bad feeling about how she's going to handle the situation. Still, I've done my bit thank goodness. The clock tells me it's too late to start any meaningful work in the office, so when I've finished my coffee, I might as well prepare one of Charlie's favourite meals for later. He's been so busy at work lately and never seems to have enough time to relax anymore. Though getting promoted to DI will do that for you, I guess.

***

I'm making stew and dumplings for dinner. We tend to have that on a Thursday when the nights draw in, because Charlie's a creature of habit and likes routine. Maybe it's to do with him being a copper. He likes order, logic, predictability - a set pattern to life. We're quite different there I suppose, as the nature of my work means that no two days are the same. But when Charlie steps in the door and smells it cooking, he says all the stress of work gets left outside. He once said that on the way home, he likes to imagine me rushing about the kitchen, pushing my 'lustrous' red hair back from my forehead with a soapy hand, stirring the stew, laying the table. Then I turn to welcome him home with a smile as wide as the sky, my jade-green eyes twinkling my love for him. That made me smile. Charlie doesn't smile as much as he once did, bless him. I couldn't believe he'd managed to wangle a month's leave to go on our wonderful trip – but he'd been owed loads of days, and Abi, his boss, practically forced him into it. The break did him the power of good. However, day-to-day work does tend to take over. Quite often his dinner ends up sitting in the oven, when he's held up at the station by one case or another.

Tonight, he's not held up, thankfully, and he comes in through the kitchen door with the smell of woodsmoke and breath of autumn on his coat.

'Hello, gorgeous,' I say. And he is, but I must admit he looks a bit weary. His lively hazel eyes aren't as bright as they should be, and his dark brows are almost always knitted together in a frown since we've been back from holiday.

Charlie gives me a peck on the cheek and grabs a can of lager from the fridge. This is an indication of his mood, as he normally has a cuddle and a chat with me. He's not even spoken yet, unless a grunt of acknowledgement counts. He sits at the table and heaves a heartfelt sigh, so I wait for him to relax and take the stew out of the oven to pop the dumplings in. Maybe the comforting aroma of our dinner and the low lights throwing a cosy fan against the bright lemon walls will cheer him. Charlie finishes his drink in record time and crushes the empty can. I raise an eyebrow and he eventually speaks, 'Sorry, Nance. I needed that.'

'Had a bad day?'

'You could say that.' He rubs his knuckles over the top of his head, making his short dark hair stick up like the bristles of a bottle brush. I notice there are a few more silver hairs at his temples too.

Nothing else seems to be forthcoming, so I sit opposite him at the scrubbed pine farmhouse table, across which so many of mine and Charlie's conversations have taken place. 'Wanna talk about it?' I hold his hand in mine.

He yanks his tie off, undoes the top button of his shirt and shakes his head. 'No. Not really. You tell me about your day.' His full mouth twists into a half smile, and he leans forward attentively, but I can tell he's just being polite.

Still, if I tell him about my momentous day, at least it will take his mind off his troubles for a while. In between checking on the dumplings, pouring myself a well-earned glass of pinot grigio and Charlie another lager – in a glass this time - I tell him about Tilly.

'Bloody hell, Nance. You've had a bit of a day too.' Charlie squeezes my hand.

'Yeah. It was a bit hairy at times, but at least I had Call the Midwife as a reference point.' I laugh as I remember how calm on the surface I was in that wood, but my insides were made of jelly. 'So now me and Alison are crossing our fingers that Tilly will decide to tell her dad, and he'll agree to the baby coming home. I can't bear to think of the little scrap being in care.'

Charlie's eyebrows shoot up. 'Well, she'll have to tell him something, as he'll be getting worried by now if he's not heard from her.'

'I think Alison was covering for her.'

'Right. Tilly's lucky to have her, and I know you don't like to think of the baby going to social services, but in the long run, it might be for the best. Tilly is only a kid herself. She's not in a good place, what with been treated cruelly by that git of a boyfriend who was married, and having a controlling father. There are lots of childless couples who would give anything to give the baby a good home.'

Was there a passing wistful look in Charlie's eye, or did I imagine it? We talked about adopting about a couple of years after Sebastian died, when the diagnosis of me being highly unlikely to ever bear another child had settled. We

27

both decided adoption wouldn't work for various reasons, the main one being that we would feel like we were trying to replace our son, which we wouldn't be of course, but it felt wrong. Though I have wondered about it from time to time. 'Hmm,' I say, in answer. 'I can see what you mean, but I think Tilly might regret it if she makes a decision too quickly.'

While I get the stew out of the oven and set the table, we talk about inviting Abi, Charlie's boss, and her partner Vicky over for a meal. It's ages since we saw them socially and we went to theirs last time. 'Yes, let's arrange it for next week if we can,' Charlie says, lighting the table candle and helping himself to a big portion of stew and dumplings. 'DCI Summercourt could do with letting her hair down a bit.'

'Abi's a bit stressed?' I ask, as I take a sip of the cold crisp pinot.

'Yeah. Not sure what's bugging her to be honest. If I say something's round, she says it's square lately.'

I blow on my fork to disperse the steam from the piping hot dumpling. 'Is that why you're a bit down tonight?'

'No. Though it doesn't help.' Charlie takes a mouthful of food and closes his eyes while he moans in appreciation. 'That is *so* good, Nance. Thanks for making one of my favourites.'

'Well, it's a Thursday in autumn. I couldn't make anything else, now could I?'

He laughs and takes a swallow of lager. 'I'm such an old stickler for routine, aren't I? Set in my ways at only forty-four years old. God knows what I'll be like when I'm sixty-four.'

'Yes, I'll still need you, and yes I'll still feed you.'

Charlie frowns. 'Eh?'

'When you're sixty-four. The old Beatles song, remember?'

'Ah yes.' His hazel eyes sparkle like warm amber in the candle light. 'I love you, Nance. And I do appreciate everything you do for me. When life is shit, I know I always have you to come home to. Means such a lot.'

My heart squeezes. 'Aw, that's lovely, Charlie. And ditto. You sure you don't want to talk about it?'

'Nope. It's something and nothing anyway. I'll be grand when I've finished this and had a shower. Then I'll get settled on the sofa with my favourite girl.' His smile disappears as he looks back to his plate and scoops up another forkful of food. I can tell he's wrestling with his worries to try and present a picture of contentment. He can't fool me though. And the sooner he tells me what's on his mind, the better.

'Charlie Cornish, we have been married far too many years for you to fob me off. Get it off your chest, or there's no pudding.'

Charlie pushes his empty plate to the side, sits back and folds his arms. 'Can't make me.' There's the shadow of a smile playing across his lips, then he grows serious. 'Okay. Remember that woman who drowned at Mawgan Porth a few days ago?'

I remember clearly, because it was so tragic. 'Yeah, it was on the local news. She'd been night swimming with her sister I think, and they'd got caught in a rough sea?

Stupid to go night swimming, but still.'

'Yep, that's her. Molly Preston.'

'So awful. She was only in her twenties, if I remember rightly? Why? Have you and Abi been involved?'

'Yeah, we have. You're right, Molly was twenty-five, and worked as a primary school teacher. Loved by everyone it seems. The coroner wasn't happy with the bruising on Molly's neck and arms, so contacted us. We questioned the sister, Leanne, younger by two years, and she said she'd tried to save Molly by grabbing her neck to keep her head up, grabbed her arms too, told her to go limp and float, but Molly wouldn't cooperate. She obviously wasn't thinking straight, they'd been drinking and they were both terrified. Molly was panicking and kept screaming that she was being pulled under by the current – she wouldn't listen to Leanne. She'd flailed her hands and cut Leanne's cheek with her fingernails, and then kicked out at her, in a desperate struggle to keep her head above water. Leanne showed us the bruises on her thighs and shins. In the end, Leanne had to just let her go and save herself. Seems feasible, yeah?

'Well, yeah…So why are you worried about it all?'

Charlie heaves a huge sigh and scrubs his knuckles across the top of his head again. 'Because I think Leanne deliberately drowned Molly.'

Chapter Three

Charlie's more relaxed now, as we snuggle up on the sofa in front of the log burner. His old blue dressing-gown smells of washing powder and his shower-fresh skin. His heartbeat's strong and steady, like our love. Pressing my nose to his chest, I inhale and close my eyes. I treasure these moments. Quiet times. The silent room, the warmth of his body next to mine, the weight of his arm around my shoulder. Here we are, sitting in our dressing gowns with our feet up, happy as a couple of pigs in muck. It could be said that moments like these, seem to be nothing out of the ordinary really, they're not exciting, or noteworthy. Yet they are. They're everything. 'I love you so bloody much, Mr Cornish,' I say looking up into his eyes.

Charlie brushes my lips with his. 'And I love you so bloody much, Mrs Cornish.'

'Feeling a bit better now?'

'Yeah. A good meal, a few beers and a cuddle with you fixes me every time.'

I squeeze his hand. 'I wish you didn't have to deal with such traumatic stuff on a day-to-day basis, though.'

'It's not quite on a day-to-day basis, thankfully. We rarely get murders in our neck of the woods, as you know.'

'Hmm, thank goodness. So, are you ready to tell me why you think Leanne killed her sister?'

Charlie puts his feet up on the foot stool and sighs. 'Yeah. Three things, really. The first thing is that the coroner says the marks on her neck were consistent with being strangled. The bruising shows that she probably had two thumbs pressed against her windpipe, which suggests she was gripped around the neck, like this.' Charlie demonstrates on me, which sends a shiver through my body. Poor Molly, fighting for her life in the crashing waves. 'And the second is that Leanne and Molly's grandmother had recently died, leaving everything to them equally. The house, a car, some savings. Their parents were killed in a car accident when both girls were small, and so they'd lived with the grandma until they both went off to uni. Leanne got a bit emotional when she told me once they'd sold the house, she and Molly had planned to use some of the proceeds to take a lovely holiday touring Australia together. They will never do that now, of course.'

'Right...how do you know all this?'

'Leanne volunteered the information - said Molly and she were devastated at the loss of their grandma, which was one of the reasons they went swimming in the moonlight. They thought it would be a lovely way to remember her, as she'd loved to go night swimming too – often took them when she was younger. Leanne admitted they were stupid to do it when they'd had a drink, but she said emotions had overtaken them.'

I look at the flames dancing in the log burner and see where Charlie's going with this. 'So, you really think

Leanne drowned her sister so she could get the house, the savings etcetera? Molly was fighting for her life – literally, but not with the ocean, with Leanne?'

'Yes. That's why Molly attacked Leanne with everything she had. She lashed out with her nails and feet, but compared to Leanne, she was smaller and certainly not as strong. Leanne is a gym instructor and does a lot of weight training.'

'Leanne shared this too?'

'Yup.'

'Don't you think it's strange that she volunteered all this information, if she thought you were onto her?'

'Yes. But maybe she thought if she shared everything, it would make us think *exactly* that.' He spreads his hands. 'A double bluff - why would she tell us everything, if she were guilty.'

'Quite cunning then.'

'I reckon so.'

'And how was she when you interviewed her?'

'What do you mean?'

'Was she breaking down, sobbing about the death of her sister for example? Two deaths, one after the other of people who were very close to her. Must have been traumatising.'

'That's the third thing. You'd think so, wouldn't you? As I said, she got a bit emotional when she talked about the holiday to Australia they'd never have, but most of the time she seemed very calm and collected. Detached, even.' Charlie strokes his chin. 'Now and then she'd do this odd nervous giggle and disguise it with a cough, right before she answered a question. It was obvious to me she was lying. I had a gut feeling, you know?'

'Oh yes. I'm quite good at gut feelings and intuition...I'm psychic, you know,' I say with a smile, trying to lighten the mood.

'I do know. And that's why I'd like to ask for your help on this one.'

Charlie and I have an agreement. I only help him out in very serious cases, as my quest is to help my community, not use my gift to work for the police solving more trivial stuff. So last year I helped solve a murder, and the year before, a missing person case. I hide a smile as I remember how Charlie used to think my psychic ability was a load of old "mumbo jumbo." After he'd seen me in action a few times, he now thinks the opposite, and would probably have me working alongside him on every case, if I let him.

I squeeze his hand. 'Of course I'll help. What does Abi think about it all?' I ask him this, because given what he said about his boss disagreeing with him earlier, I have a hunch she thinks Charlie's barking up the wrong tree.

He huffs. 'DCI Summercourt thinks I'm jumping to conclusions, and even if I weren't, we can't prove it. The bruising on Molly's neck could definitely have been caused by Leanne trying to keep her sister's head above water. Abi suggested Leanne could have been panicking just as much as her sister, and didn't know her own strength – even though she'd told us she lifted weights. Thing is, the coroner admitted it could have happened by accident too, even though he had a hunch it wasn't. But like the very knowledgeable Abi says, you can't charge someone with murder on a hunch, and it would be a bugger to try and prove in court.'

The bitterness in his voice surprises me. I hope he and Abi aren't going to fall out over this. They normally get along so well. 'Hmm. I can see that. So how can I help?'

'I have a water cup she used during the interview in my office at work. Do you think you could get a connection from it, if I bring it home tomorrow?'

I smile. 'A mug today, a cup tomorrow, all I need next is a glass for a hattrick. Okay, I'll see if I can find something useful.'

Charlie smiles back and kisses my hand. 'If anyone can, you can. And thank you.' We sit quietly watching the fire brutally expose the crimson insides of a log. As it at last shifts and crumbles to nothing, Charlie says, 'I think I was so down when I got home, because I can't help letting cases like this get to me. I get sickened by the lengths people will go to for money.' I watch his Adam's apple bob as he swallows hard. 'They were sisters, for God's sake.' He looks at me bewildered; his dark eyebrows knitted together.

Slipping my arms around him, I give him a squeeze and kiss his cheek. 'I know, I know. It's awful. And for the record, I wouldn't have you any other way. If you stop getting affected by cases like this, you'd lose a bit of what it is to be human. You'll lose what it is to be my Charlie.'

He sighs and kisses my neck. 'Thanks, Nance. Fancy making me feel even better? It's a while since we had an early night.' His kisses become more passionate as he twists his hand through my hair.

When we come up for air, I say, 'You know what? I

think that's exactly what we should do.' I stand up and take his hand. 'Make sure you empty the dishwasher and put the bin out first though.' I giggle at his downcast expression.

Charlie gets up and huffs, 'Taking the bin out? Not the kind of foreplay I'd envisioned.'

'These things have to be done.' At the foot of the stairs, I turn, give him a cheeky wink and drop my dressing gown. 'But maybe they can wait a while.'

'Now, that's more like it,' he growls. I run upstairs giggling as he comes after me.

***

Scrappy hurtles in through the cat door and threads his little body round my bare ankles, his fur damp from the Cornish mizzle. 'Yes, Scrappy. I'll feed you when I've finished my morning coffee, okay?' I look down at his expectant face, and big beseeching green eyes.

Scrappy gives a long and pitiful meow and continues his threading. 'I can see I'm not going to be allowed to relax until I feed you, am I?' Another meow confirms this, and I open the kitchen cupboard where his food's kept. I wonder how many cat owners perform this ritual every day? I'm guessing there're millions of us, all having one sided-conversations, trying to convince ourselves we're the ones in charge, when we know resistance is futile.

Scrappy fed, I'm just about to finish my coffee and toast before getting dressed and popping down to the office to write up Tilly's case in my journal, when my mobile goes off in my dressing gown pocket. Alison. Hope it's good news.

'Hi Nancy, just thought I'd give you an update.'

'Hi Alison, yes, I've been wondering what the latest is and hoping everything's okay.' I sit down at the kitchen table and pick up the last bit of toast that's somehow lost its appeal. It's cold and I've spread the marmalade too thickly. Yuck.

'Well, I think it could have gone worse, but it could have gone better too. Tilly asked me to go round and tell her dad about the baby, which I did.'

'Bloody hell, that must have been an awful job. How brave of you!' I put the toast back on the plate and take a gulp of coffee.

'It wasn't the most fun thing I've ever done,' Alison replies, with a chuckle. 'Chris was obviously in deep shock, poor guy. But credit to him, he said he wouldn't turn a child of his, or a child of hers away from his front door.'

Oh, that's lovely. So what could have gone better?'

'Well, after I explained what Chris had said, Tilly agreed to bring the baby home, but on trial. She still maintains she's not ready to be a mum. But Chris said she'd better be ready soon, because he's not going to look after his granddaughter. His exact words were, "I have neither the time, nor the tools".' There's a huge sigh on the line. 'Poor little scrap. My heart goes out to her, and to Chris and Tilly too. The whole situation is so tricky.'

'Hmm.' I think about the implications of everything Alison's told me, but something tells me it won't be as bad as she thinks. 'Everyone needs time to come to terms with it all, love. I think it will work out. It won't be easy, but they'll get there in the end. And don't forget, they will

37

probably have a health visitor or someone popping round to check on Tilly and the baby too, so they won't be alone.'

'Yeah. I've put my name down as a helper. I told the ward sister in the hospital and she was pleased that Tilly and her dad will have another pair of hands right next door.' Alison gives a nervous laugh. 'But you could write what I know about babies on a postage stamp.'

My heart twists in sympathy as I recall that Alison and her husband Jack couldn't have children. When he came to help rescue Rufus from his catnapper few years ago, the ocean of love Jack still had for his wife, even though he's in now in spirit, was almost tangible. Not for the first time I wonder why some people have to die so young. Jack was such a good man with a big heart. And dear Alison has a big heart too. 'You'll learn quickly, Alison, don't worry. It's the fact that you're willing to help that's more than half the battle.'

'Yes, I'm sure I will. Fingers crossed it will go more smoothly than I'm imagining. And you must let me pay you on Tilly's behalf, I'm sure she'd like to give you something. You're running a business after all.'

'No need. I came to you, remember, with a message from my gran. Besides, as you know, I only accept what people think my help is worth, or can afford. I doubt Tilly has money to be chucking around.'

'Well, if you're sure. I think they come home tomorrow.'

'Okay. Give me a shout if you need me.'

'I might just do that!'

After we end the call, I get dressed and pop down to the office to write up Tilly's case... so far. I have a wiggly finger of premonition poking me in the side, indicating I haven't seen the last of the new mum. From time-to-time, I look back over my cases and reminisce. That's why I always write in longhand in a proper journal. Charlie thinks a computer would be more efficient, and I'm sure it would, but I much prefer to keep a physical record of my work. Safer too. I couldn't bear it if my cases-note file got lost or corrupted. I also like the idea of having a journal, so I can look back at it in years to come. Yes, I could put a record of everything on my computer, but it wouldn't be the same. It's more meaningful somehow to write it with my favourite fountain pen, and feel the crisp, thick, pages smooth under the heel of my hand as I write. In the distant future I'll be able to remember these cases. The pages will be well-thumbed, perhaps stained with coffee and the grease of cake crumbs. It will be a real slice of the now. I'll remember the faces of those I've helped, the feelings I had, the connections I made. Memories like these can't be saved in a computer file.

Standing to a stretch, I go to the double doors and watch the clouds scudding across the pale-blue sky, chased by a playful breeze. A familiar yearning to be outside stirs in my gut, I want to be in the fresh air being chased by a playful breeze too. Maybe I'll even have a walk on the beach. Then I wonder what my bestie Penny's up to. I think it's her day off from the reception at the surgery, and decide it's been too long since we had a good catch up. There's all the news from the American holiday I haven't shared yet, either. Yes, a good old gossip and a slice of cake or two at the Cherry Trees Café is what's needed. It's not as if I'm snowed under with cases anyway, is it? Maybe I ought to put some more flyers in the local shops on my way to meet Penny. Realising I'm getting ahead of myself, I grab my phone to check she does actually have time to meet me.

'Hi, Nance, how's it going?'

A trickle of apprehension swirls in my belly. Penny's voice sounds like it belongs to someone else. It's flat and monotone, as if it's had all the energy and pep removed. Penny's normally so bubbly. 'I'm fine, just thought that it might be good to meet for a coffee and a catch up. Seems ages since I saw you.'

'Erm…not sure I can today.'

'Oh? Have I got your day off wrong?'

'No. It's just um … I have a lot on and stuff…that's all.'

This isn't Penny. I've known her for more years than I care to remember and if she didn't feel like meeting up right away, she'd just tell me straight…not give me an evasive answer. What's she hiding? 'Okay. Anything I can do to help?'

There's a strangled sob on the line and she clears her throat. 'No. I'm fine.'

'Penny, if you don't tell me what's up, I'm coming over there right now.'

'No. Don't do that!' The panic in her voice makes my stomach clench. 'I'll meet you at the café in half-an-hour.'

The line goes dead and my thoughts go into free-fall. I

hurry up the path to the cottage to get my bag and change my thin shirt for a warm jumper, all the while wondering what on earth is the matter. It must be something serious for Penny to be worried about me coming to her home. But what? There's only her and her husband Joe at home, now the kids have flown the nest. Joe would be teaching in the local secondary school at this time on a weekday. I've a feeling it's a deeply important and personal issue too. Right - apart from Joe, what's important to her? Maybe, something went wrong at the spiritualist church where she does her medium sessions? But why would that have anything to do with her house?

Could it be her niece, Morwenna, who interviewed me for her GCSE project about my psychic ability last year? Wenna, as she preferred to be called, was a headstrong outwardly confident young woman, who could be a little bit brusque, but intuition told me that was a cover for her insecurities. I slip my warm turquoise jumper on and dismiss Wenna as being the worry, because the last I heard, she was settled and happy doing A' levels. However, that could have changed. Was she in some sort of trouble and staying at her aunt and uncle's? There's only one way to find out. I lock the door and set off.

Chapter Four

On my walk into town, the autumn sun tries its best, but remains more decorative than useful - the warmth of its rays negated by the stiff breeze. I hurry along in the shade of the tiny cobbled street, and at the end, a slice of the harbour-view waits. It's like a narrow painting, except it's moving. Sun on their wings, gulls sweep in and out, alighting on rigging, and various brightly painted hulls rise and fall in a vigorous Mexican wave. The clank of halyards against masts grows louder as I approach, and once out of the street and in the harbour, the whole canvas is revealed to me in all its colour, noise and vibrancy.

Now I'm in the middle of it, I realise Padstow Harbour is not as full of bustle this morning as it sometimes is. The tourists of summer are long gone, and though it's never completely dead, there's a muted, low-key atmosphere. Unless it's all in my head, because I'm worried about Penny. Dodging round a yappy terrier straining against its lead, I skirt the harbour wall and head for Cherry Trees Coffee House. I picture Penny waiting at a table. Unlike me, Penny always looks smart, despite wearing causal clothes. Last time we met, she was wearing a crisp blue shirt and brown jeans, her biscuit-coloured hair twisted into a messy chignon. Nothing special, really, it's just that Penny has style. It comes naturally to some. The shirt reflected her eyes, the jeans toned with her hair.

As I cross the street, I see that Penny's there, sitting at a table by the window. She's scrolling through her phone and seems lost in thought. But I'm shocked to see that her smart appearance I'm used to, is no more. She looks like she's slept in the creased and crumpled grey shirt she's wearing, her hair is wild and dishevelled, while her complexion matches the colour of the shirt. She looks tired. Very tired. I walk in the door and I'm greeted by a waft of fresh coffee, warm bread and pastry, which is so welcoming. I'm guessing Penny's mood will be far from that.

'Hi Penny,' I say, as I near the table. Penny's head jerks up and a half-smile lifts one side of her mouth, the effort it must have taken to do so is evident in her empty eyes. The smile looks broken. *She* looks broken.

'Hi, Nance. I've just got a coffee, what would you like?' She begins to get up, but I wave her back down.

'No, I'll get it. And your favourite carrot cake?'

'I'm not hungry, thanks.' Her flat voice floats in the space between us on a wave of apathy and she turns her gaze to the boats bobbing in the harbour.

I get the cake for her anyway, and an Earl Grey and scone and butter for myself. The cake won't solve her problems, but it might make her feel comforted for a little while. 'There we go,' I say, over-cheerily with a Cheshire Cat smile, as I slide the tray onto the table. Penny frowns at the cake I place in front of her and is about to say something, so I head her off with, 'Just try it. You'll be

43

surprised how a bit of sugar can give you a lift.'

'Ha!' She gives me a disdainful glance. 'I'll need a helluva lot of cake for that.'

Ignoring this, I sit opposite and take a sip of my tea. 'Okay, love. Just tell me what's wrong. I know it's something big, but I have broad shoulders and give great cuddles.'

Penny's sigh sounds as if she's borrowed it from the salt wind rattling the halyards outside. 'It's Joe,' she says, then her bottom lip trembles and she takes a drink. I reach my hand across the table to cover hers, but she withdraws it. 'Don't do that or I'll crumble. I'm only just holding it together, Nance.'

Her eyes glitter with unshed tears and I have to swallow hard. 'Oh, Pen. Yeah, I know you are. Just take your time.'

'He started drinking about six months ago. Well, he's always liked a drink, but this was something else. I thought it was just the stress of being a teacher, you know? But it got worse and worse until he was drinking every night, from as soon as he got in, to him going to bed. God knows how he got through the teaching day. Weekends are a dead loss too – he spends most of Saturday in bed sleeping it off, throwing up, or both.'

'Blimey, Pen. Why didn't you tell me?' I go to take her hand again, but then remember not to.

''Cos it's not the kind of thing you want to share really, is it?' Her cheeks flush and she looks at the carrot cake on her plate. Poor Penny, she has nothing to be ashamed of.

'Hey, I'm always here for you, no matter what.' We do synchronised sipping of our drinks for a moment and I pick

44

up my scone. 'Why did Joe start drinking so much, then?'

'He won't tell me.' Penny's eyelids flutter as she tries to hold onto her tears. 'As you know, a few years ago, I told him to take early retirement and take up painting. He's fifty-seven next year and he's had enough of his teaching job. He's had enough of it for at least five-years, to be honest. His great passion is painting, and he's had a few exhibited locally,' Penny gives a quick shake of the head. 'Why am I telling you this? You've seen his work.'

I nod. 'Yeah. Joe's stuff is really good, particularly his seascapes.'

Penny nods and sniffs. 'Yeah. He said two-years back that he wanted to have a bash at doing it full-time, and I told him that if he doesn't follow his heart now, it will be too late when he's sixty-five. I'm fully behind him and even though I'm coming up to fifty-two, I've said I'll increase my hours at the surgery. Everyone knows I practically run the place anyway. Besides that, he would get quite a decent pension, even though he'd lose some for going early. He's been in the job for over thirty years, for goodness' sake. The mortgage is paid off, so we certainly wouldn't have to worry about money.'

'I remember you telling me, Pen. So why isn't he following his dreams?'

Penny's eyebrows knit together in a frown. 'Oh, he gave me some half-cocked tale about being a failure as a teacher. Said if he didn't stick teaching out until the end, he'd be throwing in the towel and he'd be letting the system beat him. He hates Ofsted, box-ticking, long hours. Poor Joe worries about the increasing social problems amongst the students, because of the lack of opportunities here. He said the kids needed more good teachers who actually cared, not fewer.'

I weigh this up as I butter my scone and think Joe has a point. 'Hmm. I get what he means, and I can see why all that could lead to him self-medicating.'

Penny's eyes grow round. 'Yeah, but a lot of that is a smoke-screen. I know my Joe, and there's another reason – something he's hiding.' She picks up a fork and attacks the carrot cake, spearing a big chunk with it. Through a huge mouthful, she mumbles, 'But what is it? The nearest I think I got to the truth, was when he said he was too old and had missed the boat with his painting, but that's not the whole story.' Penny shoves another forkful of cake into her mouth and chews it slowly, throwing a vacant stare at the counter behind me. 'If I can't get to the bottom of it soon and make him listen, he's going to drink himself to death.' Penny takes a quick gulp of coffee and covers her mouth with a napkin as if she's regretting setting that last sentence free.

'Is he home now? Is that why you were so worried that I'd come round to yours?'

'Yeah. He's at home drinking. He's been off with depression for a few weeks now, but he can't be off forever, can he? He'll have to make a decision soon…he can't carry on like this, Nancy…I can't bear the thought of coming home one day and finding him…'

The desperation in her bright blue eyes brings tears to mine, and I reach for Penny's hand. This time she doesn't pull away. 'Hey, it won't come to that. I'm here to help – you're not alone, Penny, okay?'

A shadow of a smile flickers across her lips. 'That means a lot, Nance. But what can you do?'

I pretend to be offended, and quote something she once said to me. 'What can I do? What happened to – "I'm a medium and have had the spirit view for as long as I can remember, but I don't have your bloody amazing talent, Nancy Cornish. The way you use your phenomenal gift to help people is truly amazing!" Or words to that effect.'

Penny laughs and it's genuine, joyful and music to my ears. 'And I still stand by my words, but what can you do to help Joe? If I can't get through to him, how will you?'

Yes, Nancy. How will you? Thinking quickly, I offer – 'If I find the real reason for Joe's depression, we can maybe work on it? Could you bring me something of his – or a photo of him, perhaps?'

'Could that work?'

'I don't know, but it's worth a try.'

'I have a pen of his that I grabbed to make a shopping list and a photo of him on my phone...' Penny looks around the half-full café. 'Not sure this is the right place though.'

'No, definitely not. Come to mine and I'll try to make the connection there. I made some saffron buns yesterday, so you can have one of those. The carrot cake has perked you up a bit.'

Penny's brows shoot up as she looks at her empty plate. 'I can't remember eating all of it.'

'You did, trust me.' I stand up and shrug my coat on. 'In fact, you annihilated it.'

I get a big smile. 'Thanks, Nancy.' Penny gets up and

47

gives me a hug. 'So glad we met up. You've already made feel there's more hope for Joe now.'

Gosh, I hope I can live up to her expectations. 'A trouble shared and all that.' I pull a wadge of flyers for my business - Nancy Cornish PI - from my bag and hand her half. 'Right. Make yourself useful - help me put these in the shops on our way back.'

She fans her face with them. 'It would be my pleasure.'

***

With Penny settled by the fire, Scrappy on her lap, a saffron bun and a cuppa to hand on the little side table, I print off Joe's picture and take it down to the office. I sit on the sofa with my feet up, grab my favourite old red blanket that Gran knitted, which doubles as a throw, wrap it round my legs, and get comfy. 'Now, Joe. Let's see if we can get to the bottom of you.' I lean back against the cushions, rest the photo against my bent knees, and take the gold and black fountain pen in my right hand.

Joe's eyes look out at me from the photo. Deep green, they sit on a wealth of laughter lines, and there's a warmth and depth to them which is reminiscent of his personality. I've only met him a few times, but I could tell right away that he was a lovely, caring guy.

I inhale through my nose and blow out slowly through my mouth. 'What's bothering, you Joe?' I whisper, into the silent room. Then I close my eyes and curl my fingers around the pen. The plastic case of the pen grows warm in my hand, and a familiar tingle starts in my fingers, flowing up my arm like water through a flower stem.

48

Opening my eyes, I see a series of moving images – a 'rolling film' projecting onto the back wall of a much younger Joe. He's about 10 and on a cliff by the sea, he's sitting in front of an easel with another boy by his side who looks to be about 14. They look similar. The same floppy dark hair and easy smile. I know without doubt that they are brothers. Joe's brother points at the sea, and dips his brush into a paint palette. Joe nods and copies him. Then the film stops. I blink and concentrate, but there's nothing. Damn. Opening my hand, I look at the pen and the photo balanced on my knees. Is Joe's brother at the bottom of all this? I remember Penny telling me he'd passed away about ten-years ago from pancreatic cancer, and it had hit Joe really hard. I try again to make a connection, but nothing happens. Not even a twitch in my fingers.

Blowing out a sigh of frustration, I put the pen down and then see something flicker in my peripheral vison. I sense a movement of air and then a pixilation of colours...next, Joe's brother is sitting opposite me on the other sofa. He's much older than in the images, probably in his early 50s and he's got a sad little smile playing at the edges of his mouth.

I give a welcoming smile. 'You're Joe's brother, right?'

He runs a hand through his wavy greying hair. 'Yes, I'm Terry. Joe must paint. He must do what makes him happy. There's nothing more important in life.'

'I agree, so why do you think he won't?'

'Joe thinks he's not good enough. Tell him he is, and to try again. Tell him Terry has his back, as always. Those who use failure as a weapon, are small men. Weak men.

49

Don't let him win.'

I'm about to ask what he means, when Terry does the 'off switch' and I'm left looking at an empty sofa.

Penny is nodding off by the fire with Scrappy snoozing on her lap, as I walk into the kitchen. Poor love is obviously emotionally exhausted and could do with being left to sleep, but the fresh breeze blows in with me and wakes her. She stirs with a long, loud yawn. 'Can't believe I nearly dropped off there for a moment.'

'I can. You must be bone weary with all this going on.'

Penny gives a rueful smile. 'Must admit I've not slept straight through the night for a good-few-weeks, or so.'

I sit in the chair at the other side of the fire. 'Well, at least I've made some progress. Not sure how useful it will be, but it's a start.' I tell her about Terry and what he said.

Scrappy jumps from her lap as she leans forward, her eyes bright with hope. 'That's great. I don't know what he meant, really. But Joe will, I'm sure of it.'

'Good. Will you tell him, or do you want me to pop over tomorrow and have a chat with him about it?'

A dark cloud passes across her face. 'Hmm. It would be better coming from you, but I couldn't bear for you to see him in a state. He'd be so embarrassed too…if he still cares what others think.' Penny sighs and stares into the dancing flames.

'If I come around early, say just after breakfast, he's less likely to be out of it, right?'

'Hm. But he might have a hangover from this evening. I could try to stop him drinking too much, but then he never listens normally.'

Her despairing expression makes my heart ache. 'We can only try, Penny.' I give her an encouraging smile.

'I suppose so...and thanks so much for trying to help. I can't tell you how much it means.' Penny's voice wobbles and she grabs her bag and stands up. 'Okay, I'm off now. Shall we say nine-thirty-ish tomorrow?'

'Wonderful,' I reply, and show her to the door. Waving as I watch her drive away, I wish with all my heart that her life could be wonderful too.

Charlie's early for once and has brought fish and chips as a treat. He messaged me earlier, just as I was about to make spag bol, so it was nice to have the extra time to take a long hot bubble-bath and read my book. Though I feel more relaxed now, tomorrow morning's playing on my mind, and I'm not looking forward to meeting Joe if he's in no mood to listen. Ah, well. No point in worrying about something that might never happen, as my mum would say. 'Those fish and chips smell divine,' I say, as I take the warm plates out of the oven and put them on trays. We're going to eat in front of the TV and watch a Netflix drama. Bliss.

'Not as divine as you,' Charlie says, dropping a little kiss on my cheek and shrugging out of his coat.

'You big smoothie. Flattery will get you everywhere.'

Charlie does a Groucho wiggle of his eyebrows. 'Everywhere, hmm?'

'Yes.' I hand him his tray. 'Well, almost. All the way into the living room and a seat on the sofa at least.'

He laughs and grabs a bottle of ketchup and a beer from the fridge and I follow him through, as he sits on the sofa and flicks the TV on. 'Shall we try to make the connection with Leanne's cup, after we've eaten and before we get settled for the night?'

His words throw a wet blanket on the proceedings. I'd forgotten all about that. Cold blooded murder...hardly the right ambience for a relaxing night snuggled up together, is it? But I said I'd try and I will. 'Yes, might be for the best, then we can put it behind us until tomorrow.'

After he's finished his food, he pops out to the hallway and comes back with a white plastic vending cup. 'Here it is.' I take it from him and turn it around in my fingers. 'Shall I go and put these plates in the dishwasher and have a quick shower, while you do your thing?'

'Yeah, okay. I work better without an audience as you know.' I give him a smile as he leaves, quietly closing the living room door behind him.

Now to get myself in the right frame of mind. I flick off the TV, wrap my fluffy green blanket around my knees and put my feet up on the furry grey footstool. Then holding the cup in my right hand, I close my eyes and inhale through my nose, hold for a few seconds, and blow out a slow stream of air from my mouth. Calm. Ready. The wind has died down outside, and I listen to the heartbeat-tick of gran's clock on the shelf nearby, the distant rattling of crockery as Charlie tidies the kitchen, and the creak of the beams as the old house settles in for the night. The index finger on my right-hand twitches, as a series of tiny electric shocks flows through it and spreads across my tingling palm. Then:

SNAP – an image of two little dark-haired girls, around 6 and 8 years old, playing in a sand pit. Obviously sisters. The younger one suddenly grabs her sister's ponytail and tugs it so hard the girl begins to cry. The younger one lets go, but laughs at her sister's discomfort and throws a handful of sand in her face.

SNAP – the same girls a few years older, running along a windy beach. They seem to be having fun, laughing and chasing each other. Then the younger one shoves her sister hard in the back, and sends her flying into some rocks. She laughs when the girl's nose starts to bleed.

SNAP – The same girls a few years on. The older one is sitting on a sofa with a ginger cat on her lap. The younger girl jumps up from her chair, grabs the cat roughly by the scruff of its neck and leaves the room with it. The older girl starts crying but doesn't follow.

Then nothing…

But I know without doubt, the cruel girl is Leanne, and the other is her sister Molly. Why was she so cruel to her? This is Leanne's water cup – but there's no feelings of remorse associated with the past memories I've been shown, in fact it's the opposite. There's an underlying sense of triumph. I shudder and put the cup on the coffee table, I can't bear to touch it anymore. Gives me the creeps. I hug myself and briskly rub my arms. Rarely have I had such a strong feeling about a person, just from an item they have touched. But I'm sure without a shadow of a doubt that Leanne Preston is a thoroughly nasty piece of work.

After a few more minutes and still nothing, I hear

Charlie walk across the creaky floorboards above me in our bedroom, then out again on his way to the bathroom. He's going to be very disappointed when he finds I have nothing much to tell him, other than Leanne being a horrible child and cruel to her sister. He can't pin a murder on her with that kind of information. I sigh and shut my eyes for a few moments to see if anything will come to me, but nothing will. But there we are, can't win 'em all. Maybe a hot chocolate will help smooth the way out of the blind alley I've come up against.

I open my eyes and begin to stand up, but stop mid-way and flop back down…because staring at me from a chair by the fire is Molly. Molly as I saw her on the news last week. Long dark hair, pretty green eyes and a half smile, as if unsure viewers would like to receive a full one.

'She drowned me.' The smile disappears and her eyes swim with unshed tears, which must be one of the saddest sights I've ever seen. A spirit in distress, grieving for her earthly life taken too soon, and by one who should have loved her.

For a moment I can't get words past the knot of emotion in my throat. Then I manage, 'Your sister Leanne?' Though I know the answer, I have to be absolutely sure.

'Yes.'

'She was cruel to you when you were children…I saw some of your past in my connections just now. Was she always cruel?'

'No. She sometimes was lovely to me.' Molly brushes away her tears and tries a wobbly smile. But when she

54

wasn't, she said I made her do it. I always felt bad.'

I lean forward, try to make sure she doesn't do the off switch before I've found anything out that could help Charlie. 'What happened that night when she...when you both went swimming?'

'She'd been lovely to me for a few weeks since we'd had a really bad argument, and I'd slapped her. But soon after, she apologised, was kind to me and said everything between us would be okay.' Molly pauses, a faraway look in her eye. 'Once we got in the water that night though, she changed, said I had to die. I had to pay for my betrayal, because I broke our promise...I was going to leave her you see.'

I swallow hard as I watch grief and pain pass in waves across her face. 'Leave her?'

'I was planning to get married...she...' Molly's face becomes a puzzle, starts to pixilate, fade around the edges. *Nooo. She can't go yet.* 'Find my hidden diary,' she mumbles.

Desperate, I stand up. 'Where? Where's your diary?'

'Sea cave,' she whispers...then she's gone.

'Sea cave?' I say out loud to myself as Charlie comes in.

'Sea cave?' he repeats, and flops down on the sofa.

I quickly fill him in. 'Which sea cave do you thinks she meant? There are bloody hundreds of them in Cornwall.' I throw a cushion across the room in frustration.

Charlie puts his hand up and his reasoning smile on, 'Hey, no need to get upset, love. Let's think about this logically.'

'Hmm. Because I'm clearly illogical, right? Possibly even leaning toward the hysterical?' Charlie glares at me and his mouth becomes a thin line. He folds his arms, says nothing. I sigh and flop down next to him on the sofa, slip my arm through his. 'Sorry. I'm just so sad that you were right about Leanne. How could she actually drown her own sister like that? And poor Molly seems such a nice girl...seemed. All her life in front of her, about to get married.' I swallow and close my eyes. How Charlie does his job dealing with people like Leanne, and manages to keep his temper is beyond me. Makes me admire him even more.

'I know. It's truly vile, but we've got so much more than we had before, thanks to you. If we can find the diary, there could be damning evidence we can nail Leanne with.' Charlie squeezes my hand in encouragement.

'Yeah, but it's a big if. Are there any sea caves on the beach they were swimming off?'

Charlie shrugs. 'It was Mawgan Porth, I know there are one or two small ones. If it's there, we should be able to find it.'

I picture Mawgan Porth Beach in my head... 'No, I don't think so. My gut's telling me it's not there.'

'Well, your gut's not often wrong.'

'No. But we can't rule it out.' Thoughts tumble round my head trying to form coherent ideas. 'What about any other beach associated with Leanne and Molly? Where did they live?'

'They lived with the grandma, as I said. The house is up for sale now, and our lovely Leanne is hoping to keep all the profits for herself, as you know. Should bring a pretty penny too, it being in Crantock Village.'

Immediately, my spirits rise. 'Yeah. That sounds more like it. I know for certain Crantock has quite a few big caves. You should definitely look there tomorrow.' I smile up at Charlie, glad he might have a lead.

He nods and pats my knee. 'It has the one with the woman's face carved in it too, remember?'

'Er…no. That's somewhere else.'

He yawns and shrugs. 'Is it? Anyway, I'd find it quicker with your gut on the case. Will you help me look?'

Hmm. Will I? I'd planned to relax tomorrow afternoon, after what will almost certainly be an emotional meeting with Joe. Now, not only do I have to see Joe and try to convince him that there's light at the end of the tunnel via Terry's message, I've got to go in search of a dead woman's diary in a sea cave. Great. But then Charlie's wearing his most earnest and hopeful expression, so how can I refuse? 'Of course. But as a reward, I need a cup of hot chocolate with squirty cream on top, yeah?'

With a grin, he jumps up and salutes. 'Yes, boss. On it, boss.'

Chapter Five

As I step out through the door, a dark, dismal, mid-October day sends a spiteful wind to sharpen its claws on my cheeks. I pull my parka hood around my face and hurry through the mizzle down the driveway to my car, narrowly avoiding a muddy puddle. Behind the wheel, I tilt the rear-view mirror, shove my hood back and smooth down my hair. I imagine that muddy puddles will be the least of my worries by the time I get back home again - because I'll actually *be* a muddy puddle. Or at least my brain will have turned into one, after the two lovely jobs I've got lined up. I have to be at Penny's at nine-thirty, and the car clock says I have fifteen-minutes. Can't wait.

Penny's looking through the living room window as I pull up, her face a mask of anxiety and her eyes are puffy and tearful. *Remind yourself why you do this job again, Nancy?* The answer comes straight back as I get out of the car and walk to the door. Because you have an extraordinary gift that can help people, and no matter how emotionally draining it can sometimes be, your main aim in life is to make others happy...if you can.

'Joe's not too hungover today, and he knows you're coming and why,' is Penny's opener as she ushers me through the door and into the kitchen. 'He wasn't best pleased to say the least. Said I should butt out of his life and stop interfering in everything he does.' Penny's eyes are bright with unshed tears as she turns away to run water into the kettle.

'Oh, love, I'm so sorry. I'm surprised he's still here waiting.'

'That's only because I hid the car keys.' Penny flicks the kettle on, a troubled frown furrowing her brow.

Great. I'm about to face a caged tiger...hope he's had his claws clipped. 'Right. Well, I can only try to get the message across. Not really sure how it will all work out.'

Penny tries to raise a smile, but only one side of her mouth got the message. 'I can't thank you enough, Nance. If nothing comes of it, at least you did your best.' She lifts her hands and lets them fall, looks out the window at the trees blowing in the wind. 'I've had just about enough of him, I can tell you.' I watch a single tear trace a path down the profile of her cheek and my heart goes out to her. She heaves a sigh as heavy as the grey clouds gathering above the trees and says, 'Tea or coffee?'

'Tea, please. Make one for me and Joe, and I'll take it in to him. You stay here, it might be for the best.'

Relief flickers in her eyes and she nods. 'Yes, he might say more to you without me listening in.'

Joe's in the little conservatory adjoining the living room. He's in navy pyjamas, wrapped in a green and red stripy blanket and moving slowly back and forth in a wicker rocking chair. Like his wife's a few moments ago,

59

his gaze is fixed on the tops of the tall trees at the end of the garden, as they're yanked this way and that by the petulant breeze. I'm guessing Joe's not really watching the trees, but lost in a tangle of feelings, thoughts, and memories only he can see. Not wishing to startle him, I sit down in a similar chair nearby, and set a tray of tea and chocolate chip cookies on the glass-topped coffee table.

Joe glances up at me, his expression a mix of surprise and embarrassment. A rush of blood colours his cheeks, and he looks away, self-conscious. Clearing his throat, he strokes a hand over his grey stubble and says, 'I never asked you to come, Nancy. Not being rude, but I don't need your help. Penny always thinks she knows best, but all I want is to be left alone.'

Without a word, I hand him a mug and push the plate of biscuits across the table. 'Have a drink and a biscuit, you'll feel better.'

Joe snaps his head round to me, contempt turning his normally calm green eyes into cold hard emeralds. 'Tea and biscuits will make everything alright? Jeez, I thought you were better than that, Nancy. Please just go.'

I can see the pain etched into every line and contour of his grey complexion. This is a man on the edge of giving up, and that realisation twists my gut and sends a chill down my spine. But then a strange calm settles my nerves...I'm convinced I need to let my intuition guide me. Straight talk and no punches pulled. 'No, it won't make everything alright, but the sugar will give you a little energy and the tea will warm you. I have a message from your Terry and you'll be able to consider it better if you have something inside you.'

Joe shakes his head and sneers. 'Yeah, Penny said something about that. I'm not a believer like you and her, to be honest. Oh, don't get me wrong, Penny's spiritualist church and your psychic stuff might bring comfort to those less gullible than me, but I'm a teacher and a science man.' He sticks out his chin and folds his arms. A clear challenge.

'There's a place in this world for both science and the psychic phenomenon, Terry, if you allow it. Anyway, I'm not here for an academic debate.' I pause and take a sip of tea. 'Penny told me you said you were fed up because you feel you've missed the boat with painting, and now you're too old. Teaching took over your life and you feel it's too late, or words to that effect?'

Joe gives me a withering look and shrugs.

'Terry told me it's because you think you're not a good enough artist. He said that you are, and to try again. He said he has your back as always. And this is a direct quote from him which means nothing to me, but I'm sure will make sense to you - Those who use failure as a weapon, are small men. Weak men. Don't let him win.'

Joe stares at me round-eyed in shock, and a hand shoots to his mouth as if he's trying to keep his words inside. Despite his efforts, a low moan escapes along with a river of tears and I hand him a tissue and wait. After a few moments he's composed enough to take a sip or two of tea and then he looks at me, new respect in his eyes. 'There must be something in your connections thing that Penny is always on about...because there's no way you could have known something like this, not without Terry telling you.

61

Particularly the last bit.'

'No, of course not. I offer the plate of chocolate chip cookies and he takes one. 'So what did he mean, about weak men and failure?'

He chews a mouthful of his biscuit and stares at the trees again. 'He meant our dad. Our dad always used to say I'd never amount to anything – told Terry the same. He was always the one who 'knew everything' but knew nothing, really. He was a small, weak man with no real confidence to speak of. But he hid it well. He tried to belittle people, control them when he could. Mum, Terry, me.' Joe swipes at an errant tear and drinks more tea. 'Terry never fell for it though, and protected me when he could. I wasn't as strong, because Dad made me under-confident like him. I couldn't really believe it when I got into teaching, but still I never felt I was quite good enough.'

The parallels with my Charlie's and Joe's story are so similar, I have to swallow more tea to dislodge the lump forming in my throat. I wonder how many other men, and women for that matter, have been damaged like this by one parent or another? Sometimes the mental abuse can be as bad as physical. The bruises and scars are as hurtful, it's just that they remain unseen. So sad, and so bloody unnecessary. 'I'm sorry, Joe.' I reach across and squeeze his shoulder. 'Charlie had similar with his dad.'

'Right, I see.' He heaves a sigh. 'I wish Terry were still here. He always had my back, and I could use his advice.'

'He still does, and he sent advice through me. He wants you to try again with the painting and to do what makes you happy, because that's the most important thing in life.'

Joe shakes his head but says nothing. 'Tell me why you changed your mind about making a go of it, Joe. I've seen some of your work and thought it was brilliant, and I'm not just saying that to give you a boost.'

'Thank you.' He sighs and shoves his fingers though his messy hair. 'In the spring I was painting a seascape down at Fistral Beach, but I couldn't get it right. My fingers felt awkward, stiff, and the energy didn't flow as it normally did, so I left it and went home. At first, I thought it was just one of those things and decided to try again in a few days. But the same thing happened the next time, and the time after that, too.' Joe pauses and drains his cup. 'That's when I decided I was no good…that I'd failed. All the old insecurities my dad had gifted me came flooding back, and I realised there would be no new career path. My talent had deserted me, and I'd better resign myself to staying in the classroom.' He looks at me and shrugs. 'So there you have it. The whole miserable truth.'

We sit in silence for a few moments while I consider my response. Joe's really opened up now, and I'm almost sure I can see a chink in his armour. Maybe I can persuade him to rethink his plans. 'Last spring, Joe, can you think of anything that happened which might have put you off your game?'

Joe frowns, and stares at a photo of Terry in a silver frame, sitting on a shelf across the room. Terry's on a boat, holding up what looks like a mackerel, while shielding his face from the sun with his other hand. He has a proud smile on his face, and his blue eyes are twinkling with merriment in the golden light. 'No. Quite the contrary. I'd almost made my decision to leave teaching and go in for the painting…I was going to come home and tell Penny after I'd painted that scene at Fistral…except I never did finish it.'

A lightbulb moment flashes in my mind. I'm no psychologist, but the fear of making such a big step, given his background, had obviously rendered him impotent. I tell him my reasoning and add, 'So if you admit that might be the problem, maybe you could try again and see what happens?'

'A nice idea, and you could well be right. But I need to get real and move on. I'm too old for a new start, and all that hoo ha. Truth is…I don't think my heart's in it anymore.'

My own heart sinks as I scan his woebegone expression. So close and yet so far. Then my eye catches Terry's again, and I get up and walk over to the photo. I reach for it and say over my shoulder to Joe, 'May I have a closer look?'

'Knock yourself out.'

The frame is heavy and cool under my fingertips, and I smile as I feel the simple joy of that long ago sunny day reach out to me. A warmth seeps from the frame now and into my hands and arms like a sunbeam, and there to my left by the long glass conservatory doors, Terry snaps into bold relief, like a vibrant rainbow against the backdrop of the grey October garden. He says quietly, 'Tell Joe to look at his unfinished painting again. He's mistaken. Once he sees the light, he'll know what to do.' Terry does the 'off switch' and we're immediately disconnected.

I take the photo over to Joe and hand it to him. 'Terry was just here again. He thinks you're wrong about not having enough talent, and wants you to look at the painting you abandoned again.'

Joe stares at me in surprise then back at the photo. 'But I've looked at it a thousand times.'

I shrug. 'He says once you see the light, you'll know what to do.'

Joe sits back in his chair and closes his eyes a few moments, then he sighs and opens them again. 'Okay, let's do it. If that's what my brother wants, then that's what I'll do.'

We walk into the living room and into the corridor, past Penny who's sitting at the kitchen table, head in hands. She looks up when she hears us, but I signal that she should stay where she is and give the thumbs-up. She sends a tentative thumbs-up back, but is clearly bewildered as to why I'm following her husband up the stairs.

The attic room is big, airy and full of sunlight. The clouds of earlier have gone, and there's a big patch of blue sky beyond the huge Velux window in the sloping ceiling. Oil-paint on the floorboards scents the air, and a large wooden easel stands empty under the window. Along one wall is a row of canvases, mostly seascapes, and a paint-spotted white sheet covers the last one, revealing only the corner. It's this one that Joe lifts from the sheet, and sets on the easel. Wow… Although it's unfinished, it has an ethereal quality. The seascape captures the early morning and a solitary figure on a surfboard. The figure's arms are outstretched as they ride a wave through the mist, the frothy surf kissing the shore, and most breathtaking... a golden shaft of sunlight striking a fishing boat as it sails out to the far horizon. As the sunlight through the window grows stronger, it bathes the painting in a twin echo of luminescence, and I think it is one of the most moving paintings I've ever seen. I have to blink back tears when Joe looks at me, a question in his eyes.

'Oh, Joe. It's absolutely beautiful. How could you think it wasn't?'

Bewildered, he spreads his hands. 'I don't see what you see.'

I get the feeling he's set his mind against it, because of everything he went through as a kid. The past has built barriers to the future – they've blindfolded him. 'Look at the boat, Joe.' He's already shaking his head, so I touch his arm. 'No. I mean really *look.*'

With a clatter and a scrape, he drags a rickety old wooden chair from under the eaves, sits on it, folds his arms and looks. Slowly, his blank expression finds life, as a big smile curves his lips. 'Well, I'll be damned,' he whispers, as if to himself, and chuckles, even as tears fill his eyes. Then he looks up through the window and says to the blue sky, 'I painted your boat without realising it, Terry. And that sunlight...' He stops and shakes his head, clearly overcome. He releases a big breath in a whoosh. 'And that sunlight is you sailing home.'

I stand quietly while Joe gives into his emotions and then I place a hand on his shoulder. 'Would you like me to get you some water, or anything?'

Joe shakes his head and blows his nose. 'I would like you to get something for me, but not just yet. I want to say thanks so much, Nancy for helping me to see the light. Literally.' He laughs, and I see some of the old Joe creeping back into his tired eyes. 'Our Terry loved night fishing and he'd always turn for home as the sun came up...he'd sing the old song, Here Comes the Sun as he did, and as a teenager, I'd join in when I sometimes went with him.' He nods at the painting. 'As soon as I looked at the light on the boat, that song came into my head...it was Terry's voice, Nancy. Terry's voice I could hear singing in my head.' A sob breaks free and he covers his face with his hands.

I'm finding it hard to keep it together now, but I have to, for his sake. 'Oh, Joe. I'm so glad Terry came through like that. Do you see the beauty in the canvas now?'

A nod. Through his fingers he says, 'Yeah. Yeah, it's pretty good, even though I say so myself. I've been a right bloody fool.'

'No, you haven't. It was just that weak, small man who used failure as a weapon against you. Thing is, Joe. He's not won. You have.'

Joe presses his lips together and nods vigorously. 'Yeah, with our Terry's help. He's got my back, even now. And I've not won yet, because I've got to get my head in the right place, but at least I know where I'm going...what I'm aiming for.'

'That's right. Next year at this time you'll look back on this awful period and feel relieved, because you'll be doing what makes you happy.'

Joe rubs his eyes. 'That's the plan. Thanks again, Nancy.'

'You're most welcome. And you said I could get something for you?'

'Yes. Please ask...' He takes a moment. 'Please ask my darling Penny to come up and see me. I have a lot of apologising to do.' Joe slaps his hand on the arm of the chair. 'God, I've been such a pig to her.'

'I dare say you have, but she'll forgive you because she's a wonderful woman. But you know that already. She'll be overjoyed to hear what's happened, because in the end, all she wants is for you to be happy, and I know you both will be.'

Joe nods and looks back up at the sky, so I leave him to his thoughts and go to find my friend.

Chapter Six

The sun is still shining from a clear blue sky on the journey home in the car. Joy swells my heart, and I can't help but smile as I think of how miserable I felt on the outward journey. Joe's set his feet on the right track now, and Penny was so thrilled about the change in him, I could get no sense out of her for some time. As usual, she insisted on payment, but I refused. She's more like family than a friend these days, and it didn't feel right. Thinking of family, I've to meet Charlie at Crantock Beach in an hour-and-a-half. I'll just have time to take the washing out of the machine, make a quick spaghetti sauce for later, feed Scrappy for the second time, and make a quick call to Alison to see how Tilly's doing with the new baby.

As I pull up outside Seal Cottage, I glance at the sky. Though it's sunny now, early November can be unpredictable in Cornwall. Well, any month can, come to think, but I'll need to get changed. I'll swap this checked skirt and blouse for jeans and my old turquoise woolly jumper. Wellies too. As I cross the threshold to the cottage, I do the same with my fingers, in the hope that the sea cave will throw up Molly's diary, and some of the answers that Charlie needs to get some hard evidence against Leanne.

Who hides their diary in a sea cave? Poor Molly must have been desperate to go to those lengths to keep the diary away from her sister, so there must be something about Leanne in it worth reading.

Okay, washing sorted, sauce made, Scrappy satisfied and myself appropriately clothed for a walk on the beach. I'll look out my scarf too, as it looks like it's going to be a blustery afternoon. Now…time for a quick catch up with Alison. Her number rings out for a while and just as I think it will go to answerphone, she picks up. 'Nancy, hi,' she whispers, 'Hang on a mo.' I listen to her walking through her house for a moment or two, then her voice returns to normal volume. 'Okay, I'm away from her ladyship now, so won't wake her. Nearly missed your call 'cos I'm up to my eyes in dirty nappies, sterilizing bottles and god knows what else. I only got three hours' sleep last night too.' Alison's' deep sigh says it better than her words ever could. Poor woman's clearly exhausted.

Surprised at this, I ask, 'So you're sleeping over at Tilly's to help with the night feeds?'

A humourless bark. 'No. As I told you the other day, I was going to be another pair of hands right next door. Turns out I'm very often the *only* pair, and the baby is here more than she's at home. Tilly is in a proper state. She's refusing to even try to breastfeed, which makes her worse, as her boobs are full of milk, and she's frequently in floods of tears. Mostly she takes to her bed, and neither I or Chris can get any sense out of her. Truth be told, Nancy, I think she's having a breakdown. Trouble is, if social services get wind of it, I can see the little mite being taken away. Chris

70

tries, but he hasn't a clue really, much like myself, and he's so busy at work too.'

My stomach churns as I picture the scene at Alison's, and imagining the little girl being taken away. Poor Tilly, poor baby, poor all of them. If I hadn't promised Charlie I'd meet him at the beach, I'd fly round to Alison's now and see what I could do to help. 'Really sorry to hear all that, love. If you can hang on one more night, I'll be round early tomorrow and give you a hand, okay?'

A whoosh of relief meets my ears. 'Would you? Oh, Nancy, that would be absolutely amazing.' Alison sniffs and blows her nose. 'I'm just so totally knackered.' A pause. 'But are you sure? I expect you have a hundred other things to do.'

Me? No. Just got to find a hidden diary to help put a murderer away, write up Joe's case in my journal, check there have been no calls asking for my help from anywhere, make dinner, sort the laundry and then collapse. 'Oh, you know, just the usual,' I say, with a smile in my voice.

***

Edging my car down the narrow path to the National Trust car park at Crantock, I realise I'm twenty-minutes late. Charlie's car is parked at the foot of a sandy slope which leads the way over a huge dune to the beach, and he's beside it, pacing up and down, hood up on his black raincoat, hands in pockets, totally oblivious to my arrival. Charlie always paces when he's thinking, and often rakes his fingers through his hair at the same time, but the hood prevents it today. He comes to a stop, and watches a couple

71

of surfers cleaning down their boards, but the faraway stare tells me he's puzzling through ideas inside his head, wondering which ones are most feasible.

I park next to his car and get out, pulling my woolly red hat down over my windblown curls, and raise a hand in answer to Charlie's. 'Sorry I'm late,' I say, as he pulls me in for a hug. He smells of fresh sea air and coffee. 'Had a bit of a morning, and then I had to do chores and stuff.'

'No problem, Nance. I've enjoyed a bit of time to try and get my head together,' he says into my ear as he drops a cold kiss on my warm cheek.

'What have you come up with?' I slip my arm through his, and we head up the steep sandy path over the dune.

I get a rueful grin. 'Nothing more than we had this morning. I've been looking more closely into our Leanne's life, but she's squeaky clean. Hopefully once we've found this diary, everything will change.'

'Yeah, let's hope so.' I squeeze his arm.

'I've brought a photo of Molly for you. Found it on her social media – thought it could help?'

I take it. Molly's on a windy beach, might even be this one, and she's smiling at the camera, a twinkle in her pretty green eyes, a hand to her fringe as the wind plays tug of war with her long dark hair. I smile back at her and place the photo in my pocket.

As we get to the top of the dune, we take a breather and gaze out at the dramatic panorama. A charcoal Atlantic roars into the vast shore, and along the low horizon, the stiff breeze stirs a few rainclouds into a porridge grey sky. To my right across the Gannel river, I watch a flock of screeching seagulls dip low over a chain of rockpools in their quest for dinner, and to my left in the distance by the shoreline, a dog barks at its owner, who's about to launch a ball. 'Wow. I've forgotten what a gorgeous beach this is. Must be about five-years since we came.'

Charlie twists his mouth to the side as he considers this. 'Must be. Yeah, we brought my mum for the day. And for once you were wrong last night. We had a picnic by that cave with the woman's face carved into it, remember?' He points along the beach to where it curves towards the ocean, hugged by a rocky headland and topped with undulating green hills.

'Oh yeah.' A shiver of excitement runs down my back. 'I do. And what if that cave is *the* cave.'

Charlie frowns, and we set off walking down the other side of the dune to the beach. 'That's unlikely, because as far as I remember, that cave is entirely flooded at high tide. There'd be nowhere to hide a diary.'

I answer with something that has been on my mind since Molly's connection yesterday. 'Well, if you ask me, a sea cave is a daft place to hide a diary at all. Surely it would be too damp, even if it is above the tide-line.'

At the end of the slope, Charlie jumps down onto the beach from a sand shelf formed by the wind, and then holds out his hand to help me down too. 'Well, we'll soon see. And maybe Molly was attracted to the cave with the woman's face carved in the stone, because of the story behind it.'

'Remind me of it.'

'I think it happened in the early part of the last century.

73

A woman came for a ride on the beach on her horse, but unfortunately, they were cut off by the tide. Both horse and rider were drowned. The woman's—'

'—boyfriend carved her face, a horse and a poem into the flat rock inside the cave.' I interrupt. 'Yeah, I remember it all now. Such a sad tale, and how poignant it will be if Molly's diary is in there, given how Molly herself died.'

'Yeah. Well, we'll soon find out. Come on.'

Five-minutes later, we arrive at a little horseshoe cove surrounded by a cathedral of towering wet, green, brown and black rocks - home to a few wheeling jackdaws. In these rocks, there are a few small crevices and caves, and beyond, a series of rockpools link together to shelter a plethora of tiny sea creatures awaiting the returning tide. Charlie takes my hand and hurries me to our right, and walking through some standing water, he steps into the entrance of a small cave. I follow, and we stand and stare at the smooth grey wall of the cave not far above our heads, because on it, is a simple carving of a woman's face in profile. To the left of this, is a much smaller carved figure of a horse, as if looking on from afar, but it's the poem to the right of the face which holds my attention. It was poignant the first time I read it when we came here last, but now with the added tragedy of Molly suffering the same fate, it's unbearable. I'm deeply touched, and climbing up onto a boulder, I trace each word with my fingertips, and immediately feel the deep grief and sorrow of the poor man who wrote it.

Charlie puts his arm around me and reads aloud, "Mar

not my face but let me be, secure in this lone cavern by the sea. Let the wild waves around me roar, kissing my lips for evermore." He sighs. 'Given it must be over a hundred years since he carved those words, her face isn't marred much at all, is it?'

I shake my head and think about poor Molly. Another young life cut short before her time. Glancing around the cave, I can see it's very rocky and steep, with no immediately obvious place to hide a diary above the tide line. The cave would be completely submerged, once the ocean surged into this little space. There seems to be only limpets and dripping water as company for the carved lady. 'Can't see this being the right place, Charlie,' I say to his backside as he tries to climb the slippery wall at the end.

'Nope. I thought there might be a crevice or something, but there isn't. Still, there are a few more caves on this beach. Let's have a look.'

I follow him out, then something stops me in my tracks, or should I say someone. Tiny electric shocks run across my shoulders and down the length of my arms - I know I'm not alone. I look over my shoulder and see Molly standing next to the carving, arm outstretched pointing back into the cave. But how? I didn't make a connection...then I realise that Molly's photo is in my hand. 'Where is your diary, Molly?' I ask, with a smile.

'Inside. Move the loose rock...it's there.' Then she pixilates and I'm left staring at the carving again.

'Nance? Nance what are you doing?' Charlie calls from the other side of the cove.

I beckon him over. 'Molly was just here. She said we

have to go back in and find a loose rock. The diary is in there.' I spread my arms and shrug.

'But it's soaking wet, everywhere. Nothing would keep dry in there.'

'Might as well look, now we're here.' I flick a droplet of water from the end of his chin and go back inside.

'If it's here, it can't be far, because there's hardly anywhere to look.' Charlie climbs up onto a rock and runs his fingers along a crevice between the top of the cave wall and roof. 'Ow, bloody barnacles are sharp.' He sucks his finger and I give him a tissue to dab at the shallow scratch.

'Can you feel any loose rocks?' I ask, as he returns to his task.

'Not so far.' A moment later he stops. 'Hang on, I think I felt something move then.' There's a bit of scrabbling around, a rustling of plastic, then he steps down from the rock and turns to me, a big grin on his face, a thick black bin-bag in his hand. 'Look, Nance,' he says, as he pulls an object from the bag. 'It's a tin box!

My heart leaps as I look at what appears to be an old assorted biscuit box in his hands. It's red, has a gold edging around the lid with pictures of various biscuits on the front and about 30cm square. 'Wow, let's get it open, quick.'

We go outside where there's more natural light, and sit on a couple of boulders while Charlie tries to prise the lid off. He exhales in frustration after a few moments. 'Bloody thing's not budging.' Running a thumb over a few sections of scratched metal, he says, 'Looks like Molly must have used a screwdriver or something to open it each time...and the way it's stuck on so tight, she must have tapped it down with a hammer to close it. Makes sense, as it has to be watertight.'

'Hmm. Let me see if I can find a sharp shell or rock.' There are plenty of small implements lying around in the sand, and I soon have the perfect wedge-shaped pebble. 'Here try that. Tip the tin upside down and give it a bash all around the edges with that pebble.'

It takes Charlie less than thirty-seconds to free the lid and inside, wrapped in three plastic bags is a little diary no bigger than 20cm by 25cm. Its cover is red velvet and the whole thing appears to be bone dry. 'This is amazing.' Charlie quickly flicks the pages revealing small, neat handwriting in black ink pen. 'Were so lucky it's undamaged.'

Nodding, I take the diary, pop it in the tin and stand up. 'Come on, husband of mine. The right place for reading hidden secrets is not on a damp, grey beach, with the wind whistling in our ears. Let's go home and sit by the fire with a Bailey's coffee. We'll concentrate better there.' I hold my hand out to him and he takes it, a big smile on his face.

'That sounds like a plan, Nancy.' He looks at the time on his phone. 'Nearly four o'clock. I'll call in and tell Abi I've found a lead and might not be back today. She can put that in her pipe and smoke it.'

As we make our way back up the beach, I remind myself to try and find out why Abi and Charlie aren't getting along. I mean, it's not as if I've much else on, is it?

Chapter Seven

'You'll singe those socks if you get them any closer to the flames, you crazy man.' I push Charlie's feet off the footstool which he's placed very close to the log burner, and make him shuffle his armchair further back. He grumbles and moans, but it's good humoured. 'In fact, come and sit on the sofa with me, then we'll both be able to read the diary at the same time.'

I get my own footstool, flop down on the sofa, and take a sip of my coffee. Perfect. Nothing like a Baileys coffee on a chilly evening to warm the cockles of your heart.

'Where're the biscuits?' Charlie asks, as he flops down next to me and pulls the diary out of the tin that we found in the cave.

'No biscuits. We'll be eating in a while…besides, it doesn't feel right having a jolly old time, given the task at hand.' I nod at the diary and a little wave of sadness washes over me.

Charlie pulls a sheepish expression. 'Yeah. I suppose. Okay, let's get started.'

Though the diary is small, it has lots of pages, and Molly's small handwriting means that there are three years' worth of thoughts here. Every entry is dated and underlined. Even the last one, which was a week before she died. The sneak preview I'd had of the sister's turbulent relationship as children, seems to have continued. The diary shows that Leanne was still treating her sister cruelly. Molly had written down lots of upsetting information about how she'd often been traumatised by her younger sister. One of the earliest entries from three years ago is hard to read, but we do.

I can never be absolutely sure that Leanne got rid of (killed) my pet rabbit when I was 8, or my goldfish that suddenly disappeared when I was 9, but I know she killed my cat, Marmalade. She often would say things like – "If you don't get that mangy stinky animal off my bed, I swear I'll end him and chuck him in the ocean." Or "That evil animal scratched me today when I stroked him. Talk about ungrateful. I'll show him who's boss one day." He's been missing 9 months now, so I doubt he'll be back. Whenever I ask Leanne if she has seen or heard of him, she'll always smile that sly little smile she has when she's done something evil, and use the sing-song voice that she pulls out when she's lying. And the clincher - she coughs to disguise her nervous laughter. I know 100% then that she's lying. I've known her all my life, I can always tell. My poor little Marmalade. But I can't prove it, can I? But would she REALLY do something so terrible?

Charlie jabs his finger at that page. 'See! I told you during the interview that Leanne did the cough to disguise her nervous giggle. I *knew* she was lying – this confirms it.'

'Certainly seems that way. I wonder why Molly put up with it all those years? And to kill her cat...that's just vile.'

We go back to the diary and read on. Charlie puts asterisks next to those entries which he thinks might help. A year ago, Molly writes:

Leanne dropped out of uni in her last year on a whim. Said English Lit was all too boring, and that she'd rather stack shelves at a supermarket. She didn't of course. She just lazed around at home doing sweet FA, while leeching off Gran as usual. Then a couple of weeks ago out of the blue, she begged me to help her to get the TA job that was going in my school. She'd applied for it, and would I put a good word in? That was the last thing I needed, having my sister working with me, as well as having to put up with her moods at home. But I did mention her name in passing to the head, just so I could tell Leanne I had done what she'd asked.

She didn't even get an interview, and I dreaded her response, but oddly, she was quiet about it and didn't moan to me or Gran about how unfair her life was, as I'd expected. The next day I got back from school, and noticed plumes of smoke and charred paper puttering into the air at the bottom of our garden. When I went to look what was going on, I saw Leanne throwing paper into an old tin oil-drum, and then poking it with a crowbar to disperse even more ash and smoke. Her face contorted with rage when I walked over and asked what she was doing. 'Making more work for you, big sister!' she yelled, and tipped a pile of books out of a black-bag by her feet onto the grass. My stomach clenched when I realised they were my classes' exercise books she was burning. Twenty-five of them. Year 6 SATs revision that I was going to mark this evening. I yelled at her, asked her what the hell she was doing it for, and she slapped me so hard across the face it made my head spin. I was so shocked I started to cry. Yes, she'd hit me often when we were kids, but we were grown women now for God's sake.

'You always have it so easy! Everything falls into your lap without trying.' She screamed into my face, her eyes bulging, face red, the veins standing out in her neck. 'Molly is so clever and pretty with it, Molly is so thoughtful, Molly knows how to do everything! Not like her younger, ugly sister. No.' Leanne was beside herself now, waving her arms and stabbing at the fire with the crowbar. 'Leanne is odd. Leanne can never stick at anything. She never has any friends.' My sister stopped and looked at me, bewildered, as if she was coming out of a trance.

I had no clue where all this was coming from, and I went to put my arm around her shoulder but she shoved me off. 'Nobody says those things about you, Leanne. Why do you think—'

'They do!!' She yelled. 'I heard the old bitch on the phone this morning talking to one of her friends. I always had an idea that she thought those things, but I couldn't be sure. Now I am.'

'You mean Gran?' I asked.

'No, the Queen of fucking Sheba. Yes, who else?!' was her response. Then she sat on the grass and sobbed. No matter what I did, I couldn't comfort her, then she started going on like she always did when she knew she'd gone too far – though this was a bit over the top, even for her – about how it had always been me and her against the world since

81

our parents died, about how Gran had tried her best, but she could never understand what it was like to be us. And the usual. Stuff about even though she was the younger one, she was tougher and had to protect me. Then came the apology, as always. How she was sorry, but I should have helped her get the job at my school, and she wondered if I really cared about her at all. She made me promise I would never leave her, and we'd always have each other to rely on. That no man would ever come between sisters.

Truth be told, I promised, because I was scared of her. She had a weird look about her, as if she was absent – her body was there, but her eyes looked…vacant. God knows what she would have done if I'd refused. I love my sister, and she did protect me from bullies growing up, but too often she was the bully. Leanne always said she was protecting me, trying to make me tough, but bruises and harsh words said otherwise. And now I've promised I'll never leave her. What the hell will she do when she finds out I've met someone and fallen in love?

Charlie and I look at each other.

'So this was the one she was going to marry,' I say.

'Yeah. Must be. I am a bit puzzled why this man hasn't come forward though…' Charlie rubs his chin. 'But then why would he? It was a tragic drowning, not a murder. We haven't interviewed anyone but Leanne.'

'Poor Molly. How awful that she never got her happy ending. I wonder if that's what tipped Leanne over the edge…you know, when she found out about Molly's lover? 'Possibly. But she sounds like she'd been pretty much on the edge all her life, reading these diary entries.'

We sit for a while, neither of us wanting to read any more. It's so tragic to think of a young woman, in love, her whole life ahead of her, cruelly killed like that, and by her own sister. Leanne's story is tragic too, because she's obviously seriously unwell. Maybe even a psychopath... I seem to remember that animal cruelty and killing is a common trait. I put my empty mug on the coffee table and sit back, with a sigh. 'I still don't get why Molly put up with it? She could have left any time. She had a job, and someone who loved her.'

Charlie shakes his head. 'Because of control. Leanne was obviously a master at it, and Molly had lived with it nearly all her life. The bit she wrote about Leanne protecting her, that would have been Leanne controlling her in reality. Those who are being controlled, rarely realise it. They make excuses for the ones dominating them, try to work around the bullying, try to make sense of it. Because in the end, they are supposed to be the ones who love them.'

'Yes, I can see that. It's all so sad.' I nod at the diary and squeeze his hand. 'Come on, let's finish it and get it over with.'

Molly's entry of two months ago reads:

Why does life have to be so cruel? First Rick leaves to visit his dad in America for 3 months, then Gran falls down the stairs and dies. I'm not sure I can carry on. Thank God I have Leanne to guide me through it all.

Once again, Charlie and I look at each other like a couple of meerkats on guard duty. 'She fell down the stairs? Really?' I say, incredulous.

The subtext is not lost on Charlie. 'Bloody hell. You reckon it was Leanne? I never asked how she died, not thinking it was relevant.'

'It would make sense, given what we know about her...and Leanne heard her gran on the phone saying all those things about her. Maybe she was so furious about it, she planned to get rid of her, and then she and Molly would have the house and everything.'

Charlie heaves a sigh and scrubs his fist along one side of his head. 'Yeah. But how the bloody hell can we prove it? We've nothing concrete. Neither have we proof that Leanne drowned her sister either. We have a diary, with just Molly's feelings about her sister, and her story about the things Leanne did. It's not enough. And falling down the stairs is a pretty common cause of death too.'

'Really?'

'Yeah. Particularly for the elderly.'

My gut is telling me I'm right, but it's also telling me that Charlie is too. 'Okay, let's read on with this entry and see if we can find anything more in the last few entries.'

Now that Rick's not around and Leanne is being so lovely, I think it's time to share my plans with her. When Rick's home we plan to marry, and I don't see why Leanne would be unhappy about that. We've got closer since Gran died, and while I would be moving out of here, so would she, as she was talking only the other day about us selling this place and using the profits to go on holiday and have fun. She'd have to buy another place to live, but there would be plenty of money left over from the house, and the savings, once I'd had my half. I'd still be keeping my promise to her, because surely she wouldn't see me marrying Rick as leaving her, as I'd still be here in Cornwall. We'd see each other all the time, and I'm sure she'd really like Rick, too.

In the early days he was a bit miffed as to why I wouldn't let him meet Leanne or Gran, poor love. So in the end I told him it was because Gran had some autoimmune illness and Leanne was funny about people coming to the house. I also said Leanne could behave oddly and suffers from anxiety and depression. Not sure he bought it, but I could hardly tell him the truth, could I? I can see now that all the stuff Leanne used to say about protecting me, was actually her controlling me. But I feel stronger since I met Rick, and the change in Leanne since Gran went is miraculous. At last, I pray I might get the happy ending that I only dared to dream about!

The poignancy of that renders us mute, so we move on to the last entry.

I was going to phone Rick and tell him the truth about my sister, and about what she said in response to our lovely news, but I couldn't. He would jump on a plane and be back like a shot, and that wouldn't be fair. He's only just tracked his birth-father down, and they are having such a lovely time getting to know each other. Leanne and I aren't speaking at the moment. After I told her I'd found someone and we were planning to marry, she told me I was the most thoughtless, evil, uncaring bitch of a sister, and threw my wine in my face. So I drew back my arm and slapped her. Me. The victim. I actually grew a pair and walloped her one! Maybe it was the straw that broke the camel's back.

Maybe it was because I have my wonderful Rick, and the fact that I don't feel so vulnerable anymore? Whatever the reason, I stood up for myself. And boy it felt good!

Though she was obviously in shock, there was no retaliation, no yelling. Nothing, apart from a threat. She stood there in the kitchen, round-eyed and ashen-faced, the red welt of my palm print standing in bold relief on her cheek, pointed a finger at me and said in an ice-cold voice – 'You won't get away with this. I won't let you.' That was two days ago, and we haven't spoken since. At first, I was upset, but then I started to think about all the times she'd hurt me, or something I'd loved, like Marmalade. All the times I'd felt useless, worthless and humiliated. All the times I'd pretended to Gran that the bruise on my face, or arm, was me just being clumsy, so not to upset her. All the times I'd had to lie to the few friends I'd managed to make, when they'd suggested they came over to my house, and I made a promise to myself. I said no more. No more will I allow her to dominate my life. Soon I'll be Mrs Trevelgue and she won't be able to hurt me anymore.

My sister needs help. Professional help. It's something I've suspected for some time, but never really allowed myself to fully admit. Thing is, she's such a good liar, nobody would believe me if I told them about the things she says and does. She would make me look the fool, and then the whole situation might get even worse. I don't think she'd really hurt me, not seriously, anyway. But I think she could make my life far worse than it is now, before Rick gets back and I can escape to his. Even though she's been so awful to me, she's my sister and I love her. It's not her fault she's like she is. To get her the help she needs I must be clever about this. Rick's a lawyer and he was only saying about a tough case he was working on before he left, that hard evidence is paramount. I knew this of course, but never has it been truer than now. I need evidence on my sister if I'm to get any help at all for her, and people to believe me, instead of her.

My heart thumps up the scale and I share a glance with my husband. I know we are both silently wishing that Molly is going to come up with a solution to nail Leanne. We look back to the diary entry...

This diary will be hidden in a sea cave down on Crantock Beach after I've finished this entry. There's no way I can risk Leanne finding it. There's no telling what she'd do. And I'm going to get her to admit to all the stuff she's done, and repeat her threat to me about not letting me get away with marrying Rick. I'll record it all on my phone, and hide it in the greenhouse under the old pots. She'll never find it there...hopefully. The cave is safer, but I can't risk a phone in there – if it got wet it would be useless. I won't let her win. I will get her the help she needs before she gets any worse...And it's time to fight for my future happiness. It's been a long time coming.

A sob breaks free despite me covering my mouth with my hand, and I say through my fingers. 'God this is heartbreaking. Absolutely fucking heartbreaking.'

Charlie pulls me into his arms and kisses the top of my head. 'It is. So, so sad.'

We sit in silence for a few moments letting it all sink in. Then a puzzle forms in my mind. 'Why on earth did Molly get drunk and go night swimming with Leanne? She knew she was unstable.'

Charlie considers this and says with a shrug, 'Maybe Leanne slipped a vodka or two in her drink and it went to her head? Or maybe Leanne had apologised and was being nice again – or pretending to. Molly might have believed she'd changed her mind about opposing her and Rick's relationship. She said in the diary entry that she didn't think Leanne would seriously hurt her, didn't she? Molly wanted to believe the best of her – years of control had conditioned her into that. She trusted Leanne.' He sighs and adds, 'In the end we will never know exactly what happened, I suppose.'

I nod. 'Now what?'

'Go to Leanne's and search the greenhouse, then take her back in for questioning. Hope Abi authorises it.'

That's all we need, Abi blocking him. 'Maybe I can help there. I'll speak to her. Tell her about the connection I made with Molly.' I think back a few years to when I helped Abi make a connection to solve a personal problem. She'd received hate mail at work, and told she was unfit to be in the police force. We discovered it was in fact her own sister writing the letters. The sister was a staunch Catholic and disapproved of Abi being in a gay relationship.

Charlie looks thoughtful. 'Hmm. Okay, thanks. But let's hope it doesn't come to that.'

I drop a kiss on his cheek and stand up. 'Right, that's enough misery and gloom for one night. I'll make the spag bol and then we can forget it all for a while.' He smiles up at me as I walk into the kitchen, but I can tell thoughts of everything we have just learned will be circling all night in his brain, hoping for the best outcome, like a vulture over carrion. I know this, because I've got my own vulture doing exactly the same.

Chapter Eight

Today will mainly involve going over to see Alison and the baby, to see if I can do anything to make their lives easier. I'm looking forward to it in a weird kind of way, because despite the stress of the whole situation, I'll be able to spend time with a baby again. I loved being a mum, and although it was all too short, I'll be forever grateful for each precious day I had with my Sebastian. When he was fist born, I remember being washed out and exhausted, and sometimes wished I could just have some sleep and time to myself. Now, I wish the Nancy back then could have been visited by myself now, to make sure she made every second count. But then knowledge of what was to come would have devastated her, and ruined the time she had with her boy. I sigh and wipe the toast crumbs from the kitchen table - *The past is the past, and there's nothing you can do to change it, Nancy. But you can try to make the present and future the best they can be.*

A bright yellow sun in a hard blue sky, draws sharp lines around the rooftops this morning. The muted rays of summer are long gone, and the nip in the air is more like a hefty pinch. On days like this, when sparkles of sunlight turn the navy ocean into a sequined scarf, and a mix of woodsmoke and salt perfumes the air, you can believe anything is possible. Inhaling a big breath of autumn, I jump in the car and set off. On the drive to Alison's through the narrow country lanes, I think about Charlie, and if he's got permission to look for Molly's phone. He seemed positive and upbeat this morning as I stood on the doorstep to wave him off, he even rustled a twig in a pile of red and gold autumn leaves by the gate for Scrappy to pounce on. I hope he's at Leanne's right now, and that he finds enough evidence on the phone, if it's there.

Alison waves from the window as I pull up on her driveway. She looks ten years older. Her lively caramel eyes are now dull, sitting upon cushioned bags, and her normally neat brown hair looks like shredded cardboard. Alison's bottom lip trembles as she opens the door. 'Thank God you've come, Nance. I don't think I could have coped much longer if you hadn't.'

'Hey, come on. It'll all be fine,' I say, ushering her in and closing the door behind me. I give her a quick hug and she stifles a sob as she leads the way into her homely kitchen, which today is a stage-set for a bombed-out house during the Blitz. Baby clothes are draped over every available surface – some clean, others not so clean, judging by the unsavoury aroma mingling with baby powder, and unwashed dishes piled high on the drainer. Bottles and sterilizing solution litter the countertop, and three mugs of unfinished tea, a half-eaten sandwich, and a cat bowl dot the table, like some abstract art installation.

'The baby's is asleep right now, miraculously. She

91

must have got wind of you coming.' Alison tries a weak smile, but is too exhausted to make it stick. 'Want a cup of something?'

I hold my hands up. 'No. You stay right where you are while I sort out the sink, tidy round a bit and make us a drink. Then you can go up to bed and leave everything to me.'

Immediately Alison's eyes fill. 'Thanks so, so much, Nancy.' Then she grabs a baby- wipe from a plastic pouch on the floor by her feet, and tries to blow her nose on it. 'Oh, I thought they were tissues...'She looks around, bewildered. 'What have I done with the tissues?'

'No clue.' I laugh and hand her a packet from my bag. 'Here have mine.'

Ten minutes later, the house is looking in better shape and Alison is sipping tea at the kitchen table, though she's barely awake. 'Organisation is key. I should be better at it, being a novelist, I always plan to the nth degree and know exactly where the story is going. But babies tend not to behave like characters in a book.' She does a hippo yawn and sighs.

'No. They do have a mind of their own...though I remember my friend Lucinda saying an author friend of hers never knows what's going on, and that her characters regularly take over and do some very surprising things!'

A yawn is her response.

'How long does baby sleep for normally? And is Tilly any closer to naming her?'

Alison shrugs. 'She can sleep for ten minutes or a few

hours. I can never call it. And lots of names have been discussed, but I think she's going with Ella, after a shortened version of her mum's name – Gabriella.'

'That's a gorgeous name.'

Alison nods, but I can tell she's rapidly running out of juice. A slow blink. 'Yeah.'

'Right, miss. Let's have you up to bed.' I take the mug from her fingers and pull her up from the chair. 'You'll feel like a new woman in a few hours, and I'm not going anywhere.' Slipping my arm through hers, I lead her to the bottom of the stairs. 'Where's Ella?'

'In the living room. There're disposable nappies on the sofa, and the formula is in the kitchen cupboard. All the instructions are by the microwave. The health visitor printed them off the other day and—'

'I'm on it. Off you go.' I clap my hands and shoo her upstairs. As soon as I clapped my hands, I wished I hadn't, but a thin wail coming from the room to my left, tells me it's too late, I've woken the baby. By the window is a Moses basket, and as I approach, a little fist appears, punching the air and the wailing gets louder. Ella, despite her yelling, is totally adorable. She has a tuft of dark hair, and a button nose, but I can't see the colour of her eyes, as her pink face is screwed up in frustration. She's dressed in a yellow baby grow dotted with pink cats, and the soft blue blanket with Peppa Pig's face on it, is fighting a losing battle against her kicking legs. She's gearing up for another yell, when I say, 'Hello, little one, my name's Nancy. Pleased to meet you.'

Ella immediately stops, and opens her eyes. They're

blue, but then most babies have blue eyes at her age. I think these will stay blue though, as Tilly has the same light shade. Her breath hitches as the sobs subside and she eyes me with curiosity, punching the air with her fist again and wriggling her body. I pick her up and cradle her close to me, the crown of her head with her tuft of hair is so soft, and has that indefinable 'baby' smell. Without warning, a rush of emotion surges through me like an oncoming tide, and I'm right back in a lemon and white bedroom, surrounded by cuddly toys, with my boy. My Sebastian. 'Oh Sebastian,' I whisper and close my eyes, but tears squeeze through my lashes and trickle down my cheeks. I take some deep breaths to gather my senses, and try to bring myself back to the present.

'It will all be okay, Mummy. Teach Tilly.'

My eyes fly open at the sound of a little boy's voice, and I scan the room, but my heart sinks as I realise Sebastian has chosen not to appear in person today. Bless him. Though his visit was fleeting, and his message brief, it was no less powerful. I'd been thinking about having a word with Tilly, and trying to help her accept Ella, and my boy's message confirmed that's what I should do. Relief edges grief to one side, as I think of his words. *It will all be okay.* I truly hope so, because this little girl needs her mum.

Ella wriggles in my arms and looks like she's ready to resume her complaints, so I lift her from my chest and do a 'poo sniff test' of her nappy. Hmm, not poo, but she definitely needs changing. I spy a changing mat, wet-wipes and nappies by the sofa, and lay her gently down. This isn't something she's keen on, so I talk to her in a sing-song voice, while I clean her up and put her a dry nappy on. 'Now, my little monkey. How about a bottle, hey?'

The little monkey is not exactly yelling, but she's makes one or two moans and snuffles as I sort out her bottle with one hand, while jiggling on my shoulder with the other. I sing a lullaby and coo in her ear as I do it. There's no way I dare put her down, or she'll start wailing again big time, get herself in a state and wake up poor Alison. This is something I know from experience, and neither Alison nor Tilly have that in their tool box, which of course makes looking after a baby even more difficult. Soon I think I have the bottle cool enough, but squirt a bit on my wrist to make absolutely sure. Then sitting down in a comfy armchair by the radiator, I wrap Ella securely in a blanket and offer her lunch.

Ten minutes later, it's gone, and Ella's looking at me with interest. I convince myself she's smiling at me, but I think it's probably wind, so hitch her onto my shoulder and a few gentle taps on her back confirms my suspicion, as I'm rewarded with a little burp. Okay, now what? She won't want to sleep straight away I don't think, so entertainment is needed. There's a boxed 'jungle play centre' by the door. which looks just the ticket, and I place her back on the mat while I assemble it. Luckily it takes only a few minutes, and it's comprised of a colourful padded mat, and over the top is an arch, full of dangling jungle animals. Some squeak and some rustle. There's also a plastic button, that when pressed, plays nursery rhymes. Excellent.

I place Ella on the mat and immediately her face lights

up, her arms and legs flail and kick, and her eyes grow round as she looks at all the colourful creatures jiggling above her head. I squeak and rustle them for her, and she becomes even more animated. 'You like this, don't you, Ella?' She glances at me and then back to the rustling, obviously enjoying it all immensely. I remember my mum telling me that Sebastian might be bored when he was very tiny, because he'd been changed, fed and winded, but wouldn't stop yelling. I didn't believe her at first, but we got him a play centre like this, and he loved it just as much as little Ella. Smiling, I hold a finger to the palm of her hand and she grasps it and wiggles her legs. 'Ella is a beautiful name. It is, yes it is, just like you,' I coo. Then I startle when I hear the living room door close behind me. I look round.

'I haven't decided on a name yet. Ella is just an option.' Tilly's standing there glaring at me. She's wrapped in a yellow blanket over PJs that have dubious stains on them, and mud spatters on her bare feet. Her swimming-pool eyes are red rimmed, and her long chocolate curls haven't seen shampoo for days. This poor girl is a mum, but she could really do with one herself right now. 'Where's Alison, anyway?'

Realising I have to be careful with my response, I smile and move to the side a little. 'She's having a sleep, I came round to help. Come and sit down with us. Your baby seems to love this new activity centre.'

Tilly pulls the blanket tight around herself and looks away. 'She's only days old. Too young for that.' I tell her what my mum told me all those years ago. 'Hm.' She perches on the edge of an armchair. 'How old is your son now?'

'He would have been almost eighteen...he died when he was three months old,' I say gently.

Tilly's face falls. 'Oh my god, same age as me...how sad.'

'Yes it was, but I'm lucky, because he still visits from time to time.' I tell a bemused Tilly all about my gift and she sits in silence, but I can tell she's very sceptical, as she shakes her head every now and then. So I tell her that the only reason we found her that day in Jackdaw wood, was because her mum's spirit visited me.

'You're having a laugh,' Tilly snaps, and her eyes narrow in suspicion.

'Nope. It's true. I made a connection with your Peppa Pig mug.'

An eye roll. 'Yeah, course you did. When I asked Alison what you were doing in the wood with her, she said you were just up there visiting the church, so I know you're telling fibs.' She stands up and moves to the door. 'Anyway, can you tell Alison I came round? I'm gonna go back next door to grab some lunch. Bye.'

Damn it. Alison must have kept Gabriella's visit from her, so as not to freak her out. Now I've done exactly that, and Tilly's not even had contact with her daughter. 'Look, why not stay here and I'll make you lunch? I could make some soup and a sandwich. You might keep an eye on Ell...I mean, the baby.'

She hesitates by the door, glances back at Ella, and I notice a flicker of affection pass across her face and she's transformed. Just as quickly, she's back to her tired, weary and resentful self. 'Hm. Okay, as long as you don't chat any more shit about spirits.'

I laugh. 'Promise.'

Luckily, Alison's got a well-stocked cupboard and fresh veg, so I make a vegetable soup with croutons, and a cheese and ham toasted sandwich. Every now and again, I sneak out into the hall, and peep through the crack in the living room door to see how Tilly's doing with Ella. The baby is still happily watching the colourful arch of creatures and listening to music, but although Tilly sits nearby, there's no interaction that I can see, sadly.

'Lunch is served, madam,' I say in a jokey tone as I bring the soup and sandwich in on a tray, and set it on the dining table by the patio doors. 'How's the baby?'

Tilly gets up from the floor and comes over. 'Okay, I think. She's normally yelling the place down, so I reckon you must have the magic touch.' She shrugs and sits at the table. 'Or maybe she just doesn't like me and Alison.'

'That's not true. She'll be picking up on the fact that you're both stressed out and tired. Neither of you have had experience with babies either, they don't come with a handbook, and it's a tough job. I can tell you that from my own experience.'

Tilly sighs and nods at the sandwich. 'What's in that?' I tell her. 'Right, I'm a bit hungry, to be honest.'

This passes for a thank you, and she sits and demolishes the lot in record speed. I wonder when the poor kid has last eaten. I remember Alison saying earlier that Chris, her dad, couldn't get her to eat, so this is a good sign, surely. 'You'll feel better with something inside you.' I put the empty plate and soup bowl on the tray and push it to one side. 'Have you been sleeping?' Her red rimmed eyes tell me the answer to that, but I want to get her chatting.

Shoving her fists into her eye sockets and giving them a good rub, she replies, 'Yes and no. I lie awake wondering about what the hell is going to happen to the baby...' She looks at me and away. '...to Ella. I don't know how to look after her, and to be fair, I don't even want to. Think the best thing is for her to go to adoptive parents who'll really want her and give her a good life.'

Her eyes fill and she swallows hard. All I want to do is give her a big hug, but I'm sure she wouldn't appreciate that. I say, 'Maybe you could give her a good life yourself, with help from people who know what they're doing. You have a midwife or health visitor, and she will give you information on classes and drop-in centres where you could meet other mums. And you have your dad and Alison to give you support. Me too, come to that.' I finish on what I hope is a winning smile, but I'm met with a blank expression.

'And everyone lived happily ever after, eh?' Tilly dashes away the tears with the edge of the blanket, folds her arms and looks out of the patio doors. We both silently watch a flurry of ochre and red leaves drift from the trees, and settle on the lawn like confetti.

Maybe she's a right to be angry. I did sound as if I was painting too rosy a picture, though I didn't mean to. She might not like it, but she deserves honesty. 'No. I wasn't saying that, really. It will be a hard slog, really hard, and you might feel like giving up at times. Thing is, I believe you can do it. You have to want to do it, and I reckon deep down that you do. At least give Ella a chance, please?'

Tilly's head snaps back round. 'A chance! Yeah, that's what I *would* be doing if I gave her up. Giving her a chance. What kind of life could I make for her, eh? I made a total fuck up of mine. One of the cleverest students in the school, all set to go to uni and eventually get a teaching job maybe, but what did I do? Allowed some cheating scumbag to get into my knickers, because he said he loved me. And I fell for it – how stupid was that? Not as clever as I thought, was I?' Silent tears are coursing down her cheeks now, but she doesn't wipe them away. I don't think she even notices. This is her normal right now.

I have to swallow hard before I reply. What do I say? I want to make her feel better, but whatever comes out of my mouth won't be listened to. She's not in the right frame of mind, but I have to try. I go to take her hand but decide better of it and place my palm on the table. 'Hey, you are clever. He took advantage of you, being that much older and experienced. It's a cliché, but you're not the first to end up in this situation, and you won't be the last, sadly. But it doesn't make you stupid.'

Tilly shakes her head. 'Yet here we are. I'm seventeen, buggered up my A' levels, no uni place in sight, and even if there was – what would I do with her?' She nods over at Ella who's obviously bored of being on the mat. She's snuffling in frustration and punching the air. Clear signs of gearing up for a crying fit. 'Without proper qualifications, I wouldn't be able to get a decent job, so I'd be sponging off my dad. He's not what you called exactly thrilled at having a surprise granddaughter anyway, so that scenario would be just wonderful, wouldn't it?'

She makes a good case, but things don't have to be so gloomy. 'As I said, it will be tough. But maybe you could re-sit your A'levels, and maybe defer your uni place until next year, or even a for few years more. Once Ella is old enough for nursery, maybe then you could juggle things around, and still go for your dreams. And as I also said, there are people to help you, Tilly. You wouldn't have to do it all by yourself.'

Ella interrupts with an ear-splitting yell and I hurry over to her. 'Come on, munchkin, time for another nap I think.' I walk her up and down for a few moments while she quietens a little, and my gut tells me to give her to her mum. 'Wanna hold her?' I ask, with a hopeful smile.

'Erm, I think I might pass, as she's a bit grouchy. I'm not much good with her when she's happy...which isn't very often.' Tilly's expression is apologetic, yet wistful. The wistful makes me bold.

'Here you go. Just take her and see what happens. I'm here to help.' Mindful of Sebastian's instruction I add, 'I'll teach you, don't worry.'

Tilly heaves a sigh and stands up. 'Now what?'

'Take her and hold her upright against your chest and shoulder, like I did. Firmly to make her feel secure, but not too firm.'

She does as I say, and Tilly's face soon relaxes into a smile as she rests her cheek against Ella's head. The baby wriggles and sends up a wail, and immediately Tilly goes rigid, and starts jiggling Ella, patting her back too hard. This obviously doesn't help, and the wail becomes a yell. Anxiety pinches the young woman's lips into a grimace, and she wrenches Ella away from her chest, 'Here take her back. She hates me.'

'No, she doesn't. She can detect your stress, that's all. Take some deep breaths.'

'I can't. I hate it when she cries like this, take her!' Tilly yells, which makes Ella screech all the more.

Torn between taking the baby and telling Tilly to try again, I say, 'Okay. I know it's hard, but please hold her like you did before, speak gently to her and—'

'I can't!' Tilly's shrieks are louder than Ella's now, so I step forward to take her, just as Gabriella does the 'on switch' right by her daughter's side. She's wearing jeans and a green jumper, with her dark hair in a messy bun. It's incredible how real she looks.

Gabriella blinks away tears, and hovers a hand over both her daughter and granddaughter's head. 'My poor girls,' she murmurs, and looks at me, desperation in her eyes. 'Please. Tell Tilly to sing the song I used to sing to her at bedtime, when she was little. She sang it too.'

Easier said than done. Tilly's practically thrusting her daughter into my arms while sobbing her heart out, and she's already let me know how she feels about my gift. 'Tilly, stop. Please listen!' I hold her shoulders firmly with both hands and make her look at me. 'Your mum's here and said you should sing the old song to Ella that she taught you.'

'W...what?' She says with a shuddering sigh and looks around, Ella now clasped protectively to her chest. 'You're joking, right?'

'No. She's standing to your left looking at you both and smiling through her tears. She says she loves you very much, Tilly. Ella too.' I can hardly get my words past the knot of emotion in my throat.

The wonder aflame in her eyes turns to suspicion in seconds. 'How do I know you're not making it up? Everybody probably has a lullaby they learned from a parent.'

I look at Gabriella. She wipes away her tears on the back of her sleeve and sighs. 'It's the one about the little lamb that's lost its way – Someone to Watch Over me. Tell my baby I will always be here to watch over her, and that she will be a wonderful mum. Tell her thank you for naming my granddaughter after me.' Then Gabriella starts to pixilate, rearranging bits of herself like an unfinished jigsaw.

'No. Don't go yet,' I say, but it's too late. She's gone.

'Don't tell me. You were talking to my mum?'

'I was. But she's gone now.'

I get an eye roll. 'Of course she has.' Tilly looks at her daughter who is quieter, but still distressed. 'Can you take her now, please? Or I can put her on the mat. Either way, I'm out of here.' She walks past me towards the play centre.

'Wait. She had a message for you, love.' I tell her what Gabriella said, but find I get choked up in the middle, as all my own feelings about Sebastian's loss crash into me.

Tilly's shocked face crumbles and she holds Ella close, kissing her head over and over, her tears dampening the little tuft of downy hair. 'Oh Mum,' she manages eventually, while looking out at the leaves once more, swirling on the lawn. 'Oh, Mum, I miss you so much, and thank you for watching over me.'

I sit at the table noting that Ella is now quiet, because her mum is calming down and she's holding her to her chest, while moving from foot to foot in a rocking motion. Instinct is kicking in. I smile and wipe my eyes. Thank God. Then I have to grab another handful of tissues from my bag, as Tilly starts to hum quietly in Ella's ear, and then sing the beautiful song her mum asked her to. It's punctuated by a few pauses and sniffs as she tries to keep her emotions in check, but it's doing the trick, and soon Ella's asleep.

Tilly sits at the table and gives me a wobbly smile. 'Thank you, Nancy, for everything,' she whispers. 'I'm sorry for being rude, but it all sounded properly weird to be honest…but I know you are genuine after my mum said…' Choked up again, her words are swallowed and she shakes her head.

'No need to apologise. And I hope you'll take on board what I said about Ella. I think you can make it work, if you let others help you.'

She nods. 'After today, I'm going to give it everything I have. My mum believes in me, so I have to as well.'

Unable to reply, I nod and pat her hand. This young woman has a long way to go before she gets where she needs to be, but she's stronger than she thinks, and thanks to Gabriella, she's made the first few crucial steps along the path.

Chapter Nine

My heart's singing as I zip back home through the falling leaves, the sun low in the sky, playing hide and seek through the bare branches of the trees lining the lanes. I'm not naïve enough to think that everything will be plain sailing now for Tilly and Ella, but I have a feeling that the baby won't be going to another home anytime soon. I'll call Alison later and see how things are. I left her sleeping peacefully, and Tilly playing with her daughter on the activity mat, so fingers-crossed all is well. Alison is going to be pretty shocked at the transformation in her next-door neighbour. Hopefully, she'll be able to get back to her life a little more now too.

My stomach grumbles, reminding me I skipped lunch, and I plan to rectify that with one of the freezer-to-oven Cornish pasties I made the other day. An image of a cherry scone presents itself too. *No, Nancy, you can't have both.* My past life in the café and bakery has mixed blessings. Great that I can make such delicious food, but not so great that I want to eat it all. I glance at my tummy, which is developing a little middle-age paunch. Maybe I'll go for a walk later, get a bit of exercise, and take in a visit to Mel's house by the estuary at the same time. Although she lives next door to my mum and Rory, I've not seen her for ages, and I'm dying to know if she's using her psychic gift outside the spiritualist meetings.

My mind goes back to last year when I had a strong connection to her, but didn't know why. She was helping me try to find Rory who was missing at the time, and I sensed she was a lonely and troubled young woman, but something more than that was going on. I couldn't put my finger on it. Then it all became clear when her mum's spirit visited us as we sat chatting, and I passed on her message to Mel. Mel then broke down and confessed she saw spirits too, but had been sworn to secrecy by her parents. Their daughter was having a tough time already, being the only mixed-race girl in the school. If the other children found out she was psychic, they would have had a field day. Mel was so relieved she'd at last found someone else like herself, and we became friends. She and Penny hit it off when I introduced them, and Mel helped out at the spiritualist church now and then, so she could get used to using her gift. I try to remember when we last met up, and am surprised to find that it was almost three months ago at Abi's BBQ in the summer. Mel is dating Abi's brother and things seem to be going well there. Maybe Mel could give me an insight into what's upsetting Abi lately. It would certainly help Charlie if he knew what was troubling his boss.

As I pull up outside Seal Cottage, my plans of a pasty, a walk and a visit, are put on hold when I see Lucinda's small frame, coming towards me down the side of the house from the direction of my office. She seems to have

107

grown younger since last year, looking mid-twenties instead of early thirties. Her close-cropped black hair is now shoulder length, and her honey-coloured eyes are smudged with grey eyeliner, making them seem even larger behind the tortoiseshell glasses. Softer and sure of herself, is the way I'd describe her, and when she speaks, she's lost that booming superior tone. 'Nancy! I'd lost hope of seeing you. Just popped in on the off chance.' We hug and I notice she's thicker round the middle. Then I remember her news, and hold her at arm's length.

'You're pregnant! I'd forgotten for a moment, as I've been rushed off my feet lately, and haven't had a second to myself.' She beams and turns pink. 'And don't you look wonderful.' I release her, and lead the way back down the path to the summerhouse. 'Let's have a cuppa and a catch up.'

'Are you sure you have time?' she asks, following on. 'I'd hate to interrupt, given you're so busy.'

'Never too busy for a friend. And you can join me in a pasty, if you've not already eaten. A scone too?' I chastise myself for breaking my 'only eat one of the two' rule, as I unlock the double doors.

A little while later, we're tucking into hot pasties, with a buttered cherry scone and a cup of hot chocolate waiting in the wings. 'These are so delicious, Nancy. I'd forgotten what a good baker you are.' Lucinda smiles, and dabs at the corners of her mouth with a bit of kitchen roll. 'Mind you, all I'll be fit for is a snooze after I've demolished this lot.'

I laugh and wag a finger. 'Nonsense. You're eating for

two now, as my old Gran would have said. And a snooze is absolutely necessary on chilly winter afternoons.' I take a sip of my drink and nod at her tummy. 'So, tell me all about it. How far along are you?'

'Just coming up to six months. It was a proper old shock.' Her face flushes and she shakes her head. 'Don't get me wrong. I have got the hang of things now in the bedroom department, thanks to your advice last year, but we were taking precautions.' She shrugs. 'Must be part of a greater plan.'

I chuckle as I remember Lucinda had asked me for advice, as she'd never slept with anyone before William. Her mum and gran had died, and because of her odd manner and brusque personality, she'd not had any female friends to confide in. Though she has definitely mellowed and softened around the edges. 'Life does have a way of surprising us, that's for sure,' I reply.

'We're both over the moon though. I'd never even considered having children...or a husband, come to that. I was set to go through life as an old spinster not so long ago.' Lucinda takes a sip of hot chocolate and dabs her mouth again. 'I'll have to get someone to work in the bookshop with Will, when I go off on maternity leave. Do you know of anyone?'

Mel crossed my mind briefly, probably because she'd been so recently on it when I'd arrived back here. I know she works part-time at the local supermarket, but maybe she'd fancy a change? 'I might do. I'll ask when I see her next and let you know.'

She thanks me, then brushing a few pastry crumbs from

109

her fluffy red jumper, Lucinda nods at the scone. 'Not sure I could manage that now after the pasty.' Then mischief twinkles in her eyes. 'But bugger it, I'm going to have a damn good try.'

'That's my girl. Talking of which, do you want a girl or a boy?'

'Either is fine. I've been making a list of male and female names, and I'll show them to Will once it's complete.' How very Lucinda, organised to a fault. 'But he might have one or two ideas of his own.' Lucinda bites into the scone and then covers her mouth, her eyes round. 'Oh! I almost clean forgot the main reason I came here,' she mumbles through the scone. 'Well apart from catching up with you, of course.'

I laugh. 'Let's be knowing then.'

After washing the mouthful down with a sip of hot chocolate, she says, 'William's uncle Mike is a fisherman, well, he was – retired now. But he does still have his lobster creels, because he said he'd go crazy not being on the sea at all.' Lucinda leans forward and lowers her voice as if we might be overheard. 'Thing is, he's having his creels sabotaged. Almost every week, there's at least two that have been lifted and the nets cut. They cost a fortune to replace, and his wife Debbie is doing her nut. She's saying he should pack it in, but Mike's determined to find out who's doing it, and when he does, he says he's going to make them pay.'

'How awful. Has he any idea who it could be?'

'Not really. He has lots of mates who are fishermen, but he can't think of anyone who would do such a thing.

They're a tight-knit lot in St Ives.' Lucinda grabs her bag from the side of the coffee table and pulls out a carrier. 'In here is Mike's old fishing hat. I thought you could use it to try to make a connection. You know, to see if you could get any clues as to who the culprit might be?' Her eyes are shining with excitement now, and I can tell she's taken up with the drama of the whole situation.

My 'things to do' list is growing longer by the day, and I'm worried I'll be spreading myself too thin. But it wouldn't take long to make a connection, as long as a quick follow up wasn't required. 'I can certainly try. How urgent is it though, as I do have one or two other—'

'Not urgent, don't you worry.' Lucinda flaps a hand. 'Maybe in the next few days or so?'

'Yes, no problem. I'll let you know.'

We talk babies for the next half hour and as I'm waving Lucinda off, the phone rings and it's Charlie. 'We've found Molly's phone in the greenhouse, thank God! It took long enough to get Abi to agree to going round there. In the end, I said I'd call you, so you could chat to her about your connection with Molly, but she said no need, as she believed me.'

'Thank goodness,' I say, walking into the cottage to a yowling Scrappy. 'Time for more food already?'

'Eh?'

'Sorry, talking to Scrappy.'

'Right. Well, we found loads of unpleasant information on the phone recording. Not about the murder of her gran, obviously, but she admitted to killing the cat. Said it bit her,

111

so she wrung its scrawny neck and chucked it in the Atlantic.'

My heart lurches and I scoop Scrappy up and bury my face in his fur. 'That's just so awful,' I mumble into the phone.

'Yes, Leanne's certainly a nasty piece of work. She tried to justify it by saying any animal that bites a human needs to go. She admitted to all the horrible things she did to Molly while they were growing up too, but again, justified it by explaining that she was trying to make her tough. It was the two of them against the world, and if Molly didn't toughen up, she'd be walked all over. Leanne said their gran was a worse than useless old cow, and she wasn't sad she'd died.'

I sigh and sprinkle biscuits into Scrappy's dish. 'Did you find anything on the recording about Leanne's threat to Molly, after Molly had slapped her?'

'Yes. Molly asked her what she meant by – You won't get away with this, I won't let you. And she said that Molly had promised that no man would come between them, but she'd broken the promise. So she had to pay, somehow, sometime. Molly asked her what exactly she meant by that. Leanne said that it was a secret, and it would happen when she least expected it.'

I let my breath out with a whoosh. 'Bloody hell. That should help with the enquiry, shouldn't it?'

Charlie did his own release of breath back down the line. 'You'd think so, but in the end we have nothing concrete. It's enough to raise a question over Leanne's state of mind, perhaps, but how could we prove that Leanne had drowned her sister on just that, and the fact she'd been cruel to her and killed her cat?'

Hope withers on the vine as I realise the truth of his words. 'Hmm. So, what now?'

'I'm damned if I'm letting this go. We're pulling Leanne in again for questioning. Abi said it would be pointless, but I remember the way Leanne volunteered stuff about herself last time, like she was bragging, you know? So maybe she'll say more than she intends to this time. But that's all we've got right now.'

Something clenches in my gut. I can see a good outcome to this, but I don't know exactly how Charlie will pull it off. 'All you can do is stick to your guns and call her bluff. You'll be home late then, I'm guessing?'

'Yeah, probably. Cross your fingers for me, love.'

I blow a kiss down the phone. 'Everything crossed here, sweetheart. See you soon.'

***

The evening involves more baking, freezing, and a phone call to Alison. She's over the moon that I managed to make such a great change in Tilly, and can't believe she's actually taken her daughter home. Chris apparently is similarly astonished and pleased, and Alison feels more like herself after her four-hour sleep.

'Just happy I could help. And don't forget, I couldn't have done it without help from Gabriella.'

'Of course, but Gabriella couldn't have helped without you either.'

113

'A joint effort,' I concede.

'You must come back in a few days or so and see us. Tilly can't stop talking about you, and her mind is blown with your PI stuff.'

I laugh. 'Just try and keep me away. I adore Ella.' We end the call and my mind floats back to the early days of being a mum, and I smile, even though my heart aches.

Another hour has me watching a comedy show, while ostensibly watching the clock. Nearly 10pm and no sign of Charlie. Poor love. Hope it means he's getting somewhere with Leanne. I notice the carrier bag with the hat in that Lucinda brought over, on the table by the door, and decide to try and make a connection. I can't concentrate on anything else right now, so might as well.

The hat is a blue and white striped beanie that has seen better days. I clear my mind and clasp it to my chest, take a few deep breaths and relax. Nothing for a few moments, and then a bolt of electricity shoots along both wrists and across my chest. Another beat and every nerve in my hands jump, and my fingers twitch and tingle so much, I almost lose my grip on the hat. Then, slowly, at the edges of my mind, a picture takes shape of a whitewashed cottage set on a steep road overlooking the sea. It looks a bit like St Ives…then the little harbour comes into focus and yes, it's definitely St Ives. I open my eyes, and on the back wall, watch a 'rolling film' connection of a tall, thick set man, wearing this beanie. He has a pleasant weather-beaten face, and salt and pepper curls poke out from under the hat and along his collar. Must be William's uncle Mike. As he

114

strides towards a little fishing boat, he zips up a red waterproof jacket and whistles a jaunty tune. Obviously a man happy in his work.

The next scene is Mike hauling a broken creel onto the deck. He curses and his pleasant brown eyes narrow in frustration. He's shouting something that the wind snatches at, which I think is 'Bastard, not again!' and kicks the creel along the deck, furious that his catch has been taken and someone has sabotaged his work once more. He turns the boat for home, thoroughly dejected.

I think that's all I'm going to get, until the playing card effect grabs my attention with a :

SNAP – A boat under the stars in an ink-black sky. Gloved hands hauling up a creel. A lobster is pulled from it and thrown overboard.

SNAP – the thick netted rope is snipped to pieces, with what looks like small bolt croppers.

SNAP – A woman's moonlit silhouette outside a whitewashed cottage.

SNAP – A woman's face. Her expression sad, yet determined. She wipes a tear …and then nothing…I'm looking at my living room wall again.

I take a moment to come back to myself and try to process what I've seen. This is a puzzle. Why is she sabotaging the creels, if she isn't taking the lobsters? Why is she so sad about it? Is she ashamed? Has she got a grievance against Mike? Even if she has, why wouldn't she keep the catch?

It's too late to ring up Lucinda and describe the woman to her, so I decide to get my pencils out, and try and sketch

115

her likeness before it fades from my mind's eye. This method has never failed in the past, and I'm hoping this time won't prove the exception to the rule. An hour later, I'm looking at a woman in her late fifties, or early sixties, greying hair styled into an asymmetric bob, and thick dark eyebrows sit above cautious olive-green eyes. Yes, that's the woman I saw...her nose could do with being a bit longer, but overall, I'm pleased with the likeness.

'Who are you, and why are you sabotaging poor Mike's creels?' I ask her. The woman doesn't answer – there's no gut feeling, no inkling, nothing. Yawning, I shove the sketch pad to one side and look at the time again. Just gone eleven. No good messaging Charlie, he will be home when he's ready. Scrappy looks up from his chair by the fire, and gives me a silent meow. I smile. 'No more food for you, mister.' I give him a stroke under the chin and make my way upstairs. Let's hope tomorrow will bring some answers for Mike, and hopefully for my Charlie too.

Chapter Ten

I wake to the sound of rumbling, followed shortly afterwards by the weight of Charlie's arm flung across the top of my head. Sliding out from under it, I realise the rumbling is the ridiculously loud snoring coming from underneath the duvet, tucked around his head. How the hell can he breathe swaddled up like that? About to untuck him, a swift kick to my shin and a low moan makes me think again, and I slip out of bed and pad across to the ensuite. Poor Charlie must have been exhausted when he crashed into bed next to me in the early hours. I vaguely remember it, but was too sleepy to speak to him. I wonder if he managed to get any more information from the loathsome Leanne?

I pull the flush and examine my reflection in the bathroom mirror. Tired and pale is my assessment. Maybe I'll ask Penny about the tinted moisturiser she always uses. I could do with perking up a bit, but then we *are* heading for winter. Hmm. I think I look old. Red hair, green eyes and pale skin might suit some younger women, but when you're forty-four a few added crow's feet under the eyes can tend to make you look a bit washed out. I yawn, splash water on my face and then smooth a finger over my wrinkles. A smile curves my lips, because I can almost hear my gran clicking her tongue against the roof of her mouth, and saying – *You can't hold back time, maid, no matter what you do. Live your life and stop worrying about things you can't change.* She's right. I need to count my blessings and keep this smile on my face.

Over breakfast, I pull out the sketch I did last night and look at the woman's face again. Allowing my mind to focus on her cautious olive-green eyes, I wait to see if anything will come to me. But no. Nothing. I don't even feel a remote inkling about who she is and why she's sabotaging Mike's creels. The kitchen clock tells me it's still too early to phone Lucinda, so I pour more coffee and find myself doodling on a clean page. I'm surprised to find a little while later, that I've drawn some cows in a field, a horse and some geese in a large farmyard and farmhouse. The hills behind them look a little familiar, but I can't immediately bring the setting to mind. Why have I drawn all this, and where is it? My hand moves over the page again and quickly sketches a gate with the beginnings of a sign fixed to it. I want to write the name of the farm, but it won't come to me. It's there, hovering in my mind, but it's jumbled, just out of reach. I think it begins with a K, but that's all. I write the letter K on the sign and then push it to one side. No good forcing it. Hopefully it will come to me at a later date.

I'm still puzzling over the farm picture, and wondering if the sketch is actually anything important, or just a mindless sketch, when Charlie comes into the kitchen, his hair stood on end as if he's put his fingers in a socket.

There're dark circles under his eyes and he does a hippo yawn. 'Morning, love. Any coffee going?'

'Yep. And a bacon sandwich if you want one?'

I get a lopsided grin as he pulls his dressing gown on. 'That would be bloody marvellous, Nance. Can't remember when I last ate.'

'Any joy with Leanne?' I ask, as I set a mug of coffee in front of him.

Charlie takes a grateful sip and nods. 'Yeah, thank God. Let me wake up properly and I'll tell you all about it.'

I quickly stick bacon under the grill and cut some thick slices of homemade bread, while Charlie alternately sips coffee, yawns, and scratches his head. Though I'm dying to hear all about his interview, I know I'll get no sense out of him until he's had his coffee and woken up a bit. A squirt of brown sauce over the bacon and the sandwich is ready. Although I had cereal and toast earlier, my mouth is watering a bit as the delicious aroma of coffee and bacon fills the kitchen. Maybe half a slice of bread with that extra little rasher I put on the grill 'by mistake' wouldn't hurt. The truthful side of me asserts that I put an extra rasher on, with the full knowledge that I was going to eat it all along, so I tell it to shush.

'Okay, then,' I say, sitting opposite him at the table and taking a bite from my half-sandwich. 'Wor hapren?'

'Wor hapren?' Charlie repeats with a grin. 'Nor soor you're spleaking English. Didn't your mum ever tell you not to speak with your mouth full?'

I smile, swallow my food, and dab brown sauce from the side of my mouth. 'I said what happened?'

'Wiv wor?' He asks, with his own mouth full.

'With Leanne. Stop messing about, I'm dying to know.'

Charlie finishes his mouthful and takes a swig of coffee. 'You aren't gonna believe this, Nance, but she confessed to the murder of Molly and her grandmother!' He sits back, eyes dancing while he watches my incredulous expression.

'Shut up. You're having me on!'

'No. It's true.' I have to wait a few moments until he demolishes more of his sandwich. 'At first she just laughed, when I suggested she'd made good on her threat to punish Molly for letting a man come between them. I kept taunting her with the phone recording, and the diary, but she folded her arms and said I had Jack Shit on her. That it was all just supposition, that the conversation on the phone between her and her sister didn't incriminate her at all, apart from in a 'cat murder', and we had no evidence to suggest that she harmed Molly. All true, sadly.'

'So how come she confessed?'

Again, I have to wait while Charlie finishes eating, and I pop the rest of my half-sandwich in my mouth as he pushes his plate away. 'Abi pulled me out of the interview and said we had to let Leanne go. I knew she was right, and so went back into the room, about to do just that, when I suddenly had an idea.' He looks a bit sheepish and won't meet my eye. 'Not sure you'll approve, but it's done, and we got the result we needed.' Charlie shuffles on his chair and pokes a few breadcrumbs round his plate.

'Let's be having it then.' I take a sip of coffee and wait. 'He knows I don't really approve of fibs and white lies to get a confession, and imagine it's something along those lines.

To the table he says in a rush, 'I ended the interview, and as I was showing her out of the building, I just mentioned that Molly had appeared to you and told us the truth about how she died. That's how we found the diary and phone.'

My mouth drops open in shock and I shake my head at him. The tips of his ears have gone as pink as his cheeks, and he looks like a naughty schoolboy, as well he might. 'Charlie. How could you, without asking me first? You know how I feel about my gift being used like that. It's not a side-show.'

He holds his hands up in surrender. 'I know...but nobody else was around to hear it, and I couldn't bear her being allowed to get away with murder. Literally. I had to try something.'

'Hm. What did she say?'

'At first, she said I was making it up, until I told her what Molly had said when they were in the water together on the night she was killed.'

I fold my arms and give him a hard stare. 'Refresh my memory.'

'Molly said that Leanne told her when they went swimming that fateful night, that she had to die for betraying her with Rick...that she'd broken their promise.'

'And then what?'

Charlie heaves a sigh. 'She almost collapsed, and I sat her down on a chair in the corridor. She was sobbing and said she never meant to go so far, but she couldn't bear

Molly leaving, after everything she'd done for her. Leanne actually believed she'd made Molly stronger, by 'protecting' her all those years, punishing her for her mistakes and making her see sense. She was fed up of always being blamed for things too, and feeling second best to Molly. She also said she can't help herself sometimes, when she sets out to do something bad, she never intends to go so far, but a red rage overtakes her and she can't stop.'

I let out a long whoosh of breath I hadn't realised I'd been holding, and with it, comes the exasperation with my husband I'd felt a moment ago. I suppose he can be excused a little, if he's got a murderer locked up. 'Right. Okay, I suppose I can forgive you. But I'm still not very happy about it, Charlie. We could have at least talked about it beforehand.'

At last I get eye-contact. 'I'm so sorry, love. Thing is, I had no idea I was going to mention Molly before the whole thing was out of my mouth.' He offers a wobbly smile. 'I put it to her that she killed her grandmother too, while she was in a confessing mood, added that she might not have intended to do that, either. Straightaway she admitted that she'd pushed her gran downstairs.'

My stomach turns over. 'Right…what a horrible, evil woman. But like Molly said in her diary, Leanne needed professional help. Too late now of course.'

'Hopefully she'll get it in prison,' Charlie says with a sigh and drains his coffee mug.

I watch him take our plates and mugs over to the dishwasher as I process everything he said - and then a puzzle pops into my mind. 'Hang on. You said nobody heard you tell Leanne about Molly's spirit appearing to me. How did you explain her sudden change of mind to Abi and everyone? Didn't Leanne tell them what you'd said to her?' I can just imagine the whole police station talking about me behind my back. Okay, I know some will know about my gift, because I've helped with cases in the past, but we have always kept it low key.

'Erm...' Charlie begins and turns away from my gaze, busies himself at the sink. 'I... er, kind of told Leanne she mustn't say anything about it. You know, when we went back to the interview room to do the recording of her confession? Just that she should say she'd had a change of mind, and wanted to set the record straight about the two murders to get the guilt off her chest.'

His body language and tone of voice reveals that he's still hiding something pretty important. Something he knows will annoy the hell out of me. 'And why would Leanne just do as you said, hm? Just go along with it, without an argument?' He doesn't answer, just constantly wipes down the draining board, even though it doesn't need it. 'Charlie?' I say in my best assertive voice.

He turns round and looks at the ceiling. 'Because I said if she mentioned anything about Molly's spirit visiting to anyone, anyone at all, at the station or in court later, Molly wouldn't be at all pleased with her...in fact, she'd be furious. Molly needed to rest in peace and not have people talking about her...there'd be no telling what Molly would do if she was angry.' He smirks at me, actually smirks. 'I've never seen anyone so terrified in all my life. She went the colour of this.' He shakes a carton of milk I'd left out

123

on the worktop.

I jump up from the table and shout, 'Charlie! It's not funny! How could you tell such lies? This isn't some bloody game you know? Spirits aren't to be used to scare people half to death, no matter what those people have done.'

Immediately abashed, he loses the daft grin and comes over to me, but I brush off his embrace. 'Hey, Nance. I'm sorry, but if it hadn't have been for Molly, and you of course, Leanne would have walked.'

'Yes, I get that, but I feel you went behind my back...I feel uncomfortable with that, Charlie.' I step back and stare into his eyes, which are full of guilt and an apology.

He spreads his hands and gives his head a little shake. 'What can I say? I *am* truly sorry, and I promise I won't do anything like that again before I've talked to you, okay?'

I look away, fold my arms.

'Okay?' He puts a finger under my chin, lifts my gaze to his. 'Okay, Nance? Please, I promised, yeah?'

Wordlessly, I slip my arms around his waist, lay my head on his chest and listen to the thud of his steady heartbeat. It calms me, and I hold him tight. I know he means what he says, bless him, but I do worry about helping in the future. One thing's for sure, I know there is no way I want to become more involved with working with the police than I already am. Last year, both Abi and Charlie suggested I came on board more, and I did waver, but this has made my mind up. My gift is to help people, yes, but it's all to do with making connections offered willingly, and to a positive end. The last thing I want is the whole thing turning into a charade, a point of gossip, entertainment and even ridicule.

I step out of his arms and fix him with a hard stare. 'If you ever do anything like that again, Charlie, I swear that will be the end of me helping out on cases, no matter how important they are. Do you understand me?'

He nods and pulls me to him again. 'I do. And I won't ever do it again.' He looks deep into my eyes. 'Now can we forget about all that for a moment and go back to bed? I have an hour or so before I go in to work...' He lifts my chin and gives me a kiss that spreads a warmth through my body.

'I suppose so. If you promise to be good from now on.' I give him a cheeky wink.

'Now, what's the fun in that?' He laughs. 'I promise to be good after this next hour or so,' he murmurs after kissing me again, and then he leads me upstairs.

Chapter Eleven

After Charlie has gone to work, I have a shower and decide to ring Lucinda, then write up the Leanne case notes in my journal. It's great that she's been caught, but my heart still stings when I think of the way it happened. Never mind. Charlie has promised faithfully that he'll never do anything like that again, without discussing his plans with me first. Scrappy leads the way through the carpet of amber and gold leaves, and waits at the summer house for me to catch up. Maybe he thinks there's some of his favourite salmon and tuna in the cupboard in there, and a comfy spot for him on the fluffy grey cushions I bought in the January sales. 'No idea where you get your ideas from, my gorgeous boy,' I say, as I tickle him under the chin and let him inside.

The temperature inside reminds me it won't be too long before I can have a rummage in the January sales again, and I switch the heater on. Scrappy's looking pointedly at the cupboard and I quickly give him a dish of his favourite food, before filling the kettle and having a look at what delights are left in the biscuit barrel. A few broken ginger nuts and one chocolate digestive don't fill me with joy, to be honest. Must get some more from the house later. Case-note writing has to be done with tea and nice biscuits. It's the law.

I take my tea and broken biscuits over to the sofa and set the mug on the coffee table. Scrappy finishes his food, then leaps onto the comfy cushion and begins to knead it, make biscuits on it, or play the piano on it, as I prefer to call the padding-paw action cats do. Just as I'm about to open the journal and begin, my phone rings. It's Lucinda. I'd forgotten all about ringing her! 'Hi, Lucinda. I was about to ring you,' I say, with my fingers crossed.

'Saved you a job then.' She laughs. 'I was wondering if you have had time to try a connection with Mike's hat?'

Plumping the cushions behind me, I settle back into them and say, 'Well, yes and no. I have seen who the creel culprit is, but I have no idea what they're up to.' I tell Lucinda about the woman not keeping the catch, and looking sad as she stood by a moonlit cottage at the end of the connection.

'A woman? That is surprising, there's not that many fisherwomen,' Lucinda replies. 'What did she look like?'

'Late fifties, or early sixties, greying hair styled into an asymmetric bob, and thick dark eyebrows, olive-green eyes. I sketched her, but still couldn't get an answer as to who she is, and why she's doing it.'

There's a long pause on the line and then, 'Oh God. I hope I'm wrong, Nancy, but based on that description, I think I know who it is. Though why on earth would she sabotage Mike's creels?'

'Who do you think it is?'

'No earthly reason why she'd do it...' Lucinda mutters, as if she's forgotten I'm there.

Impatient to know her suspicions, I interject, 'So *who* is it?'

'Sorry, Nance. I can't get my head around it, but I think it's Debbie, Mike's wife.'

I'm incredulous. 'His wife? But why would she do that?'

'I have absolutely no idea.'

'Do they have a happy marriage?'

'Yeah. Been together nearly forty years, always seem good together.'

'Doesn't make sense.'

'Nope.'

Something must be going on with them that we don't know about. I ponder a while and then say, 'Maybe you could go and have a chat with her, Lucinda?'

'Oh, I don't know. I'm not very good with people I don't know that well.'

'How about William?'

'He's not one to stick his nose in other people's business, even though they are his relatives.'

The silence on the line speaks volumes. 'Do you want me to see if I can get to the bottom of it? I could call her?'

'Oh, would you? That would be wonderful. I know if I got involved, I'd just make it all worse…though not sure a phone call would be the right thing, given the unorthodox way you found out about what she was doing. Maybe a face-to-face?'

I think about a trip to St Ives of an hour or so there and back, plus the time spent with Debbie. 'I wouldn't be able to go for a few days. I wanted to pop over to see Mel, and I have baking, plus case study write ups to do.'

'Yes, that's fine. I'm sure a few days won't make a difference. Debbie was busy yesterday apparently, and she only does it a couple of times a week. It's costing them a fortune as you know, because Mike won't give in. Dear, oh dear. What a pickle.'

'Okay. Give me their address and phone number, and I'll get onto it as soon as I can.'

A few moments after I we end the call, I'm reaching for my journal when my phone rings again. Blimey, I'm in demand today. It's Mel. 'Hey, you. You must be psychic; I was going to phone you later!'

Mel bursts out laughing. 'I am psychic, don't you know,' she says in a fake posh accent.

'I do. That was my hilarious joke.'

'It was so funny, you should be on the stage.' Mel chuckles.

'So how are you? Things okay?'

'Yeah, I was just thinking that we haven't seen each other for a while and it would be nice to catch up.'

'I was thinking exactly the same!'

'We must be psychic.'

'You reckon?'

'Ha. So are you doing anything today? I could make us lunch round at mine.'

'That would be lovely. I have a few case notes to write, and then I'll be over about noonish. That okay?'

'Perfect. See you then.'

After we say goodbye, I pick up my journal once again,

129

and make a mental note to ask Mel about the maternity cover for Lucinda's shop. Also, to see if she could try to find out what's bothering Abi.

I pull up outside Mel's at twelve-fifteen, and notice that both Mum and Rory's cars are missing from next door's driveway. I was hoping to pop in for a chat before I went home. Oh well, never mind, I only saw her last week. I walk up the path to the grand, white detached house overlooking the estuary, and take a deep breath of pungent autumn scents flavoured with a dab of the Camel and a salt kiss from the Atlantic. Before I can knock, Mel flings open the door and ushers me inside. Unlike Rory's, which is as grand inside as the outside of the house, Mel's is much more homely and welcoming.

'I do love this place, Mel,' I call over my shoulder from the living room as she busies herself in the kitchen. It shares the same estuary view from the picture window in the living room, as Rory's house. Mum tells me she can lose track of time just staring at the ever- changing scene, and I can see why. I look around the room and am reminded of my first impression of the place when I first visited. Tasteful décor, and plain furniture. It's a bit like walking into an IKEA store. There are a few open books piled up on the coffee table in front of a modern blue pine-legged sofa, but everything else is in its place.

Mel pops her head around the door, her long beaded braids clicking together as they whip the wooden door jamb. 'I love it too. Never get bored of the view. Tea or coffee?'

'Tea please. Can I help?'

'No. Just sit down and I'll bring it through.'

A beautiful black and white cat pads into the room from the hallway, and leaps onto the sofa beside me just as I sit down. 'Lola, how are you?' Lola rubs her head against my hand and starts to purr like a traction engine. 'I expect you want some lunch too, huh?'

Mel comes in with a tray of sandwiches, little sausage rolls, crisps, two mugs of tea and a slab of fruit cake, and puts it on the long pine coffee table in front of me. 'She always wants lunch, even though she's already had it, don't you, little one?' Lola bumps her head against Mel's outstretched hand, the cat's big green eyes showing a keen interest in the sandwiches.

'Same as my Scrappy.'

Lola sets a paw on the coffee table. 'Oh no you don't, madam.' Mel's conker-brown eyes twinkle with merriment and she laughs, showing the cute gap in her teeth as she whisks Lola off to the kitchen. 'Help yourself to crab sandwiches,' she adds, closing the kitchen door after setting a dish of food down for Lola.

'No wonder Lola was interested. Crab sandwiches are my favourites.' I pick up a triangle of homemade wholemeal bread, heavy with white crabmeat in mayonnaise, and bite into it. Delicious. 'Oops, sorry.' I dab the corner of my mouth with a napkin. 'Where are my manners? I should have waited for you to sit down!'

'We don't stand on ceremony at this house. Fill yer boots, as my mum used to say.' Mel sits opposite on a matching chair and piles her plate high.

There's a short pause while we do justice to the delicious lunch, and my mind goes back to last year, when Mel's mum appeared to tell me that she and her husband were wrong to suppress Mel's gift. Back then, poor Mel had no friends and rarely left the house after her parents died. But looking at her now that she's accepted and embraced her gift, she's transformed into a completely different person. She's no longer the lonely young woman who jumped at her own shadow when I first met her. I'll be forever grateful that I have been a small part in that transformation, and feel blessed anew that I too have the gift.

'You seem like a changed woman from last year. It's great to see.' I smile and pick up another sandwich.

'That'll be the fact that I'm not hiding my gift anymore, and possibly because of the love of a good man.' She wipes her mouth and gives me a dreamy smile. 'In fact, I'm sure of it. Sometimes I wake up and wonder how I ever lived my life without him.'

'Oooh, tell me more.' I didn't know things were quite so serious with Abi's brother Anthony.

Mel's eyes light up. 'I adore him. We're inseparable lately, well, apart from when we're at work. In the evening he's either here, or I'm at his. We're talking about moving in together.' She claps her hands together, her whole face beaming. 'Makes sense for him to move in here, as this house is much bigger than his two-bed flat.'

I'm so thrilled for her. Happiness is flowing from her in waves. 'Wonderful!' As I say this, the distant sound of children's laughter and the thump of little feet on wooden floors comes to me. Wow. That's never happened before…a connection to the future, unlooked for. My gift will never cease to amaze me. I'm overjoyed that Mel and Anthony will be blessed with children.

She frowns as she crunches into a crisp. 'You have a very weird look on your face all of a sudden.'

'I always look weird.' I laugh and take another sandwich. I'm not going to divulge what I know, because discovering you're going to be a parent, should be a precious and private experience. Mel's still looking at me, a puzzle in her face, so I add, 'I was just thinking about how nice it would be to have a wedding, here in the garden next to the river.' *Nancy Cornish, you big fat liar.*

Mel's eyes grow round. 'Well, you must be psychic, because we have talked about that very thing! Maybe next year… we need to see how it goes first.'

'Oh I have a feeling it will go very well, my dear.' We munch away in silence for a few moments while I think about the best way to approach the Abi issue. Best just go for it, I think. Pushing my plate to one side I say, 'How do you get on with Abi?'

'Really well, she's lovely.' Mel picks up a knife and points it at the cake, a question in her eyes. I nod and she cuts a thick slab. So much for my good intentions to eat less.

Trying for a nonchalant tone, I say, 'Yeah, she is. Not sure if she's quite as happy as she used to be though.'

Mel raises an eyebrow. 'I thought the same. She's lost her sparkle a bit. What do you think's up?'

Through a mouthful of delicious fruit cake, I mumble.

133

'No idea, but she's making Charlie's work-life miserable. Always blocking and arguing for no reason.' I raise a finger. 'This goes no further though, right?'

'Poor Charlie. No, I won't say anything…wish I knew why though.'

'Mm. Me too. Maybe you could do a bit of digging?'

Mel looks doubtful. 'Not sure we know each other well enough for a heart-to-heart.'

'No…but maybe try and make a connection with something of hers, and see where it takes you?'

'I can't do that.' She sits back and brushes crumbs from her cream Arran jumper. 'Spirits come to me and often don't make much sense when they do. You're the genius of the psychic world.' She grins and sips her tea.

'You don't know until you try. I learnt all my stuff as I went along. And even now I have no idea how some things happen. As I told you before, my gran said what we have is a gift, a blessing and an honour. We don't always get it right, and sometimes we get messages meant for others, or half formed, muddled, like radio waves that don't quite connect. Allow your mind to stay open and believe anything is possible. Works for me.'

We look at each other for a few moments, and it feels like we are making our own connection of firm friendship. Then Mel says, 'Okay. I'll promise I'll try, but no guarantees, yeah?'

'I can't ask for more. I'd do it myself, but I think Abi would be on her guard with me a bit. She's obviously going through some stuff she's not that keen to share.'

We spend another hour or so talking about nothing in particular, and Lola joins us, stretched out, bathing in a patch of sunlight next to the French windows. I make a move and Mel walks me to the door. But just as I say goodbye and step through it, I remember I'm supposed to ask her about Lucinda's maternity cover. She's immediately interested.

'That would be fantastic. I adore books and bookshops. As you know, I used to work in the library. But the supermarket is only part-time and a bit of a chore, to be honest. I still have a little nest egg from my parent's will, but I do need to supplement it. Working in Port Isaac would be great too – might even see Doc Martin!'

I give her my best withering look and say, 'You do know he's not real, Mel?'

'He's not? Oh, my goodness, I had no idea,' she replies, deadpan.

Laughing, I give her a hug and turn to leave. 'I'll let you know the dates of the maternity cover and arrange for you to meet Lucinda. And don't forget, keep an open mind about our gift's possibilities.' I raise a hand as I walk away.

'I will. See you soon, Nance!'

I've only been in half-an-hour when the phone rings again. Buggeration, who is it now? I have a starving cat to feed, food to prepare, laundry to take out of the dryer, and a hundred other chores. Alison. Immediately my heart squeezes, I hope all is okay with Tilly and baby Ella.

'Alison, everything all right?'

'Yes, it couldn't be better.' Her buoyant mood is almost

tangible and relief spreads through me. 'Tilly is doing a brilliant job with Ella and I'm practically redundant. I even found time to do a rough draft of a few chapters of my next book!'

'That's the best news!' I hug myself and flop down on the sofa.

'It is. We were wondering if we could pop over for a visit tomorrow? Tilly wants to show you the new outfits Chris has bought for his granddaughter. He chose them himself, and Tilly is obviously over the moon about that. He's definitely thawing in his attitude to being an unexpected granddad.'

'How lovely. When, tomorrow?' I had hoped to visit Debbie in St Ives, but I don't want to say no if I can help it. Tilly needs all the encouragement she can get.

'Afternoon? Say, around 1 to 2pm?'

That would mean I'd have to squeeze things in tomorrow, rather than taking my time trying to win Debbie over. She'll have to wait until the day after. 'Okay, that sounds perfect.'

'Fab. Okay, we'll see you then, Nancy!'

I find myself smiling as I tackle the downstairs loo. Not because it's my favourite job, but because I know young Tilly is on the right track with her daughter now. Being a PI is such a privilege and makes me feel like I'm really using my gift to its fullest extent. Helping my community is so rewarding, and I'm grateful every day that I can help somebody. Be it in a big or a small way. Penny and Charlie often chastise me when I tell people I don't need payment for my help, because I have to put food on the table. But the truth is, I'd do this job for absolutely nothing. I spray the mirror and wipe it clean, and see my gran over my left shoulder beaming at me.

'Gran! Lovely to see you as always.'

She nods, and immediately swaps her old self for her young. She has a bump under a floral maternity dress, and tenderly cradles her tummy. 'New life is everything, Nancy. You deserve your happiness.'

'Thanks, Gran. I'm so thrilled for Tilly.' I smile back at her.

'Not just for Tilly. You'll see.' Gran blows a kiss and does the off switch.

I'm left with a warm glow, and as I finish up and go to put the kettle on, I wonder what she meant when she said not just Tilly? A quiet voice mutters in my head, a*ll will become clear in the fullness of time, maid.*

Chapter Twelve

Charlie and I snuggle up together on the sofa and cover our legs with the charcoal fluffy throw we have draped over the back of it. I'm not the greatest fan of chilly late autumn evenings, but cosy times like this makes them much more enjoyable. We've had a nice meal, a glass of wine, and now we're about to watch a new series on Netflix. Simple pleasures. And Charlie told me that the not so lovely Leanne will most likely go to prison for a very long time, when her case comes to court. Hearing this made me happy that justice had been done for poor Molly and her grandma, but at the same time, I can't help feel a little sorry for Leanne. She obviously had issues since she was a child, unsurprisingly this was made worse after both her parents were killed, but nobody had realised she was struggling. If they had, maybe things would have played out very differently, and Molly and her gran would still be here with us.

'Penny for them?' Charlie whispers in my ear.

'Just thinking about how sad Leanne's case is. Wish her problems had been spotted before it was too late.'

'Hmm. Yeah, I guess. The main thing is she's off the streets and won't be able to harm anyone else.'

I close my eyes, lean my head on his shoulder and he runs his fingers through my hair. 'Well at least I've been able to help a very troubled young woman, maybe even changed her life, if that doesn't sound too big-headed.'

'Young Tilly?'

'Yeah. She's coming over tomorrow with Alison and baby Ella.'

'Great.'

'Even Gran popped by today to say new life is everything, but then she was a bit cryptic. She said I deserved happiness, and I thought she meant because I'd helped Tilly. Then she said not just for Tilly. Odd.'

'You often get odd connections, love. I wouldn't ponder too much on it. Now are we going to watch telly, or not?'

'Yep.' I watch Charlie fiddle with the remote and wonder how he's been getting on with Abi these last few days. I decide not to mention that Mel will try to find out why she's been acting out of character, as he might tell me to keep my nose out. My husband can be a bit stubborn when it comes to work relationships. He likes to think he can sort out any problems by himself. Just as he's about to press play, I ask, 'Have you been getting on any better with Abi recently?'

'Not so you'd notice.' He sighs. 'It's not just me either, others have said what a snappy bugger she's becoming lately. They all give her a wide birth, and at this rate she'll have no friends in the workplace. Yes, I know she's the boss, but she's well liked...or was. Wish I could fathom it.'

I almost tell him about Mel, but bite my lip. 'Yeah.

Well maybe we'll have her and Vicky over for dinner soon. See if I can't suss her out.'

'Yeah, good luck with that. I doubt she'd accept, to be honest. Right let's watch this before it's time to go to bed.'

The next morning dawns cold and bright. I smile as I gaze out of the kitchen window at the grand view over the rooftops of Padstow, to where the distant Camel Estuary glints like a sapphire in the silver autumn sunshine. I adore days like this. A hard blue sky, crisp air, and an absence of shimmer projects a clear outline of buildings, trees and water. Right, time to get busy...

By noon, I've managed to get a batch of baking done. Scones, bread, eclairs and chocolate chip cookies, should go down well this afternoon with Tilly and Alison. I've also got my case-notes up to date and had a chat on the phone to Penny about Joe. He's doing so well already and is talking of going back to school next week. He's also talking about making this year his last, and by next September, he will be a retired teacher and embarking on a new career as a painter. Penny is over the moon and so am I.

Okay, time to have quick sandwich now before my guests arrive. While I make it, I wonder about meeting the creel thief. I think tomorrow might be the best day to go to St Ives and try to talk to Debbie. I've no more jobs on the horizon, but I noticed quite a few of the flyers advertising my business I put in the corner shop the other day had gone, when I popped in for milk this morning. If I don't go to see her tomorrow, there might be more local jobs to do, and she'll get pushed further down the list. The weather's supposed to turn in the next few days too, with high winds and rain forecast. Best get it done while it's fine.

Scrappy alerts me to the arrival of my visitors. He stands up from where he's been watching the world go by on the windowsill, jumps down and runs to the door, tail up.

'Who is it, Scrappy? Alison and Tilly?' I ask, as I pick him up and move him out of the way. He meows in response and immediately runs back to the door. 'Come on, monkey, how can I open the door with you in front of it?'

Eventually I open the door and am greeted by a wail from baby Ella. Tilly's got her wrapped in a beautiful rainbow sling, and I can just see a tuft of dark hair poking out of the top. Tilly looks transformed. Her hair is glossy and swept into a messy topknot and her light-blue eyes are alert and bright, having lost the dark circles that were under them. Her complexion is fresh, her cheeks pink, and she beams me a 1000-watt smile which is contagious, because both Alison and I mirror it. 'Hello! We're here at last,' she says, giving me an awkward hug because of Ella squished between us.

'We were dropped by a neighbour about a mile away, as she was coming past here today. We decided we fancied a walk, and it was so lovely to be out in the fresh sea air,' Alison says, hugging me too.

'That's wonderful, but is the neighbour collecting you?' I ask, leading the way inside. 'I can take you back if you like?'

141

'No, Dad's coming to get us once he's finished school,' Tilly replies, as I take her coat. 'He wants to thank you personally for changing our lives.'

My throat thickens as I see her eyes moisten, Alison's too. 'What a lovely thing to say.'

'It's true.' Tilly dabs at her eyes with the sleeve of her fluffy green top. 'Once I told him that Mum's spirit had come to help, he was a different man. I expected him to say it was a load of rubbish – your gift, I mean...like I did at first.' She looks apologetic. 'But he didn't. His aunty had the gift, apparently, and so he was completely on board straightaway.'

'It was as if Chris completely changed his views once Gabby had visited. I think it was as if she had reached out to him too, in a way. But he's not a man to share his feelings much, is he, Tilly?' Alison says, pink-cheeked. Why is she embarrassed?

Tilly laughs. 'Nope. Dad is not a man who wears his heart on his sleeve, to say the least.'

'Right, let's get you comfy.' I lead the way into the living room and they sit down on the sofa. Ella wriggles as Tilly unwraps the sling, but doesn't look like she's going to cry. Unlike me. An unexpected wave of emotion surges through me as I gaze at her little face. Her eyes are open wide with curiosity, and she's impossibly cute, dressed in a turquoise and yellow striped baby grow, complete with a gorgeous lemon jumper with a pink heart in the middle. I kneel at Tilly's feet and take one of Ella's tiny hands. 'Hello, little one. Who's the cutest child in the world, eh?'

Alison leans forward and ruffles the baby's hair. 'She

so is. And now she's sleeping well, she's allowing her mummy to feel more human again, aren't you? Yes. Yes, you are, sweetie.' Alison pulls a face and tickles Ella's tummy.

'I noticed that her mummy is feeling more human again. In fact, I would go as far as to say stunning,' I comment, and smile at Tilly.

She turns beetroot. 'I don't know about that. But yes, I certainly feel more like my old self the past few days. I've had some good sleep and good food. And the main thing is that I know that my mum's on my side, thanks to you, Nancy. I can't tell you how grateful I am.'

Tilly's eyes fill again, so I stand up and put my hand on her shoulder. 'Hey, it was my pleasure. Now, who's for homemade chocolate eclairs and maybe a cookie or two?'

Alison's hand shoots up, quickly followed by Tilly's. 'Ooh. Yes please!' Alison grins. 'I'll come and give you a hand.'

As we busy ourselves in my kitchen, I notice Alison seems different too. Yes, she's had some sleep and washed her hair since I last saw her, and that makes a hell of a difference, but there's something else. I keep taking surreptitious glances at her as I put the cakes on a plate and get the mugs out of the cupboard, while she fills the kettle and chats on about baby Ella. Her hair, normally bang straight, has a little curl through it, and she's wearing more colours. She has on light jeans, a crimson jumper, which hugs trim figure, and yes...make up. Alison normally just wears a bit of lipstick and maybe eyebrow pencil, but she

143

has added subtle eyeliner and a touch of mascara. I glance down at my well-worn floral shirt and leggings and feel dowdy in comparison.

'You're so clever making these, Nancy.' Alison nods at the eclairs. 'Do you ever miss working at the café?'

'Sometimes, but I do lots of baking and always seem to have takers. I freeze some, but take some to the community larder and various friends and relatives. I need to watch what I eat though, as I have a middle-age spread starting.'

'I'm sure you don't.' Alison says kindly, as she pours water into the teapot.

'You look absolutely wonderful, I've noticed. Your hair is gorgeous and make up too.'

A pink blush rushes up her neck and cheeks. 'Oh, thanks. Just thought I should make a bit more effort with myself. I'm normally just in baggy old jumpers and jeans.'

As we carry the things through, I wonder if she's making an effort for herself, which is great, but could it be for another reason? Or another person? My intuition is sending my imagination a few messages, but I ignore it for now. Time will tell.

'Wow! Those eclairs look fantastic.' Tilly takes one, narrowly avoiding having it knocked from her grasp by her daughter's flailing fist.

'Looks like someone's gearing up for a yell. She hungry?' I ask, pouring the tea.

'She'll be getting that way. I'll just demolish a few of these and then I'll feed her.'

We talk babies for the next ten minutes, and Alison and I can't help but share a look, as Tilly is as good as her word. Three eclairs are made to disappear in that time and she's looking at the cookies too. Oh, to be seventeen again with a metabolism of a whippet. Ella has quietened, but that's probably because her mum is bouncing her on her knee and singing to her. The transformation in Tilly is unbelievable. Her parenting instincts have kicked in big time, and she's totally in tune with her baby.

'Okay, young lady, time for a feed I think, before you start getting fractious.' Tilly drains her cup and settles back on the cushions. This puzzles me, because I was just about to put the kettle on for her formula. Maybe Alison has got the bottle in her bag…then all becomes clear, when Tilly unzips her top and directs Ella's mouth to her breast. The infant latches on and settles to her feed contentedly. Wow!

'You're breastfeeding,' I say, stating the obvious, but I'm still shocked. 'That's amazing in such a short time!'

Tilly's face is full of pride as she nods. 'Yeah. I tried it myself, but it was hit and miss, so I popped to the clinic and the nurse explained what to do in no time. Ella is thriving on it, and there's no faffing with bottles and stuff. Win-win.'

'It's great, isn't it?' Alison says, taking a cookie from the plate. 'And when we've finished eating, we'll show you the lovely outfits her granddad has bought.' If I'm not mistaken there's another flush starting on her cheeks, and she can't hold my gaze. My instinct tells me it's right, and I can't argue with it this time.

Half-an-hour later, there's an array of adorable outfits on the table, each one carefully chosen with a loving eye.

'Your dad certainly has a good idea what will be practical, yet lovely too.' I pick up a woollen lemon dress covered in ladybirds, with matching socks. 'And he's got different sizes for her as she grows.' My eye falls on a pair of red jeans with blue patch pockets for when Ella is around three months old. Sebastian had a similar pair, and the old familiar pain of his loss gives me a poke in the chest. Unthinkingly, I pick them up and hold them up to the light, imagining my boy in them.

'They are SO cute,' Alison says. I nod and hand them to her while pretending to fluff up a blue pom-pom on a white woolly hat, to get my emotions under control. I used to be able to manage them much better, but lately I'm a mess. God knows why.

'And this is for you, Nancy. Once again, thank you so much for everything.' Tilly hands me an envelope and a pale-blue cardboard box tied with a navy bow.

I look at her in surprise and open the envelope. Two hundred pounds. 'You didn't need to do that. My gran told me you were in danger, so I would have looked for you anyway. You didn't actually ask for my help.'

'I know. And it's not much, in comparison to what you've given me. You probably saved my life, acted as midwife, and then brought my mum to me.' She nods at the box on the arm of my chair. 'Open it, then.'

I open it and gasp at a delicate teardrop-shaped emerald pendant, suspended on a silver necklace. 'Oh, my goodness, it's stunning.'

Tilly beams and shifts Ella to the other breast. 'I'm so glad you like it. When I passed it in the shop the other day,

I thought it matched the colour of your eyes.'

'That's so lovely. But I don't want you spending money on me.' I'm aware that she'll need every penny and I'm guessing she doesn't have much to start with.

'It's from my savings.' She gives me a direct look. 'I wanted to, okay? So just say, thanks, Tilly and put the damned thing on.'

I laugh. 'Thanks, Tilly.' Alison helps me fasten it and I look in the mirror. Yes, it does match my eyes. Right now, I can't tell which is sparkling the most, them or the emerald.

A little later, Ella's fast asleep on my sofa, bolstered by some cushions and covered with my throw. She looks so peaceful, one hand up by her ear, the other tucked under the cover, and her tiny mouth puckered, as if she's dreaming of having a feed. Tilly's phone beeps and she announces her dad will be here shortly, so I put the kettle on for more tea and bring the scones out to butter. There are a few eclairs left too, so we'll be fine. I won't have more though; I'd never eat my dinner when Charlie comes home.

Everything's ready just as the doorbell sounds, and Tilly runs to let her dad in. As they come back down the corridor, I hear her say, 'Shh. Ella's just gone off, so we're in the kitchen for a cuppa, okay?'

I quickly look into the living room to check Ella's not fallen of the sofa, which would be a miracle, given the cushions she's got around her, and turn to greet the tall, broad shouldered, bearded man with stunning turquoise eyes. His dark curly hair is streaked with silver, as is his

147

beard, and I'm dazzled by a wide welcoming smile as he steps forward and holds out a hand. 'Hi, Nancy, I'm Chris.' I take his hand, and he clasps it in both of his. 'I can't tell you how utterly grateful I am that you came to my daughter's aid when she was unconscious in the woods, and again the other day too. How wonderful that you have the gift.' His voice breaks on the last word and he swallows as his eyes grow moist.

'It's my absolute pleasure, Chris.' I watch as he goes over to greet Alison and drops a kiss on her cheek - which turns them scarlet - then pops his head through the door to look at his granddaughter. What a lovely man. I must admit he is nicer looking than I was expecting, and I tell myself off for having had a stereotypical image of a stuffy chess-playing teacher, who was a bit grumpy and set in his ways. Though to be fair, Alison did say he was controlling, that's why Tilly couldn't tell him she was pregnant. Maybe the reason was that he just couldn't cope after his wife died. Perhaps he became over-strict to compensate for being a single-parent responsible for a teenage girl. He certainly seems relaxed and affable now.

'Nancy loves her necklace, Dad,' Tilly says, sitting down at the kitchen table.

Chris turns to me. 'It certainly looks perfect, and as you say, matches her eyes.'

My cheeks are in danger of becoming as pink as Alison's, so I say a quick thank you and busy myself with the tea.

As we eat the scones and chat about Chris's job, Ella, Tilly's plans for the future and my gift, I notice the heated glances passing between Chris and Alison like flames chasing each along dry kindling. My hunches were correct. It's Chris. This is why she's changed. She's smitten by him, and he certainly seems very interested in her too. I wonder if they're seeing each other? Alison catches me giving her a knowing look, and mid-sentence, she stutters to a halt and takes a sip of tea.

Ella startles us all as she sends up a yell from the living room, so Chris and Tilly go in to see her, while Alison and I clear away. I'm glad I've got her on her own, and waste no time trying to find out what's going on. I half close the door to the living room with my foot, and then in a low voice, drop in causally as I carefully stack the dishwasher, 'Chris seems such a lovely man. I must admit I was a little surprised, given what you'd told me about him being so controlling.'

Alison's mouth drops open. 'Yeah, well that was before I got to know him properly,' she says, defensively. 'He told me he'd made a mess of things after Gabby died, and he was being overprotective, because he didn't have a clue about how to raise a teenage girl.'

My suppositions were correct then. 'Yeah, I did wonder. Because he seems a really nice guy.' She nods and avoids my eyes, picks up a cloth and wipes the side down. 'Nice that he confided in you too, especially as you said earlier, he doesn't share his feelings much.'

'Hm, well he does sometimes, about certain things...but not about others.' She throws the cloth in the bowl and folds her arms. 'Oh, I don't know what I mean. Ignore me. Let's go in and see Ella.'

149

'No. let's talk about *your* feelings.' I look through the door to check what's happening, and see Chris and Tilly are playing with Ella on the sofa. 'It's obvious you and Chris really like each other. Has anything happened between you?'

Alison's shy brown eyes flit away from mine like a couple of nervous sparrows. 'How is it obvious?'

'By the way you look at each other, and the way you blush every time you mention his name.' I give her an encouraging smile and indicate we should sit back down at the table.

'Do you really think he likes me?'

'Absolutely.'

Her whole face lights up. 'Oh Nancy, I'm so glad,' she whispers. I thought he did, but I wasn't sure. There's been nobody since my darling Jack died, and I'm very much out of practice when it comes to reading signals from men.'

I pat her hand. 'That's understandable. But if as you say he's rubbish at showing his feelings in certain areas, then he might be feeling exactly the same as you – can't read the signs. He's lost his wife, and has been struggling. Then there was the whole Tilly situation to deal with. Maybe his heart couldn't take a rejection right now, if he told you how he felt and his feelings weren't reciprocated.'

Alison nods as she considers this. 'I guess. Then we're stuck.' She shrugs.

'Why? Surely not because you have some outdated idea that men have to be the ones to make the first move?' I wink to show her I understand, if that is the real reason.

'Kind of is.'

'Well let me tell you that you're a strong, passionate, attractive woman who is going to take the bull by the horns and tell him how you feel. Later this evening, if possible. I promise you, it won't be in vain.'

A hand flutters uncertainly to her mouth and her eyebrows shoot up into her fringe. 'Do you mean that a spirit told you?'

'No. My gut did.'

'Oh, I don't know Nanc—'

'Well, I do. You can do this. And when you have, get on the phone pronto and let me know.'

We burst out laughing, just as Tilly, Ella and Chris come into the kitchen. 'What's tickled you two?' Chris asks, a smile on his face.

'It's a secret,' I tell him, deadpan. 'If we tell you, we'd have to kill you.'

Chapter Thirteen

The turn in the weather is here quicker than forecast. Through the bedroom window, I watch an army of bruised clouds driven by a brisk wind gathering over the fields, ready to resume battle. Their overnight fight is evidenced by a huge puddle on the patio and a twisted and battered forsythia shrub, clinging to a rose bush for protection. I almost shut the curtains and get back into bed, but I have to go and see Debbie in St Ives. Can't wait. Charlie had an early start and I barely stirred when he left an hour or so ago. I never used to be so tired. At one time I would have leapt out of bed and made us both breakfast, while he showered and got ready. I sigh. Must be getting old.

I'm just finishing breakfast and girding my loins for the trip to St Ives, when the phone ringing is a welcome distraction. I am so not looking forward to travelling in this weather, and no idea what reception I'll receive at the other end when I get there. I'm guessing it won't be favourable. I smile when I see it's Mel calling. Wonder if she's found out anything about Abi.

'Hi, Mel, what's new?'

'Nothing good. Oh, Nance. I'm so worried about your mum.'

The panic in Mel's voice sweeps through me and the smile slides off my face. I sit down on a kitchen chair with a bump. 'Mum? Why, what's happened?'

'Well, I was thinking about your suggestion about trying to make a connection with something of Abi's this morning, and then I found one of your earrings when I was sweeping the kitchen floor. It must have fallen out when you were here the other day.'

'Okay. Yeah, I wondered where it went.'

'So, I thought I'd practice with that first. I sat quietly by the window, looked out at the estuary and took a few deep breaths. Then boom. I saw an image of your mum lying in some grass, she'd got blood on her cheek and seemed to be unconscious. Then nothing. Then as I was about to put the earring down, I saw some cows, possibly horses, then it went blank.'

My heart rate rockets up the scale, and I grip the edge of the table. 'Oh my God! Where was she? A field, a farm, bloody Bodmin Moor?'

'I don't know, Nancy.' Mel's voice trembles. 'I wish I did.'

I realise I'm on the edge of losing it and it's not Mel's fault. 'Sorry, I'm just worried. Did you go next door to check she wasn't at home?'

'Yeah, just now. There's nobody there, and she's not answering her phone.'

'Rory's not there either?' Even as I ask this, I remember he's gone to spend a few days with his brother and wife in Exeter. Mum didn't go with him, because she's busy with the new choir she's set up.

'No. His car wasn't there and—'

'Yeah, sorry, not thinking straight. He went away for a few days.'

'Right. And I was going to say, but your mum's car *is* there…'

'What?' I jump up and pace the room trying to think calmly. 'Have you looked in the garden, you say she was lying in some grass. Maybe she fell in the garden and hit her head or something.'

'Yes, I checked everywhere. She's not there, Nancy. And that wouldn't explain the cows or horses.'

Mel's trembling voice indicates she's close to tears and I need her to stay calm. 'Okay, okay. Listen. This is the first time you've tried to make a connection, well done for making it, by the way. But it could have been a bad one. Maybe it isn't real. Or mixed up with another one about animals. Maybe it's a message that was meant for someone else…' I stumble to a halt, aware I'm talking rubbish. I can feel Mum's in danger.

'Yeah, maybe.' Mel sounds about as convinced as me. 'Maybe you can try and make a connection?'

Instinctively I know that wouldn't work. 'We can't always see things that are personal to us. Gran once told me that.' I pace some more and then it hits me. 'Can you come here? Bring the earring. If we both try, then maybe we'll get something?'

'Yes, of course. On my way!'

'Okay. I'll try calling her, and please hurry.'

In the fifteen minutes it takes Mel to get here, I've

154

called Mum's number twenty-odd times. I know it's probably futile, if she's unconscious somewhere, but I need to be doing something, anything to find her. Mel comes in like a bat out of hell, her eyes are wild and she pulls me into a hug that would crush a boulder.

'Oh God, Nancy. I'm so sorry I couldn't find anything more out about your mum.'

'Hey, if it wasn't for you, we wouldn't even know that she was in danger. I'm so grateful to you, love.'

Mel sniffs away a tear and nods. 'Okay. Let's get comfy and try to find her. I need to calm myself first.' She walks round my kitchen shaking her hands and exhaling long breaths.

'We might be better on the sofa.' I lead the way through to the living room and we sit side by side for a few moments, inhaling through or noses and exhaling through our mouths. I'm about to inhale again when Mel shrieks and my eyes fly open.

'Where's this!' She's gripping my sketch-pad, with the drawing of the farm with no name that I doodled the other day. She must have picked it up from the footstool.

'I...I don't know. I just started doodling it and then couldn't bring the name of the place to mind. It feels a bit familiar but—' I suddenly see what she's getting at as I stare at the cows in the field and the farmyard. I'd almost forgotten I'd drawn it. My blood runs cold. 'Shit. Do you think my mum could be here?'

Mel spreads her hands. 'It's possible! In fact, more than likely. I mean, why on earth would you sketch this, and then a few days after, I see your mum unconscious and then

155

some cows?'

'Or horses.'

'Or both, it wasn't exactly clear, as I said. You've drawn a horse in the farmyard.'

I stare intensely at the letter K on the gate, but I still can't think of the rest of the name. I'm still as clueless as I was when I first drew it. 'God this is so frustrating.' I look at Mel, then back at the drawing. 'Let's try to use this to connect with where mum is. I don't think I'll be able to do it alone, because it's too personal to me. We'll both put our hands on the sketch and see what happens. Let's concentrate on the letter K, okay?'

Mel nods and we both grasp the sketch pad and concentrate. There's nothing at all , then I see a quick moving image of man – a farmer I suppose, wandering amongst the geese and tending the cows. Then nothing. I open my eyes to find Mel's are still closed and she's nodding her head. Her eyes fly open and she whispers with urgency, 'Write this down. Grabbing the stubby pencil, I hold it poised above the sketch pad as she dictates, 'K E N' she stops and pinches the bridge of her nose between forefinger and thumb. 'Um...Y...' She shakes her head. 'No, it's not Y.' I put a line through it and wait. 'Okay, first it's W, then Y, then N.'

I repeat what she told me back to her. 'KENWYN, yeah?'

'That's it.'

We both stare at the black graphite letters on the white page for a few moments, and she shrugs. I have nothing. Never heard of that name.'

Unfortunately, it isn't ringing a bell with me either, so I grab my phone and Google Kenwyn Farm. Immediately I'm rewarded with a little red marker on a map, and my memory wakes up and spurs me into action. 'I know where it is! I thought I recognised the hills on my sketch. I never knew what it was called, but used to go past it every time Mum and I walked the coast path from here to Harbour Cove, and sometimes onto Trevone. The farm overlooks the cove. Come on!'

My heart's racing as I fly to the cupboard for my car keys and snatch my coat from the hook. 'Mel, grab a bottle of water from the fridge and that throw from the sofa. Mum will need both.'

Mel does as I ask, and hurries after me slamming the door behind her. 'Don't you think we should call the ambulance before we go?'

I've already considered this. 'Not yet, because what if she's not there? We'd look pretty stupid when they arrived if she wasn't.'

She shoves her arms into her coat and gets into the car beside me. 'Okay, but I have a very strong feeling that she's there somewhere.'

'Me too. But let's be sure, eh? It's only ten-minutes' drive.' Breaking all speed limits we arrive in less, and I leap out of the car, push open the gate and run up the driveway. It's like running into my sketch and feels very surreal. Just before I get to the front door of the farmhouse, a gaggle of geese come round the corner of a barn and make for me, necks outstretched looking quite aggressive. 'Oy, shoo!' I wave my arms which stops them for a few seconds, and then they advance again.

'Aaargh!' Mel yells from behind me, and I turn to see her flapping the throw at them as she charges forward. This does the trick and they turn tail feathers and run.

'What the bleddy hell are you two playing at!' A ruddy-faced farmer demands, stepping out of the front door, hands on hips, a frown on his brow as deep as the furrows in his field.

He's the one I saw in my brief connection. Late forties, brown curly hair, navy overalls, a square chin which is at the moment thrust out in a belligerent fashion, and bushy dark brows over steel-grey eyes. 'Mr Kenwyn?'

'Yeah?' His eyes narrow in suspicion and he folds his arms.

'Sorry we frightened your geese, but we believe my mum is here somewhere on your land lying injured. Either cows or horses might be involved...' My voice trembles as I realise how weird this sounds.

Mr Kenwyn raises his eyebrows. 'You *believe* she's here? What make you think that?'

Mel and I share a worried glance. There's no way we can tell him the truth, or he'll shoo us off his land quicker than Mel shoed the geese. Coming to my rescue, she says, 'I had a bit of a premonition. I have them sometimes and I saw this farm in my mind's eye. Nancy here's mum was in it. It's all a bit hazy, but her mum's not answering her phone and her car's at home, but she's missing.'

It's a half-truth, but seems less outlandish than the whole-truth – just. Mr Kenwyn gives us an incredulous look, as well he might. 'So do we have permission to search, please?' I ask.

His eyes dance to each of our faces and away. Then he sighs as he considers my question. 'Only if I come with you. But I gotta say, this all sounds a bit odd.'

'Thank you!' I squeeze his arm and he pulls his neck back, and grunts a response, obviously unsure how to take me.

'Cows and horses, you say?' We nod in unison. 'Mm. Well, we'd best look in top field. Quicker on my tractor too. Come on.'

Five-minutes of bouncing about in the tractor-trailer amongst some bales of hay takes us to a long sloping field overlooking the ocean. There are about ten black and white cows here, and two chestnut horses in the adjoining field. Farmer Kenwyn switches of the engine and turns to face us. 'I hope you're wrong about your mum, Nancy. Because cows don't like people they don't know walking through their field. They can band together and chase intruders.'

My stomach turns over as I imagine mum being trampled. 'I don't think she would have walked into the field…I mean why would she? She's a country woman and knows not to. She was probably walking the coast path along here like normal.'

Sympathy floods his face which makes my stomach turn again. 'Short cut,' he says simply. 'Coast path is waterlogged at the moment. Might be a bit tricky to follow. There's a sign up to say to take a detour to a longer way, but sometimes people think they know better and trespass across my land.' He jumps from the tractor and offers his hand to help us down. 'I really hope your mum turned back, cos as I say. The cows ain't happy with a strange face.'

I'm glad of his hand, because my legs feel like jelly thinking of what might have happened to my mum. Maybe Mum had a stroke or a heart attack and wandered into the field in a panic. I take a moment to steady myself, before we follow on after the farmer, who's hoisted a bale of hay across his shoulders, and striding up the field. The cows all lift their heads as one, and come hurtling down the hillside towards us. Mel grabs my arm at the same time as I grab hers, and we hurry to the side of the field to give them a wide berth. We needn't have worried, as the cows are only interested in the hay that Farmer K is spreading around the ground. He fetches another bale from the tractor, and soon the animals are all munching contentedly.

'Right, best get searching about while they're having their grub,' he says, coming over to us.

'Thanks so much for helping us, Mr Kenwyn,' Mel says, with a smile.

He nods. 'Call me Ken.'

'Really? Ken Kenwyn?' Mel blurts. Even though I was thinking it, poor Ken must get this all the time.

'Yes. My parents had a great sense of humour. Now, let's spread out – don't forget to look under the hedgerows.' Ken strides off to the left, so I take the right and Mel heads towards the top of the field.

A few minutes later, the bruised clouds I noticed earlier start haemorrhaging water in biblical proportions. In seconds I'm soaked through, and my trainers squelch through the grass as I walk. Twisting my sodden hair into a scrunchie, I cup my hands to my mouth and yell 'Mum! Mum, it's Nancy!' I cock my head to one side, but all I hear is the driving rain, and Mel and Ken shouting Mum's name in the distance. Soon Mel comes towards me wiping the rain from her face.

'Nothing across the top, Nance. You carry on up this side and I'll go to the bottom, okay?'

'Okay,' I manage, though I know I'm close to tears. She pats my back as she passes and I set off again. This seems like a fool's errand. Why the hell didn't I call Charlie and see if he had any ideas about how to find her? Psychic connections can be invaluable, but they're not always accurate, are they? Maybe Charlie's crew could track her phone or something. Five more minutes and I'm calling him.

'Mum! Mum are you here? Mum!' I squelch along looking under hedgerows and in the ditches. Nothing. Tears are mingling with the raindrops running down my cheeks now, and I tell myself off. *This not helping, Nancy Cornish. Not helping at all!*

I stop at the top right-hand corner of the field, and wonder why the hell I'm searching up so far in this direction? Why would Mum have gone up here? The coast path is down to the left of the field by the sea. I'm about to go over to join Ken on the left, when something stops me. I get a tingle down my spine and an answer. Given that she was in the cow field for some inexplicable reason, and not ill with a heart attack or something like I surmised, she might have had to run away from the cows. And if they had been charging from the bottom left, Mum would have run up and away. So maybe it's not such a silly place to look. No stone unturned, Nancy.

There's a deep ditch a few feet away, overgrown with a tangle of brambles and nettles. 'Mum!' I call as I edge nearer to a spot less overgrown. 'Are you there? I stop and listen.

'Mmm. Uurgh.'

My feet have wings as I rush towards the sound. And there she is, half covered in undergrowth, her ashen face peeping from the black hood of her anorak, her lips a thin slash of pink trying to form words, eyelashes flickering but the lids remain closed.

'Mum! Oh my god, Mum!' I kneel, reach into the ditch and gently take her wrist. Her pulse is weak and she's chilled to the bone. She moves her head towards me and under the hood, I can see matted blood thick in her blonde hair.

Her eyes open at last and as they find my face, recognition flickers in their green depths, then they become vacant and her lids droop again. I let go of her wrist, stand up, windmilling my arms and yell, 'Mel, Ken! I've found her! She's alive. Call 999!!'

Mel and Ken raise their hands in acknowledgement, they say something to each other, then Ken pulls a phone from his pocket, while Mel speeds towards me like a greyhound.

I kneel back down and take Mum's hand as Mel joins me, her face a mask of concern. 'Oh thank god, Nance.' Mel gives me a quick hug and then leans into the ditch to

162

put her fingers on the pulse in Mum's neck. 'Weak, but there. Hell, she's so cold...' She looks at me. 'Do you think she's been here all night?'

This thought has been whirling around in my head, ever since I saw how pale, cold and injured she was. 'I'd say so, yes. It's only 10.30am now, so she wouldn't have got this cold already, because Mum would have been unlikely to come out walking much before nine-o'clock-ish.'

Lost in our own thoughts, we sit vigil, watching Mum's face. I try to speak to her but tears overtake me. Everything is still in the grey silence, apart from the pelting rain and I send up a prayer as I hold Mum's hand and Mel holds mine.

Ken arrives with the throw and water. 'Not conscious then,' he says, gently covering Mum with the throw, though it's futile, given the weather.

'Not now. She was briefly, when I shouted her name, but it was just moaning. She didn't say anything, then fell into unconsciousness again.' Sympathy swims in Mel's eyes, and as Ken pats my arm, unable to stop myself, I burst out sobbing.

Mel pulls me into a soggy embrace. 'Hey, don't worry, it will all be okay. Karen's a tough old bird and the ambulance will be here soon.'

'Hope she can't hear you saying 'old bird'. She'll have your guts for garters, as my gran used to say.' I try a wobbly smile, but it won't stay put.

Ten minutes later, we hear the siren growing ever louder, and I send up another prayer as the paramedics run up the rain-soaked field towards us.

Chapter Fourteen

Mum looks so much older than her sixty-nine years as she lies supine in the hospital bed the next day. Her complexion blends with the starched white pillows and she's unmoving, almost corpselike. So much so, that when I first walked in here, I feared the worst. Thank goodness the steady, constant beep of the heart monitor tells me she's far from that. She's out of intensive care but on a drip, and an oxygen mask covers her mouth and nose. The doctors weren't one hundred percent sure if she would make a total recovery, because of the head injury and concussion, but after a brain scan, they are now pretty confident. They will know more when she wakes.

Glancing at the big clock on the far wall, I can't believe Charlie, Rory and I have been at her bedside nearly all day on rotation, as only one person at a time is allowed in ICU. After a sleepless night waiting to hear from the hospital, we were so relieved when they said we could see her. Rory too. He raced back home from his brother's in Exeter, totally distraught and spent the night at ours. Since we were told we could visit, the hours have flown by. Mum's had nurses and doctors in and out during that time, Charlie, Rory and I have been out for a breath of air and a coffee.

But mostly I have been sitting here, holding her hand, glad of every twitch and tremor, reliving a thousand happy memories from my childhood and after.

A kaleidoscope of colour, laughter and joy, is how I'd sum up life with my mum and dad. I couldn't have wished for better parents. Little snippets of my past whirl in my mind. Days on the beach, walks in the countryside, trips to the cinema, visits to Gran's, school concerts – me on stage, them in the audience encouraging me with beaming smiles. And love. Lots of love. Dad's loss hits me again and I squeeze Mum's hand. Please let her be okay. I know the doctors say she probably will be, but I don't like that word 'probably.' I much prefer the word 'certainly.' I can't bear to lose her. Not after Sebastian, Gran and Dad. Then for what feels like the umpteenth time, I feel tears pushing behind my eyes, and dash them away with my sleeve, just as Rory puts his head round the door for his turn at the bedside.

'All okay? No change?' Rory's browny-grey hair is a bird's nest, due to the constant raking of his fingers, and there are a flock of crow's feet gathering around his kind blue eyes. Poor man hasn't slept a wink either. I think back to last year when he'd been at such a low ebb and gone missing, and had to be rescued from the eighty-foot hole of a collapsed sea-cave. I remember thinking then about the fragility of life, and what drove Rory to the edge of that hole. What drives us all. We humans are all a bit like mobile phones. If we're taken care of and recharged, we tend to thrive, and are useful. If not, we grow weak and eventually our battery dies. Since then, my mum has been his battery charger, and he hers. I'm so glad they found each other.

I give him a watery smile. 'Yeah. She's just the same.' His mouth droops down at the corners, so I add, 'But I think she might have a bit more colour in her face than she did when you saw her last.'

Rory brightens, comes in and studies Mums face. 'You know what, you're right. She's definitely got pinker cheeks.'

I stand and shrug my coat on. 'I'll go and find Charlie. Give me a shout if there's any change.' I pat his shoulder as I leave.

Charlie and I are finishing yet another coffee an hour later, when my phone rings. It's Rory. 'Nance, a few minutes ago your mum started fidgeting and mumbling. So I buzzed for the nurse. She came in with a doctor and he said it looked like Karen was waking up and shooed me out. They said they'd contact us when they had done tests and stuff.'

'Oh that's brilliant…I think.' "Tests and stuff" bring worries of the unthinkable to the surface, so I replace them with ones of Mum sitting up in bed chatting away and eating chocolates.

'Course it is, love. It will all be fine,' Rory says, with a chuckle.

'Were in the café, Rory, if you want to join us while we wait for news?'

'Yeah. I'll be right there.'

Rory ends the call and I grab Charlie's hand. 'I didn't

say anything to Rory, but what if Mum isn't okay? What if she's brain damaged, or disabled…or…' A sob cuts my words off and I slump against Charlie's shoulder, tears pouring unchecked down my face.

'Hey, hey. Now listen to me. You're emotionally and physically exhausted, so thinking the worst. Not surprising with the grief you've had losing loved ones over the years. But the docs reckon your mum will make a recovery. It will be fine, sweetling. I've a good feeling in my gut about this.'

Bolstered by his words, the use of his pet name for me, and the strength of his arm around my shoulder, I blow my nose and say, 'Charlie Cornish. Are you saying you are relying on intuition? "Feelings" instead of facts? Surely not.'

He moves back a little so he can see my expression. 'Okay, you're normally the one with the razor-sharp intuition, and a load of other unfathomable skills, but today you need to listen to me, right?'

He lifts my chin and looks into my eyes. I kiss him and snuggle back under his arm. 'Thanks, love. I'm sure you're right.'

Rory comes over all smiles and joins us. It's hard to stay gloomy with him and Charlie cheering me up, and soon I'm beginning to allow tentative rays of hope to shine light into my darkest corners. We order tea and cake, and just as I put the last morsel of a cherry slice into my mouth, my phone lights up and I almost choke when I answer it to find it's the doctor. Charlie and Rory stare round-eyed at me while I take the call, their hope for good news tangible in the space between us. My heart's beating loud in my ears as I process the news, and joy spreads warmth through my bones. 'Okay, yes. Thanks so much, doctor.'

I put the phone on the table and Charlie and Rory ask in unison, 'What did he say?'

I take a deep breath, swallow tears of happiness and reply, 'She's okay…Mum's gonna be okay! Let's go and see her!'

The corpse has gone and my lovely mum has taken its place in the bed. She's propped up on a wall of pillows and looks a bit frail, but her cheeks are certainly pinker, and her eyes light up as we pile in. The doc says we can all go in for a little while, then we have to go and leave her to recover. The tests and checks have all come back fine and all she needs now is rest. A plump, dark-haired nurse is doing Mum's blood pressure, and looks up as we enter. 'Right folks. Ten minutes, and then you'll have to go. I'll be round to check that you've gone, okay? If you're still here, I'll shoo you out.' she gives us a wink to show us she means it, but in a nice way, and then leaves.

Mum holds both arms out to me and I give her a long, but gentle hug. 'I can't tell you how happy I am to see you lot,' she says, a tremor in her voice.

'Oh, Mum. You had us so worried. Thank God, you're …' A lump rises in my throat, so I just shake my head and sit back down.

Rory hugs her next. 'Happy to see you looking more like yourself, Karen, love.' Wiping away a tear, he smiles. 'You gave us a right old shock.' He kisses her cheek and nods at the dressing on her left temple. 'How's the head?'

169

'A bit sore, but they have me on painkillers and a rehydrating whatsit.' She points at the drip.

Charlie kisses her cheek. 'What the bleddy heck were you doing anyway, woman? You should know not to walk through a field full of cows.'

'Well, I went for a walk, as I often do on coast path the other lunchtime – took my sandwiches.' She pauses and frowns. 'Wednesday…must have been, 'cos the nurse said today is Friday.'

A shudder runs through me. 'Good god, Mum. You were in that ditch from Wednesday lunch, until we found you yesterday?' I imagined she must have been there overnight, but I'd hoped she'd gone late afternoon, not lunchtime.

'Yeah, must have been.' She gives us an incredulous look. 'And as to the cows, young Charlie, yes, I know not to walk through cow fields, but I didn't see them. When I realised the path was flooded, I was going to turn back and then I glanced across the field. I saw horses in the next one, but no cows. It was only when I was already halfway down the damned field that I saw them gathered in a dip near the bottom. They saw me and came charging up.'

'Ah, that explains it then,' Charlie says, with a sigh.

'So they came and knocked you over?' I say, taking her hand. 'It's a bloody good job you weren't trampled on. Could have been much worse, despite your head injury.'

'As far as I can remember, one of them barged into me and sent me flying, and then I was kicked by one of their hooves as they ran past. Must have rolled into the ditch…' Mum stares into the distance. '…seem to remember waking at some point and trying to stand, but I felt terribly nauseous, and it'd been raining, so I slipped in the mud and fell backwards into the ditch again.'

'And there you lay until Nancy and Mel found you,' Ralph says. Mum nods. 'It's a wonder the endless phone calls didn't wake you, though.'

Mum looks a bit sheepish. 'Erm, it might have run out of juice.'

'Mum! How many times do you have to be reminded.' I turn to Rory. 'Rory, you're great at making sure Mum's physical and mental battery is charged, can you do the same for her damned phone?'

Mum frowns and then bursts out laughing. It's such a joyful infectious sound, that we can't help but join in.

Chapter Fifteen

The kitchen at Seal Cottage is flooded with November sunshine a few weeks later. I'm not fooled by the blue skies and fluffy clouds sailing above the rooftops, though. I stuck my nose out earlier to take the recycling down the path, and an icy wind nearly bit it off. My daily phone call to Mum has reassured me she's going from strength to strength, though Rory has promised he won't let her do too much. Apparently, she wanted to do a 'spot of gardening' yesterday, but he managed to persuade her to wait a bit longer. I'm so thrilled she's come on so fast. After a three-day stay in hospital, she came home to be waited on hand and foot by me, but mostly by Rory and Mel. She wants for nothing, and though she moans, I can tell she's enjoying being thoroughly spoilt. I'll pop in and see her tomorrow, as it's been a couple of days, but today is earmarked for that long-overdue St Ives visit to see Debbie, the creel wrecker.

There are literally hundreds of things I'd rather do, but I promised Lucinda I'd try to help, and I will. Debbie has been particularly busy last week with not one, not two, but three creels ruined. She's obviously getting more desperate, and if I don't get to the bottom of why she's doing it soon, I can see it ending very badly between her and husband Mike. And this is what keeps me going. If someone can be helped, then I'm there, no matter how awkward or upsetting it might be.

I stack the breakfast things in the dishwasher and go into the hall to pull on my winter boots and my parka with the fur lined hood. Then, popping my head around the living room door, I say to my little ball of fluff who's sprawled upside down on the sofa, 'Okay, Scrappy, Mummy's going out for a few hours. Be a good boy.' Scrappy opens one eye, meows and turns the other way. Not a care in the world, that one. It's alright for some.

The dark branches of the trees lining the lanes are spread like warning fingers, stark against the blue sky and green fields. Maybe they want me to turn back for home and the cosy warmth of my kitchen. I could make some cakes and pop them over to Penny's. Now wouldn't that be nice, Nancy? A good old chin-wag with Penny about what happened to your mum and a proper catch up about Joe? Yes, it would be. But she's probably working at the surgery today, and Debbie won't be put off again. *Just get it over with for goodness' sake.*

Traffic on the A30 is light, and soon I'm inching my car through the narrow streets of St Ives. Debbie and Mike live near the harbour, and after I've parked my car, I walk down the hill, taking in the gorgeous view of the little white and brown cottages tumbling down to the water. The yellow beaches frame the scene, and the headland or 'island,' topped with its 15th century chapel, stands sentinel above all else. If I had my sketchpad, I'd draw it. Looking at my phone, I follow directions to a little whitewashed cottage on a steep hill, not far from the harbour. This is it. This is the cottage with the sad and guilty looking Debbie outside it that I saw in my connection to Mike's hat. The door is red with a silver knocker, a black number 38 above it. I raise my hand to lift the knocker and take a deep breath. Then I go no further. What if Mike's here? Why the hell didn't I think of that before? I don't want to talk to Debbie in front of him. Hopefully I can persuade her to stop, and he need never know.

There's a low wall overlooking a little carpark to my left, and I hurry over to sit on it while I think what to do. My PI skills are pretty poor right now, and I chastise myself for rubbish planning. Then I cut myself some slack. I've been worried sick about Mum lately and not thinking straight. Is there any wonder I'm not firing on all cylinders? I pull out my phone, intending to call Lucinda and ask her if Mike is normally at home at this time on a weekday. She might not know, but it's all I've got right now. Hell, Debbie might not be in either. Heaving a sigh, I'm about to call Lucinda, when the door to the cottage opens and a tall, thick set man, wearing a red woolly hat comes out. He has a pleasant weather-beaten face and salt and pepper curls poke out from under the hat and along his collar. It's Mike. His soft brown eyes sweep over me, and he nods and gives me a little smile, before heaving a rucksack onto his shoulder and striding away down the narrow, cobbled street.

Phew! I wait until Mike turns a corner and then hurry

over to the cottage again and lift the knocker and bring it down. The sound of metal on wood echoes through the house and the door is quickly opened by a woman in her late fifties, or early sixties, greying hair styled into an asymmetric bob, and thick dark eyebrows over olive-green eyes. The brows lift questioningly as she takes me in. 'Debbie Roskilly?' I ask.

'Yes?' she closes the door slightly, obviously unsure.

'You don't know me, but I'm Nancy Cornish, a friend of Lucinda and William's. William, your nephew?' I cringe. She obviously knows who William is.

'Yes? Are they okay?' She frowns.

I see the worry in her eyes, and imagine she thinks I'm the bringer of bad news. 'Yes, absolutely fine. It's just that I'd like to have a bit of a chat with you. It's to do with Mike. Is it okay if I come in?'

'Mike?' The frown deepens. 'Um, well I'd like to know more of what this is about…'

And why wouldn't she? I have an idea. 'How about you call Lucinda and she can vouch for me, I completely understand why you don't want a complete stranger in your house.' I brandish my phone and give her a hopeful smile.

Debbie loses the frown, but shows me she's still wary as she folds her arms and steps aside. 'That's okay, go through to the kitchen.'

Seal Cottage isn't a mansion, but this place is tiny. The corridor from the front door to the kitchen is short and narrow, but the kitchen itself, though small, is homely and bright. It's whitewashed like the outside, and built of thick Cornish stone. A proper old fisherman's cottage. There's a

175

range along the far wall, an open fire, and a long characterful wooden table similar to the one we have, centre stage. On the walls are pictures of various boats in the harbour and at sea, with Mike at different stages of his life smiling proudly on each of them. One by the back stable door is of both Debbie and Mike on the deck of a boat at sea. They're impossibly young, wearing bright orange sou' westers, and drenched through. Arms about each other, gazing into each other's eyes adoringly, they don't seem to mind about the weather.

'A lovely photo of you and Mike, Debbie.' I smile and point to it.

Her face softens. 'Yeah. That was our first boat. We'd only been married a few months. Happy times.'

On the back wall is a large family photo of three teenagers, a boy and two girls with Debbie and Mike in the middle. 'Those your children?' A bit of a lame question, but I need to lighten the awkward atmosphere.

A dismissive nod. 'Yeah, all grown now.' She pulls out a chair at the kitchen table and indicates we should sit down. 'I'm not interested in small talk, Nancy. Are you going to tell me why you want to talk to me about Mike?'

'Yes.' I dredge up what I hope is a confident smile, though it feels a bit forced, because my confidence levels are rock bottom. This is a bit like the day I talked to Tilly about her mum visiting, but at least she knew me a bit. I've just rocked up out of the blue to poor Debbie's front door and...Oh blimey. How do I start?

'Anytime now would be good.' The frown is back and she draws her lips into a tight pucker.

176

I heave a sigh. 'Okay, Debbie. There's no easy way to explain all this...but Lucinda asked if I could help William's uncle Mike find out who is vandalising his creels.'

Debbie's eyes widen and a pink hue creeps up her neck like a spring tide. 'Why? Are you a police officer, then?'

I smile. 'No. But my husband is, funnily enough.'

'So why didn't Lucinda or William ask your husband?' She sniffs. 'Come to think of it, why didn't they ask Mike first, before poking about in his business?'

'Thing is, Debbie. I'm a PI...not a private investigator, a psychic investigator. In order to help people, I'm sometimes able to make connections with objects belonging to them, and they sometimes tell me things about that person. Often loved ones who have passed away come through to me at the same time, you know, to help point me in the right direction.'

Debbie shakes her head and glares at me. 'Are you for real?'

I hold my hands up. 'Yes. I know how that sounds, but it's the truth. I don't expect you to believe me, without evidence. So, I'll tell you that I made a connection with Mike's hat, and I know who's been sabotaging his creels.' I watch the red tide on her neck turn crimson and seep into her cheeks. 'I'm here to help if I can. Just to have a chat with you to try to get to the bottom of it.'

I see a flicker of relief in her eyes at the mention of help, and then they narrow with suspicion. 'All this is bleddy nuts. And why the hell would you need to talk to me? Shouldn't you be talking to your copper husband, if you know who's doing it?'

My eyes slide to the kettle. 'Look, shall we have a cuppa and talk about it, Debbie?'

'No. I'd like you to leave please.' She stands up and folds her arms.

I remain seated. There's no way I'm giving up yet. 'I'm sure we could sort it out if we put our heads together. Mike need never know.'

Debbie thrusts her chin out, her eyes blazing with anger. 'Never know what!'

Do I say it? Or should I get her to? 'You know exactly what I'm talking about, love.'

'Don't 'love' me. I haven't a sodding clue what you're on about! You knock on my door, tell me you're a psychic detective or something, and come out with a load of crap. As I said. I'd like you to leave. Now.' Debbie walks back up the little corridor and opens the front door. I can see I have little choice but to follow her. She's in no mood to talk, and would probably deny everything, no matter what I said. What a shame, the errand was for nothing.

As I walk down the corridor, I'm drawn to a little black and white photo in a gilt frame of a woman and a child on a beach. The child's making sand castles. Instinctively I know the child is Debbie, even though she has her back to me. My fingers trace it as I pass, and electricity shoots through my hand rooting me to the spot. Immediately a woman who looks very much like Debbie, though her hair is swept into a pony tail does the 'on switch' by the door and gazes at Debbie so tenderly, my heart aches. She's wearing a blue woollen dress and a floral apron. It's her mum, the woman in the photo. She looks at me and smiles.

'Hello, thank you for coming,' I say gently.

Debbie glares at me. 'Thank you for coming? What the fuck is the matter with you? Just get out of my house!'

Debbie's mum shakes her head. 'What language! I taught her better than that. How rude.'

'She's in shock I think…er?'

'Margaret, people called me Maggie.'

'Maggie.'

Debbie's colour drains and she follows the direction of my eyes. 'Who…who are you talking to?'

I sigh. Your mum, Debbie. She's standing right next to you and she says she doesn't like your language.'

Debbie half closes the door and leans heavily against the jamb. 'No…no, you could have found out my mum's name and… be making the whole thing up.' Her voice is trembling and she sounds about as convinced of her words as I am.

'Why would I, Debbie? I have nothing to gain.'

Maggie's clucks her tongue against the rood of her mouth. 'Tell her to stop being a silly sausage and to listen to you.' Maggie folds her arms over the floral apron. 'Be her own woman. Don't leave it until it's too late like I did. I told her this on my death bed.' Her eyes fill and she hovers her hand over her daughter's shoulder. 'Tell her she'll always be my sunshine.' Then she does the off switch, and I'm left staring at the wall.

Great. I wish spirits could communicate directly, because this is the second mother and daughter connection I've been involved in recently, and it's killing me. Debbie's

179

looking at me with a mixture of irritation and sympathy as tears well up in my eyes.

'Let's go and sit back down, Debbie and we'll talk about—'

She shoves herself away from the wall and folds her arms almost a carbon copy of her mum a few minutes ago. 'No. I want you to explain why you're upset, and all this stuff about my m...mum.'

'Might be better sitting down? You look a bit shaky.'

'Tell me now, or you can leave.'

I tell her. Then have to act quickly as she slumps against the door and slides down it. 'Hold on to me, Debbie. It's been a shock, come on, lovely. Let's get you to the kitchen and we'll have a cup of tea.'

She mutely does as I ask, thankfully, and a little while later we're sitting at the long scrubbed-pine table with steaming mugs of tea in front of us. I watch her face as she stares unseeingly through the half-open stable door. I can imagine memories of her mum are playing in her mind, and maybe one or two of how she's sabotaged Mike's creels. 'I was always her sunshine, right from when I was old enough to sing it with her,' she tells the patch of blue peeping through the clouds outside. Then she turns to me. 'The old song, you know? You are my sunshine...'

Her attempt at singing ends abruptly as she's overcome with emotion. 'I know it. My dad used to sing it to me...' I take a gulp of tea to swallow down my own tears.

Debbie's eyes slide from mine and then back, her expression apologetic. She goes to say something and then closes he mouth again. Then she blows her nose and sets her shoulders back, her chin lifts in a determined manner. 'Firstly, I'm sorry for being so rude, Nancy…but you have to admit, asking me to believe that you're a PI was a bit out there.' She smiles and her face is transformed. I go to reply but she holds up a finger. 'Obviously I know that you're telling the truth now, after you told me what my mum said. There's no way you could know.'

'Yes. And I understand it must have been a huge shock. This is the second time recently that a deceased mum has come to a daughter's aid. With a poignant song too. It's very emotional for everyone. Me included. The strength of a mother's love never diminishes, even after death.' I don't tell her about Sebastian. She doesn't need to know and it would only reduce me to a blubbering wreck.

Debbie blows her nose again. 'So, the bit about you finding out who is vandalising Mike's creels is true too.' She heaves a sigh. 'I feel so ashamed.'

I pat her hand. 'It will help to talk about it. If I know the reason why you're doing it, then we can think of a way forward.'

Debbie takes a sip of tea. 'If I followed Mum's advice I wouldn't be in this mess. I used to sit by her bedside when she was ill…she had cancer.' She takes a moment and lifts her eyes to the sky again. 'One of the last things she said to me was, be your own woman, Deb. Don't be like me at your dad's beck and call all your life. Do the things that makes you happy. Follow your dreams.'

My heart squeezes. 'Maggie was unhappy then? With your dad?'

Debbie shakes her head. 'No, not at all. They loved each other. But it was what you might call an old-fashioned marriage. He went out to work, she stayed at home – did all the domestic stuff. It was how they'd both been brought up. Neither of them really questioned their roles, but Mum said as she'd grown older, she felt like she'd missed out on life. She'd told Dad, but he either didn't get it, or didn't know what to do about it. Mum told him she wanted to do something different. Maybe volunteer in the library part-time, as she loved to read, or do an online class, or join a walking group, or all three. Thing is, my dad thought she was just getting bored with him and got a bit narky. So, for a quiet life, she dropped her ideas, and then she got ill.' Debbie shrugs. 'It was all too late.'

'That's so sad. Is your dad still with us?'

'No, he went six-months after her, in his sleep. I reckon he died of a broken heart…he was hopeless without her.'

My throat thickens again. This is tragic. 'So sorry, Debbie. Is all this linked to you and Mike…to the creels?'

'In a way, yeah. Because I've been following in Mum's footsteps. Not totally – I've always worked outside the home. And nowadays I have a part-time job in the charity shop, but all my married life, I've done most of the domestic stuff, and looked after the kids. Both of them left home a good ten years back, got kids of their own now. Mike and I always said we'd travel once he'd retired. See a bit of the world. I'd told Mum that was my ambition, and she said I should make bloody sure it happened.' Debbie's voice cracks and she gets up to run cold water into a glass.

I'm guessing I know the reason for Debbie's behaviour.

I remember that Lucinda told me that Mike was only partially retired, as he'd go mad if he wasn't at sea some of the time. When she comes to sit back down I say, 'I think Mike changed his mind, didn't he? About your travels?'

She nods and sighs. 'Yep. He came up with some rubbish about not spending our nest egg because who knew what the future held? We'd be silly to blow it all on travel, as things are so uncertain with the economy these days. He said we would need security in our later years, and his part-time lobster fishing would add to the savings. When we'd got a bit more saved, we could think again.'

'Hmm. And when you got more savings, he still didn't want to know?'

'Correct.'

'Sounds like the sea's in his blood.'

'Yeah. But what about our dreams? Or should I say, mine? I don't know if Mike ever really wanted to do anything but be on his stupid boat. He might have liked the idea of travelling, but the reality...' She shrugs.

'So, you went to desperate measures, hoping he'd pack fishing in if his creels kept being damaged?'

'Yeah. Stupid really. It just made him dig his heels in even more.' Debbie raises her hands and lets them fall. 'God knows what the answer is. I've just about had enough and I can see the years I have left to me being eaten up. I don't want to die with regrets, like my mum did.'

Silence grows between us as we ponder this. Eventually I say, 'If it were me, I'd tell him how you feel about it all. Really make him listen. Make him know you're serious, and determined to go travelling.'

Debbie stares into my eyes, yet I can tell she's far away. Then she nods slowly, a smile finding her lips. 'You're right. I have tried before, but maybe not hard enough...' Her olive eyes deepen to a fiery jade and she thumps the table. 'And you know what, Nancy? If he says no, I'll bleddy well go on my own!

On the way back up to Padstow, I can't help but smile to myself. After all my trepidation about the visit and the rocky start when I first met Debbie, intuition tells me that I can mark it down to a success. Debbie says she'll tell me how it all goes with Mike, and by the determined look in her eye, I'm sure she's going to stick to her guns. Too many women of a certain age have put their dreams on the back burner, only to have the flame go out completely in the end. I'm so lucky that I'm following my dream now. I suppressed my gift for too many years, but once I took the huge step of 'coming out' as a psychic and completely changing my life, I have never been happier. Well, I have when my boy was with us, of course. Thoughts of Sebastian lead me to Tilly and Ella, and my heart swells with happiness. Also, I think about Alison. I wonder whether she's told Chris how she feels yet? I must call her when I get back.

Chapter Sixteen

A cheese toastie for lunch, I think. Kicking the door closed behind me, I walk into the warmth of Seal Cottage and shrug off my coat. Yes, definitely a toastie. I've not had one of those for a very long time, and it's just the thing for a cold November day. Maybe I could have a cuppa soup too. Not very nutritious, but great comfort food. And fast. I'm starving and so I can have the soup while I'm making the toastie...might put a bit of red onion in with the cheese too. I absently hum a merry tune while I boil the kettle and chop the cheese. It's a few seconds before I realise what I'm humming. *You are my Sunshine.* A big grin finds my lips, and I do a little dance as I move around the kitchen.

Moments later, Scrappy bursts through the cat door like a missile, and demands lunch too. 'Okay, Scrappy, let me just sort out my toastie, eh?' Me at the kitchen table, him on the floor by the sink, we both tuck into our food, while through the French doors, the winter sunlight dapples through the trees, swaying in the breeze to a silent melody. Contentment wraps me in a hug and I sigh. Simple pleasures. As I'm putting the last morsel into my mouth, my mobile phone rings faintly from my pocket in the hallway. I'm always leaving it in my coat, must try harder.

Hurrying to claim it, I see it's Alison. Great minds think alike.

'Hi, Alison. I was going to phone you after lunch.'

'Saved you the bother, then.' She laughs then clears her throat. 'Thought you might like to know my news.'

The excitement in her voice gives me goosebumps. 'If it's what I think it is, I certainly do!'

'What? That they have a sale on at Mackerel Sky in Mevagissey?

'Oh, ha ha.' I cross my fingers and wait.

'Last night, I plucked up courage and told Chris that I had feelings for him. At first, I thought I'd done the wrong thing, because he burst out laughing. I tell you, Nancy I was gobsmacked.' She chuckles.

'Blimey. Not the reaction you'd expect.'

'Nope. But then he apologised when he saw my face, and said he was laughing with relief, because he'd been gearing up to say the same thing to me!'

'Yes! I knew it. I'm thrilled for you, Alison!'

'I'm thrilled for me too.' Her giggle is girlish and infectious. 'Though I am a bit apprehensive, as there's been no one since my Jack, and no one before him, either.'

'Hey, I can see that. But Chris will be in a similar position, and you don't have to rush things.'

'That's exactly what he said. We should take it slowly and see what happens. Mind you, having said that, we went for a drink after our chat, hugged at the end of the night, and it ended up in a snog!' She bursts out laughing.

'You shameless hussy, Alison.' I laugh along with her, and then we end the call. Another success story. How marvellous.

An hour or so later, I get ready to go out to Mum's. I hadn't intended to, but I have nothing pressing, which is both a good and bad thing. It's nice to have time to please myself, but on the other hand, nobody has responded to the new leaflets I put in local shops to advertise my services. Perhaps there will be something in the next few days. Mum's partial to my cherry scones and I slip a tin of freshly baked ones into a carrier, give Scrappy a kiss goodbye, grab my coat, check I have my phone and head out.

It's still bright and sunny on the brief drive to the edge of the estuary, but I'm mindful that the days are growing shorter and will only stay an hour or so. I'll pop into Merryn's the butchers on the way back, and get some of Cecil's special sausages for dinner. I smile as I remember how I helped him find the missing ingredient of those sausages, with the help of the spirit of his deceased wife a few years ago. He's such a lovely man, and he's making a go of things nowadays with Linda, someone else I helped. They were both very lonely and they make a great couple. I'm pleased to have had a small hand in getting them together. Wish he'd let me pay for the sausages though, but he won't hear of it.

Mum flings open the door before I can knock. I'd hoped to surprise her, but she must have seen me pull up on the drive. She looks back to normal, now. In fact, better than normal. She's had more blonde highlights put through

187

her neat bob, and paired a soft red roll-neck with black jeans. 'Nancy! Why didn't you tell me you were popping over?' My reply is redundant as she pulls me into a tight embrace, my face squashed up against her shoulder.

At last released, I say, 'I didn't plan to, but I had some free time and thought I'd pop over for an hour.'

'Lovely. Come on in out of the cold.'

'No Rory, then?' I look round the door to the living room as she leads us into the kitchen.

'No. He's gone to Merryn's for some sausages.'

'Ha! Great minds.' I hand her the carrier containing the tin of scones. 'I'm going to pop in there on the way home.'

Mum looks in the tin. 'Scones! My favourite. Shall I put the kettle on.'

'Thought you'd never ask.'

After we've chatted about the ill-fated day in the cow field, and how well she's doing now, Mum says, 'Right. I'm glad you're here, because I'd like to run something by you. Do you think I'd be any good working in a shop?'

'A shop?' To be honest I can't see mum behind the till in a supermarket. She tends to get bored quickly, and though she'd get to meet people, I don't really think it's her. 'What kind of a shop?'

Mum gives me a big smile. 'Well, I met this lovely girl, Sennen, in the Cherry Trees Café the other day. She was here with her friend Jasmine. You know Jasmine, daughter of Sally, lives up the road from you?' I nod. 'Anyway, Jasmine, Sally and this Sennen were having lunch and we got talking. Apparently, she has a gorgeous art shop which she owns in Polzeath. She's an artist and so talented. I saw photos of her work on her phone. Anyway, she's pregnant, and needs someone to help part-time. I said I might think about it.'

A faint bell rings in the back of my mind. 'I think I vaguely remember seeing Sennen with Jasmine a while back, when it was my birthday in the pub. She's pregnant? Nice.' It occurs to me that I seem surrounded with news of women who are pregnant, or have had a baby lately.

'Well?' Mum's got her head on one side scrutinising my face.

'Well, what?'

'Do you think it would be a good move for me, working in the shop?'

'I think it might suit you, as it's an art shop. I know you like to dabble now and then.'

'Yeah. And guess what? Sennen told me she'd teach me to throw a few pots. She has a potter's wheel in the back, and the pieces she makes are incredible.'

Mum's eyes are afire with excitement, and that warms my heart. It's not so long ago that I was terrified of losing her. 'Wow. I can just see you and Rory acting out 'that' scene from ghost. I laugh as her cheeks turn pink.

'Er, I don't think so. But yeah, I reckon it would be right up my street. I wanted to get your opinion though, so thanks, love.'

I'm so pleased Mum is happy now. She looks so content and confident. A strong woman who knows her mind and heart. Mum endured a few rocky years, after losing Dad, and then that awful time she had with Guy. Let's hope the cow-field debacle is the last rotten thing to happen for a good while. Gran used to say bad luck came in threes. Well poor Mum's had her three, thank you very much. 'You're welcome.' I stand up and collect the crockery. 'I'd best get off if I'm going to get to Cecil's before they shut.'

'Okay, love. I'll pop round in a few days, for a cuppa if you're not busy. Message me.' There's a knock at the door, and she goes to answer it.

'Hey, Nancy,' Mel says from the front step as I walk towards her along the corridor.

'Hi there. How are things?'

'Okay. I saw your car and wondered if I might have a word?' Mel's brows knit together and her soft brown eyes look a bit troubled.

'Yeah, sure. Wanna go to yours?'

'Yes. I won't keep you long.'

I turn to give Mum a hug, noticing the curious look she throws Mel. I expect she'll want chapter and verse on what's bothering her neighbour later. 'Bye Mum.'

'Bye love. And remember, message me.' She inclines her head towards Mel's back as she walks away towards her house. 'Looks a bit fed up.'

I nod my head and shrug, before hurrying after my friend.

Stepping into Mel's bright kitchen, I decline tea, explaining I have to get to the butcher's before it closes, so she leans against the counter and gets straight to the point.

'It's Abi. Me and Anthony went over there for dinner last night, and I paid particular attention to her behaviour because of what you said. And yeah. She's a right moody Judy. Snapping at Vicky for the slightest thing, and not joining in conversation much. When she'd gone to the loo, I asked Anthony what he thought was up, and he said had no idea. We were going to mention something to Vicky, but she looked pretty fed up already, so we kept quiet.' Mel fiddles with one of the beads on her braids and looks out of the window.

'Hm. This sounds worrying. Charlie thought it might be stuff at work getting to her, but if she's like it at home too, she must really be down.'

Mel nods. 'I went to the bathroom later, and sneaked Abi's silk scarf in with me. She'd taken it off and draped it over the back of a chair earlier in the evening.'

My heart lifts. 'You made a connection?'

She rolls her eyes. 'Sadly not. I'm no Nancy Cornish. I tried to get something from the scarf, but nothing. Nada.'

'Never mind. It'll come...and it worked when we tried together, remember?'

'Yes, but I want to be able to do it by myself.' Mel pouts and I have to hide a smile.

'It will come.' I give her a quick hug. 'Patience, young Skywalker.'

She laughs and then walks me to the door. 'So, Nancy. Will you try and find out what's wrong with Abi? I feel she's really troubled, and now Anthony is worried about her too.'

I nod. 'Yeah, but not sure when, or how.'

'Well, she's home now. She told us last night she wasn't feeling too good and would be taking today off.'

Abi has taken a day off? Hell, things must be bad. That woman is at the station before everyone gets in, and last to leave. I don't say any of this though. Mel is already worried. 'I might pop by then, after I've been to get these damned sausages.'

We say goodbye and I drive to town, pondering on how to tackle Abi. She's not the most open person in the world, and hides the truth of her feelings very well. Must be the police training.

***

Cecil is his usual chatty self, and insists I take a few pasties that his daughter-in-law has made for the shop. 'Take 'em for the freezer if you don't eat them tonight. Nobody will buy them now, as we close in half-an-hour. Fresh made today, mind. They're are almost as good as yours, maid,' he says, with a cheeky wink. 'But I won't let her hear me say that. She'd have a headfit!'

I laugh. 'Only if you're sure, Cecil.' I pick up the pasties and the packet of sausages. 'How much do I—'

Cecil holds a sausage-like finger up to silence me. 'Nancy. Do we always have to have the same old discussion every time you come in here?' His ruddy cheeks become plump apples as he smiles. 'I told you. Them sausages are free for life, after what you did for me.'

'But the pasties?'

'A gift.' Now be off with you.' He smooths his navy and white striped apron. 'I have to go and make myself look beautiful for a certain lovely Linda.' Cecil flutters his eyelashes, which sets me off again.

'Lovely Linda is lucky to have you. Give her my love, won't you?'

'I will, my dear. Mind how you go.'

Mind how you go... Yes, I'll have to, if I'm to get anything from Abi. Gently does it, I think. The car clock tells me it's almost five-o'clock as I pull up outside Abi and Vicky's in Rock. Vicky works unregulated hours, as she's a journalist, but I think she's sometimes home at six-ish as far as I remember, so I'd better be quick. It's even more unlikely that she'd confide in me, if her partner was there. I've only been to their new place once before, and now with its 1930s curved white walls, standing at the top of a sweeping driveway in the winter dusk, it looks even grander than last time. Rock is one of the most expensive places in Cornwall to live, but the girls could afford it, once they'd sold their respective homes and bought this one together. Abi's is the lone car at the top of the drive. Good. I pull up next to it and get out. There's a cosy glow coming from the kitchen window, and so I hurry round to the back door which overlooks the long, ordered garden, sweeping to the beach and estuary beyond.

Abi opens the door to me, and I'm surprised in the difference in her. An image of the first time I saw her surfaces. A slightly built, tallish woman with blonde bob and elfin features hurrying down the garden path towards me. She was wearing black trousers and a smart red shirt, her stunning blue eyes sparkling with life. It's been a few months since we last met, but even so, under the baggy grey sweatshirt and joggers, I can see she's lost quite a bit of weight. Her cheekbones just sharp in her heart-shaped face, and her eyes resemble a stormy ocean. The blonde bob is longer now, and in messy unkempt spirals. 'Nancy? Everything okay?'

'Yeah, I was in the area, so just thought I'd pop in and see you. It's been a while.' I try a bright smile, mindful of the fact that she's trained to spot fake behaviour a mile off. My cheeks grow hot, which doesn't help my act.

A slow nod and a narrowing of the eyes. 'Right.' She doesn't offer to ask me in, and the space between us is solid, awkward.

Unable to keep the bright smile on my face any longer, I say, 'If you're busy, don't worry. I should have called.' I take a step back, and look over my shoulder at nothing in particular.

'No, come in.' I've had warmer invitations, but she turns and leads the way inside, so I follow.

The kitchen is a stunning creation of chrome and scarlet, with a scattering of spotlights to soften the edges. It's equipped with all the latest must-have gadgets, as that's Abi's thing. She loves new technology, which feels at odds with her choice of house. It all seems to work though, the 2020s rubbing shoulders with the 1930s. 'So how have you been?'

Abi perches on a tall stool and leans her forearms on the scarlet countertop. 'Oh, you know...' She nods at the stool opposite and I climb onto it. 'Wanna coffee, or a G&T?'

'I would love a G&T, but I'd better not, as I'm driving. Coffee would be nice, thanks.'

She nods, slips off the stool and presses various buttons on a state-of-the-art coffee machine which growls into action. 'Made you a latte,' she says a few minutes later, pushing a mug towards me, and then goes to the fridge. I watch her make a huge gin and tonic, and her slow deliberate actions and careful steps around the kitchen tell me it's not her first today. Back on the stool, the ice cubes tap together as she swirls her drink, then takes a long swallow. Exhaling she says, 'That's better.'

Again, an awkward space builds up between us, so to halt its progress, I say, 'How's Vicky?'

'Peachy.' Abi takes another swallow and burps, her eyes staring straight ahead over my shoulder.

'Good...and how's work?'

'Look, just tell me why you're here, Nancy and cut the bull.'

I'm taken aback by both her words and the annoyance in her eyes. I don't know what to say. 'Er...not sure what you—'

'You know exactly what I mean. You come to see me at home at 5pm. Why on earth would you expect me to be in? I would normally be at work.' She pushes her fingers through her messy hair. 'So this leads me to believe you've been speaking to either Charlie, my brother, Vicky or Mel. Maybe all of them. Maybe they all think I need a visit from the resident psychic investigator.' She turns her bottom lip down and flutters her eyelashes. 'You know, just to try and find out what's the matter with poor little Abi.'

I can't hold her piercing gaze, so look into my coffee mug, wondering how to handle this. Deciding honesty is

195

the best policy here, I say, 'Okay. Yeah, I came specially to see you. A while back Charlie mentioned you weren't yourself at work, and then more recently, Mel said she was worried about you. You're moody, not yourself at all. As a friend...' I look up from my mug and see her eyes briming with tears. I take her hand and she lets me. 'As a friend, I wanted to come and check on you. See if there's anything I can do.'

I pull a tissue from my pocket, as tears roll down her cheeks. She blows her nose and takes another drink. 'Maybe you're the best person to talk to, given the way you helped me a few years back. You know what my background was like. What my parents were like.'

Only too well. They were very religious and were in vehement opposition to sex before marriage, abortion, and homosexuality, to name a few. They were exacting in their demands of all three of their children to be perfect and attain the highest goals. As a teenager, Abi had hidden the fact that she was gay from them, as she knew what it would mean. She broached the subject with her priest, and had been told it was a ridiculous phase. Then her sister, who was a novice nun at the time, had blackmailed Abi, threatening to 'out her', if she didn't resign from her job. Thankfully, Anthony had stood up for her, and things had settled down a little between Abi and her parents, though the relationship was far from great.

'Yeah, I do. Has something else happened with your mum and dad?'

Abi sniffs and blows her nose. 'No. They are still as delightful as ever. Slightly right of Genghis Khan, and as

196

about as tolerant of the beliefs of others as the Spanish Inquisition. So, nothing's changed there. But they are at the centre of it - my whole background.' She looks up at me and notices the puzzled frown.' Right. Let me get to the point. You see, it's about me and Vicky…we want different things for the future. She wants a child, and is talking about sperm banks. The thought of it bloody terrifies me.'

I had no idea what I was expecting, but it certainly wasn't this. More baby news, everywhere I look. 'Have you never wanted children, Abi?'

A deep sigh. 'Oh, I want them. I love babies. But this is me we're talking about. Me, whose parents completely fucked my head up, who controlled and directed me from the word go. I have a lot of baggage because of them, Nance. And I mean, a lot. I'm always pushing myself, feel things are never good enough, that I'm not enough, in oh, so many ways. I thank god for the day Vicky walked into my life, but can't imagine why she stays. And if I tell her I don't want kids, she'll walk right back out again. Oh, maybe not now, but she will, eventually.

Her face twists in anguish and she looks into her glass. 'Hey, let's get things in perspective, love. If you want children, then that's half the battle. More than half. There is always a way around things. And let me tell you, I know exactly why Vicky stays. You're a wonderful, caring, lovely woman, a loyal friend, and a fair and diligent police officer. Someone who goes the extra mile to get the bad guys.'

Abi blinks away standing tears. 'Thank you. But I'd be no good as a parent, Nancy. I'd hate to make a mess of their lives, like my parents made of mine. It wouldn't be fair.'

I shake my head and take her hand again. 'But you wouldn't, if you have Vicky alongside you to discuss every move. Have you told Vicky about your fears. I'm guessing you haven't?'

'No. I said I couldn't give her an answer right away, as I needed to think. That was a few months ago…and whenever she brings it up, I say I need more time. She's getting pissed off with my reluctance to discuss things, and our relationship is suffering. My work life too. I'm like a bear with a sore head with colleagues, because the baby question is always there in the background, nagging away at me. Then all the shit about me being a rubbish person piles in, and I end up snapping at everyone.'

We sit in thoughtful silence for a while and then I say, 'Look. The only way around this is to tell Vicky exactly what you told me. She'll understand, and you will work through this, believe me.'

'I don't think it will be as easy as that.'

'No. It won't be easy, but I know you'll get there.'

'You've had a vision or something?'

'No. But I can try and glean something, if you like?' She nods and holds my gaze. 'Okay. Keep hold of my hand, and we'll see if anything comes to me.'

I clear my mind, take a few deep breaths and close my eyes. The silence in the room grows, save for the ticking of the huge kitchen clock on the far wall, and the whisper of the wind through the trees outside the window. Then a rolling image of Vicky and Abi with a little girl about two-years-old in a pushchair, and a boy about six-years-old, comes at me full of vibrant colour and energy. Abi's pushing him on a swing and laughing, her head thrown back, carefree. Then it ends, and I open my eyes and smile.

'Well? Did you see something?'

'I did. But I'm not telling you the detail, because I want your future to be a surprise.' Abi starts to protest, so I hold up a finger. 'Suffice to say, that you will make a wonderful parent and you will be happy. Very.'

'Really?' Tears chase each other down her cheeks.

'Really.'

Abi throws her arms around me. 'I can't tell you how relieved I am. Thanks *so* much, Nancy.'

'It's my pleasure. Now talk to that woman of yours, tonight. Okay?' I shrug my coat on and turn towards the door. Best get going.

'I will talk to her as soon as she gets home, promise.'

'Great. Let me know how it all pans out.' I give her a quick hug, and then hurry to the car.

I drive home with a smile on my face. Thank goodness Abi and Vicky are going to be happy again. As she said, it won't be easy, but now she knows I've seen a positive future, it should help them both work through it all. My stomach growls and an image of sausages and mash in onion gravy wafts into my mind. Maybe I'll make an apple crumble too. Okay, maybe that won't help the middle-age spread, but I feel I deserve a treat tonight.

Chapter Seventeen

The next morning brings with it wind, rain and a miserable grey light that cloaks the garden and seeps into my soul. Why I'm so fed up I have no idea. Okay, the weather isn't the best, and I'm not great with winter, but I was so happy last night, pleased with myself that I'd helped Abi and Vicky. Why I'm so low now is a mystery. Even Charlie asked if I was okay before he went off to work this morning, and as he's on autopilot before he's had at least three coffees, he normally never notices anything. Thinking about it, my moods have been a bit up and down lately. Nothing too serious, but I'm not usually prone to feeling down. I put in an extra slice of bread to toast, and make a cuppa while I have a puzzle over why I'm sometimes such a moody Judy, as Mel would say.

Fortified by toast with thick butter and homemade marmalade, my brain presents me with a possible answer. The fact that Lucinda, Tilly, and now Abi's lives are very much geared towards babies fills me with joy, yet there is a little shadow of sadness tagging along behind as well. My boy was with me for far too brief a time, and maybe I'm resenting that fact. Why did Sebastian have to be taken? What had he done wrong, what had I or Charlie done? We were good people, always tried to help anyone. So why us? I take a sip of tea and admonish myself. There is never rhyme nor reason to things like this. Why not us? There's no grand plan that says bad things never happen to good people, is there? I sigh and wonder about more toast. Sebastian's death is something I will never 'get over,' but it's been a long time since he left, and I have learned to live with it. So why is the fact I'm surrounded by baby news getting to me now?

Toast is not the answer, because my tummy will be the size of a mountain if I keep this up. Comfort eating is never comfortable in the end. Neither is wallowing, so get off your bum and do something, woman. I wash up the few breakfast dishes and ponder on what I should be doing as I wipe the worktops down in the kitchen, and then head upstairs to get dressed. Maybe I need to consider advertising on Facebook, because those flyers don't seem to be working. That could be another reason as to why I'm out of sorts. No work coming in means no income and idle hands. Idle hands lead to boredom, and boredom leads to being more fed up, and being more fed up leads to comfort eating and…I catch sight of my frowny face in the bedroom mirror and shake my head. Sort yourself out, Nancy. You should be patting yourself on the back for all the good things you've done lately and all the people you've helped, not tearing yourself down.

A little twinge and ache in my tummy reminds me that the whole thing could be hormonal. I might be due on my period, though they have been all over the place for a while too. In fact, I can't remember when the last one was. The reason for this whispers 'helpfully' in my ear, as it has been doing for some time, so I tell it to shut up. The big M will not be allowed into my life until it's absolutely necessary. I slip on a pair of black jeans and find that I can hardly zip them up. Maybe it *is* absolutely necessary? I exhale and look at my face in the mirror. Pink cheeks as a result of the struggle with the jeans, and shiny resentful eyes as a result of maybe realising I *am* actually starting with the damned menopause.

As a great believer in thinking that talking to someone who has experience of the problem you might be having, I decide to take the bull by the horns. Perhaps Mum would be the one to chat to...or possibly Penny. I'm due a catch up with her, and she only recently went through the whole thing herself. Luckily, it's her day off, and if I give her a quick call, I might be able to meet her for lunch. Lunch. Thinking about food again. Is this a symptom of the menopause? I know putting on weight is. Opting for a comfortable soft blue jumper to disguise my too tight jeans, I put a brush through my hair and hurry downstairs to give Penny a call.

My mobile is in the pocket of my coat *again* and almost out of charge or 'gas' as Charlie says. It's been in there since last night, and there's a missed call from Debbie. Maybe the menopause makes you forgetful too. I plug the phone in by the sofa in the living room, flop down onto it and press return call. 'Hi, Debbie, sorry I missed you.'

'That's okay, Nancy. I just wanted to give you a quick update. I'm happy to say that Mick and I are on the right track now. I toyed with the idea of keeping what I'd done

202

to his creels a secret, but in the end, I knew honesty was needed. I expected a huge row when I told him about the sabotage, but after the shock had hit home, he was just strangely quiet and very sad.' Debbie sniffs. 'Eventually, he said he was so sorry I'd had to resort to such drastic measures. And...'

Debbie's quiet sob halts her words, and I say, 'Hey, don't worry about telling me. It's still quite raw and—'

'No. No I want to tell you, because what he said was lovely.' She clears her throat. 'Mike said I was the most important thing in his life. Well, me and the kids, and he would do anything to make it right. He said that he'd been selfish and unthinking, and it was time it stopped. So, in the spring we're going travelling for six-months. Not sure where yet, but wherever it is, it will be bloody fantastic!'

Through an ear-to-ear smile I say, 'That's such good news. I'm so thrilled for you!'

'Thanks, Nancy. And thanks so much for your help. God knows what would have happened if you'd not shown up and let me have my lovely mum's guidance. I've never needed it more.' There's another sniff and some nose blowing. 'I have given some money to Lucinda to pop to you, as she only lives nearby, I know. Mike sends his thanks too – though he was a bit shocked to hear about your special talents, I must say.' Debbie chuckles.

'Yes, it can take a bit of getting used to, this PI stuff. And thanks for the money. I'll keep up to date on your travels via Lucinda. Bet she and Will are thrilled for you both too.'

'They are. And would you mind if we kept in touch? I

feel like you're a friend now.' Her words come out in a rush. 'Seems silly after the way I behaved, and we've only met once but...'

I stop her with, 'Of course. I'd like that too. Keep me up to date, yeah?'

'I will. Thanks again, Nancy.'

Debbie's news has given me a lift and suddenly things don't look so gloomy. Penny said she would love to meet for lunch, too, so I do a bit of dead-heading in the garden, feed Scrappy for the third time today, and check my reflection in the hall mirror. I shrug on my coat and am about to add a bit of lip gloss, and head into town, when the doorbell rings. Lucinda's standing there with a huge smile on her face. Then her honey eyes sweep my attire, telling her I'm dressed for the outdoors, and the smile falters. 'Nancy, you're off out?'

'Yes, off to meet my friend Penny for lunch. But come in for a mo.' I step aside and wave her in.

'You sure? I won't stay long, just dropping some money to you from Debbie.'

'Yeah, thanks. She called earlier.' I close the door behind us, and we go through to the kitchen.

'Isn't it fantastic news?' Lucinda says, pushing her tortoiseshell glasses up to the bridge of her nose. 'I must admit, Nancy, when you told me you thought the creel wrecker could be Debbie, I didn't think it possible. But desperation makes people do odd things sometimes, I suppose.'

'It does. And I'm so pleased it ended well.' I note that

while she's been talking that she's been cradling her bump, stroking it lovingly. 'I nod at her tummy. 'You're cooking away nicely there.'

'Yes, he or she is doing a jig at the moment. Want to feel?'

Her happy face full of pride is literally glowing, and I reach out to put my hand on her belly. Just as I do, I feel a rush of envy and a mix of feelings crash into each other, as tears fill my eyes. What the hell is wrong with me? I look down and concentrate on the little life I can feel moving under my palm, and joy takes the upper hand. 'Oh, Lucinda. How wonderful.'

Lucinda's small hand finds mine, and she peers up into my face. 'Hey, Nancy. Are you okay?'

I sniff and dab my eyes. 'Yes, just emotional about a whole new life starting.' This is true, but Sebastian's loss is there too, twisting my gut, reminding me that my time as a mother is long gone. And maybe I'm beginning the menopause now…it's too much.

'Aw. Yes, it is truly amazing.' Lucinda leads me to a kitchen table and sits me down. Head on one side like a curious sparrow, she asks, 'Are you sure that's all it is?'

Hell, is everyone psychic these days? 'I consider saying yes, all is well, but then out comes, 'Feeling your little one move made me think of my Sebastian. It seems like forever since we lost him, and only yesterday at the same time.'

It's Lucinda's turn to get tearful. 'Oh, Nance. It must be so hard. You did tell me, but I can't remember why you couldn't have more children?'

'Complications of his birth meant that it would be

extremely unlikely that I would conceive. I had an emergency C-section which left me with uterine scarring, and I've only one fallopian tube.'

She frowns. 'Sorry to hear that...but I've heard of people having babies with just the one.'

'Yes, but it didn't happen for us. We thought about adoption briefly, but decided against it. It didn't feel right.'

'What a shame. You were a wonderful mum, I bet.'

I smile through my tears and see her copy me. 'I wasn't bad.' We hold each other's eyes for a few seconds and then a take a breath. 'Right. No good wallowing here. I have to go and see Penny. And it is truly wonderful to see you happy, Lucinda. You've not had it easy, I know.'

'Thank you, Nancy. And once again, if it hadn't been for your help when I lost my gran's precious book, I would never have met Will again.' She rubs her tummy. 'And this little one wouldn't exist. You've helped so many people with your phenomenal gift.'

'Thanks, Lucinda. I needed to hear that today.'

A smile. 'Right. I'll be off, then.' I follow her to the door and then she stops and touches her forehead. 'My brain isn't switched on right these days. I haven't given you the money from Debbie and Mike.' Out of her bag she pulls a brown envelope. 'There you go. £200, Debbie said.'

'That's lovely, though I only saw her the once.' Not sure if I'll ever get used to people paying for my help, but then we have to eat.

'She was happy to give it, Nancy. And Mike says can he have his hat that I gave you to make a connection with? It's old and battered like him he said, but it's of sentimental value.'

'It's right here.' I take it down from the coat peg by the door and hand it to her. 'Please keep me posted on things, and let me know when you might want to see Mel to have a chat about maternity leave.'

'I will. In fact, just give her my number and we can chat direct.' I get a quick peck on the cheek. 'Bye, Nance. See you soon.'

As I wave her off, I think of all the people who now know each other because of me and my gift. It's a wonderful community of different personalities and backgrounds, but they all seem to gel together somehow. As I lock the door and set off into town, contentment grows in my chest. Let's hope it stays around.

Chapter Eighteen

It's stopped raining and the afternoon sky is opening its grey curtains little by little. The winter sun feels as if it's trying to peep through in patches here and there, but I'm not sure it's quite up to the challenge. Penny is sitting at our usual table by the window in the Cherry Trees Café, gazing out at the boats in the harbour, They are bouncing up and down on their moorings, as if impatient to be off. I wave as I hurry across the road, and she lifts a hand in acknowledgement.

'Hi Nancy,' she says, as I bustle in. 'I ordered us a pot of tea while we decide what we want. She nods at the red and white stripy pot and cups on the table in front of her. 'Hope that's okay.'

'Lovely. I could murder a cuppa.' I shrug my coat off onto the back of a chair and sit down. 'It's been one of those mornings, you know?'

Penny frowns and fiddles with the collar of her pink shirt. 'Oh. Nothing too awful I hope?'

'No. Well, yes and no...' I stop and consider my menopause worries. 'No. It's not too awful really. It's something that is inevitable, but upsetting, nonetheless.' Then remembering the contented feeling I had just before I left the house, I take a breath and smile. 'There was a lovely thing happened this morning too. Well, two actually. Debbie, someone I helped lately rang to thank me, and then, another friend, Lucinda, came over who's having a baby. You remember, I helped her find a lost book a while back?' Penny nods. 'Anyway, I felt her baby move and…'

Unexpectedly my throat closes over, and all I can do is shake my head when Penny asks, 'Hey, what's wrong, Nance?'

I sniff back tears, angry that I'm getting so emotional again. 'God knows. Well, I think I do know, actually. That's one of the reasons I wanted to come and see you,' I blurt. Penny looks at me, concern in her calm blue eyes. Why can't I just say what I mean, instead of bubbling over, like a pot on a stove?

'Look. Just take a minute.' Penny pours us both a cup of tea and pushes one towards me. 'Have a drink and relax.'

We do synchronised sipping for a few moments, then I take a deep breath. 'I think I might be starting with the menopause,' I say to the teapot. Why I can't look my friend in the eye, I don't know. It's nothing to be ashamed of, and she's been through it herself.

'Oh, love. No wonder you're upset. It's a bit of a shock, isn't it…kind of creeps up on you.' Penny pats my hand.

The waitress picks that moment to come over and ask if we are ready to order. We both shake our heads, then I change my mind. No point in pondering over the menu, I know exactly what I want. 'Actually, can I have one of your giant pasties, please?'

209

Penny's eyes grow round. We'd always said we'd never be able to eat even half of one, because they were so massive. 'Flippin' 'eck, Nance. You sure?'

'Yeah. Fed up of worrying about my ever growing belly – might as well go the whole hog for once.'

The waitress chuckles. 'Life's too short to not have a blow out now and then, eh?'

'Exactly.' The waitress' hazel eyes full of merriment give me the seal of approval.

'Well, I can't go giant,' Penny says, 'but I'll have a normal sized one to keep you company, mate.'

'Coming up,' the waitress says, with a smile.

'So, Nance. What made you realise you might be starting then?'

I sit back fold my arms and reply, 'Piling weight round my middle, sporadic periods and then no period for,' I calculate where we are in the year, 'must be two months at least. Irritable, moody, not sleeping great on occasion, more tired than normal, overly emotional...that will do for now. And being surrounded by babies every way I turn recently, hasn't helped. It's brought the loss of Sebastian back big-time, and now I think I'm in the menopause, it makes it all even worse. I know it shouldn't, because I've known for years I can't have kids anyway, but it does. It's like the final nail in the coffin. Stupid, I know.' I look at the boats engaged in their endless dance with the sea and shake my head.

'It's certainly not stupid. The menopause is a huge thing for us, Nancy. Psychologically, emotionally, physically, mentally, all the 'allys'. We all go through it, and have similar experiences, but it's unique to each and every one of us. Nobody can tell you how you should be feeling, or how to get through it.' Penny squeezes my hand and I see her eyes are moist as I look back at her. 'I'm here to help if I can, and offer advice, given my experience, of course. But we're all different.' She laughs, and smooths a stray hair back into her neat chignon. 'My mum sailed through, hardly affected her at all. I was a wreck for years.'

'You hid it well then.'

'We do, don't we? We women are supposed to just get on with it. Yes, I know there's more discussion about it all nowadays, and celebrities have written books, etcetera. But we're constantly bombarded with messages about what it is to be a woman – how we should look, dress, behave, god knows what else. And we're all put into little boxes according to age. Once we've become menopausal, we maybe see ourselves as less of a woman. Less attractive, less sexy, less confident...just less.' Penny shrugs. 'We need to fight against all that, and in the end, the world doesn't stop just because our periods do. I didn't really talk to Joe about it much either. He didn't know what to say – just comforted me when I was down and said he loved me. That's all I needed, really. You talked to Charlie?'

'No. I didn't really admit it to myself until this morning. I've sort of known for some time it couldn't be anything other than the menopause, but I pushed it all away, hoping it would disappear. I'll have to tell him sooner or later.'

'It will all be fine.'

'Hm. What were your symptoms, then?'

'Hot flushes, irritable, put weight on, knackered, moody, heavy periods, mostly. Hot flushes were worst I think, especially being a receptionist at the surgery. I'm sure people used to think I was embarrassed. Well, you would, wouldn't you? If I was booking them in, I'd be reading the computer screen, and my bright red face would make some uncomfortable, because I'm sure they wondered if I knew all about their intimate personal problems!' Penny laughs.

I laugh with her. 'Yes, I can see how that would work.' We drink our tea and I'm glad I came. Penny's fighting talk about not accepting the bombardment of media messages has helped. I'm nothing if not a fighter. She'd definitely put my mind at rest a bit. 'Sounds like it's the menopause then for me. Well, apart from hot flushes and the period thing. You had heavy ones, mine's buggered off.'

'Yep. But as I said, we're all different. You should definitely come to the surgery for a check-up, though. It wouldn't go amiss to have a bit of an overhaul.'

'I'm not one of those boats out there, Pen.' I nod through the window. 'You reckon I might need my barnacles scraping?'

'Ha! Maybe. Seriously though, it might help. The doc will run a few tests and maybe give some advice. I went on HRT for a bit, but it didn't suit me. It might work for you though, and as far as I can see, the more information you have about this, the better.'

Penny's making a lot of sense, but there's a little worry at the back of my mind that wants to come to the front. Penny must see lots of illnesses in her job and will know some of the symptoms. 'You don't think it could be anything else, do you? You know something bad...so you're suggesting I go for tests?'

I get a withering look. 'No, Nancy. I suggested it so you could get advice and a check over. Now, let's talk about something else. Our pasties are on their way.' She smiles as the waitress sets our plates down, and looks askance at mine. 'Bloody hell, Nancy, if you eat all that, you'll need a crane to get you home.'

The pasty is so big, it sticks over the rim of the plate at both sides, and I think ordering this giant might have been a bit rash. 'Hmm...well, I'll give it my best shot.'

We eat in companiable silence for a few minutes, agreeing that the pasty is one of the best we've ever tasted, then Penny puts her head on one side and gives me a searching look. 'You know you said you missed Sebastian, and that all the baby news, coupled with the menopause made you realise you'll never be a mum again?'

'Yeah, but I don't really think that, I—'

'Why not adopt?'

That brings me up with a start. One, because it's a ludicrous idea, and two, because I was only talking to Lucinda about it earlier. 'Adopt?'

'Yeah.'

What a crazy idea. 'No. Me and Charlie decided against that, years back, and we're too old now anyway.' An image of Charlie's wistful expression comes to me, the time we were talking about Tilly maybe giving Ella up for adoption. What was that all about?

'No, you aren't. I know a couple in their fifties who

213

adopted.'

'Really?'

'Yeah. Why is it a crazy idea?'

I shake my head and break another bit of pasty off in my fingers, while a snatch of Gran's words from her recent connection whispers in my ear. She'd appeared to me pregnant, and said something about new life is everything, and I deserve my happiness. Could it be this? Is adoption what she meant? I look into Penny's questioning face and say, 'Because Charlie would think it's too late to become parents again, as do I. And what would Sebastian think?' As soon as I said those words, I wished them back in. Heaven knows what Penny made of them.

'Sebastian would be pleased for you, love. Ask him if you're not sure. There will be an answer.'

I should have known she'd get it. The depth of her understanding warms my heart. She doesn't think I'm silly at all, but then she's a medium and used to my world. Suddenly, for some reason, the idea of adoption doesn't seem so crazy after all. Maybe Charlie and I weren't ready all those years ago, but maybe we are now. Maybe the time is right, now. I heave a sigh. 'I'll see, Pen. I might broach it with Charlie soon. There's a lot I have to deal with at the moment though.' I give her a cheeky smile. 'Baby steps.'

'Indeed. But it seems to me that you being surrounded by babies at every turn is a blatant message, Nance. A message that says it's time to give a child a loving home and wonderful future with you and Charlie. What do you want, a neon sign, complete with flashing lights around the edges?'

'It might look nice in the garden?'

Penny narrows her eyes and nods at my plate. 'Finish your pasty, while I order that crane.'

***

My footsteps are lighter on the walk back to Seal Cottage than they were on the way into to town earlier. Penny's chat has been a real tonic, even though she did throw up the idea of adoption. Certainly not something I thought I'd be considering when I got out of bed this morning. But she's right. Everything does seem to be pointing in that direction. Babies here, there and everywhere, even Gran's cryptic connection. I think about discussing it with Charlie, but doubt tiptoes in and makes itself at home.

Even if I'm right, that he had been wistful about the idea of adoption recently, it might just have been a passing regret that we hadn't gone for it. The reality of having a baby or child in our lives in our mid-forties might not be at all what he'd want. Or me either. We're both settled in our careers, have a comfortable life, and what on earth would I do about Nancy Cornish PI with a baby in tow? I adore what I do, so it wouldn't work, would it? No. In the café with Penny, the whole idea hadn't sounded too crazy, but now it's just me, on my own with my thoughts, it feels like just that. An idea.

On my way past Merryn's, Cecil leaps out of the doorway onto the pavement in front of me brandishing a boning knife. 'Bloody hell, Cecil! What are you doing? You scared the life out of me!' I put a hand on my chest, and take a breath. My heart's going like the clappers.

Cecil puts the knife into the big pocket of his black and white striped butcher's apron, his expression apologetic. 'Gawd. Sorry, Nance. I forgot I was holding the knife. Just trimming some pork chops when I saw you crossing over the road, and I remembered I needed to ask you something.' He laughs, his blue eyes sparkling like chips of sapphire in his florid complexion. 'Should have asked you when you came in the shop for sausages recently, but forgot.'

Calmer now, I'm able to see the funny side of things. 'Right. What's it about?'

'Come through and I'll put the kettle on. Talan's minding the shop.' He turns to go inside, but I've had enough tea for a while.

'I won't if you don't mind. Just been to the café, Cecil, and I have stuff to do. Can you tell me out here?'

'Yes. It won't take long.' He folds his arms over his ample stomach. 'It's my sister, see. Her name's Yvonne. She needs your side-kick help.' A cheeky wink. Cecil's always said side-kick instead of psychic. I always answer him in the same way too. It's like our little in-joke.

'That's hilarious, Cecil. You should go on the stage.'

'I might just do that one day,' he says with a grin.

'How can I help her?'

'Well, Yvonne's going to be a granny soon. Can hardly believe it, as she's my little sister. You never think your little sister will become a granny one day, do you?'

'No. I don't suppose you do.' I move to one side to let someone past. Cecil was never great at getting to the point, and people are having to edge round us on the pavement.

216

'She's been waiting long enough, mind. Her daughter, my niece, Bella, is in her late thirties. Lovely girl. Got married two years back. We never thought she'd get pregnant though, her being one of those high flyer types. She's a lawyer, you know. Or do we call 'em solicitors? You get confused with all those American TV shows...'

Cecil rambles on about which TV show he likes the best, while I think about neon signs pointing to yet more babies. Why am I not surprised? Then I hold my hand up, halting his ramblings. 'What exactly does your sister need my help with, Cecil?'

He chuckles and shakes his head. 'Sorry. Here's me going on and on. I know you have things to do.' I give him an encouraging smile. 'Okay. You see, our grandma was a great knitter. There was nothing she couldn't make. Often she wouldn't even use a pattern.' He taps his temple. 'Had it all up here, you know. Clever, she was. Thing is, she had lots of patterns that our Yvonne had after she died. Yvonne is a keen knitter too. So when she knew she was going to be a granny, she went to get the baby clothes patterns, but she's lost em.'

'Oh, that's a shame. Where did she keep them?'

'In the shed. Had a big plastic box of 'em but they were gone.' Cecil's eyes grow round and he raises his hands to the sky. 'Poof! Gone.'

'I see. And she wants me to help her find them?'

'Got it in one.' He jabs a sausage finger at me. 'Hang on a mo, I'll just pop back inside to get her address and phone number.' I pray that he doesn't get waylaid by a customer and be missing for ages. Luckily my prayers are

217

answered, as moments later he's back with a bit of paper which he hands to me. Sticking a stubby pencil behind his ear, he says, 'Thanks, Nancy. I've written down her information on there. Hope you can help our Yvonne. She was really looking forward to making hand-made baby things.'

I smile. 'I'll certainly do my best, Cecil.'

'Proper job. Babies are such a precious gift, aren't they?'

'They are indeed.' I put the paper in my pocket and take my leave.

Hurrying away along the pavement, I think about Cecil's words again. A gift. But do Charlie and I really want to receive one? We'll see.

Chapter Nineteen

Two days after I met with Penny, Charlie rang to say he'd be home around six and so we can eat at a reasonable time for once. He's been so busy at work, dotting the I's and crossing the T's to make sure all the evidence for Leanne's trial is as it should be. Then there's a new case he's working on – an aggravated burglary of a shoe store in Truro. Why people would want to steal shoes, I have no idea. Maybe the baddie is a centipede. It's not funny really, because the poor security guard defending the store is in hospital, and it's touch and go whether he will make it. Poor Charlie. His job is hardly a bundle of laughs, is it? But then again, he said that Abi is much more like her old self, so that's a bonus. I'm so glad I could help her.

Because he's up to his eyes, and a plethora of other reasons, I've been dithering about tackling the adoption topic with him. But it should be sooner rather than later, and this evening I've more-or-less decided is the sooner. I wipe the kitchen worktop down and rinse the cloth, while doubt creeps in to keep me company. Hmm. Maybe this evening is a bit too soon – particularly because I'm still unsure about it all. It's a pretty new idea, to say the least…besides, I haven't asked Sebastian yet.

Home-made chicken goujons, savoury rice and salad is on the menu I decide, and I take out some chicken breasts and give them a good bash with a rolling pin. My hands seem to work on auto pilot, as I think about the times Sebastian has visited me over the years. He's come to me at different ages, but never older than about eight. I wonder if he'll come to me in the future as a teenager, or even as a man? Even though he's gone, those visits are so precious to me. Maybe he's living another life somewhere. Somewhere where he grows up, just as he would if he were here. It seems possible, or why would he show himself at different times of his development? Even though I have a wonderful gift, I know very little about the spirit world, or what happens to the spirit after our bodies die. But then I'm not alone there, and in a way, I'm not sure I'd want to know. Perhaps we will all be let into the secret when the time comes.

Okay, breadcrumbs next. I wash my hands at the sink and stare out through the window at the dark garden. Night has almost fallen, and as I reach up to pull the blind, through the pane, I see the reflection of someone behind me in the kitchen. A little someone. My boy. I turn around and my heart swells as he smiles at me. My Sebastian is here and he looks around thirteen or so now, dressed in black jeans and a white T-shirt. My breath catches in my throat as I see how much like Charlie he's becoming, apart from the eyes. He has my green eyes, but his hair is the exact colour of his dad's and his jaw is becoming squarer like Charlie's. Suddenly it's all too much, as a barrage of what if's, regrets and longing hammer into my mind, and a sob breaks free as my eyes blur. I quickly wipe my tears away with a tea-towel as I don't want to miss one second of his visit, but he folds his arms over his chest and says, 'Don't cry, Mummy.'

'Oh, my love. I miss you so much. Are you...are you happy?'

He gives a serene smile, but doesn't reply, just holds my gaze with an intensity I can hardly bear, then he says, 'A baby. A baby sister. She will come and be loved too.'

Oh hell, this is breaking me. I wipe my tears again and swallow hard. 'A sister, you mean for you, and a daughter...for us?'

'Yes. I love you, Mummy. Tell Daddy the same.' Then he raises a hand and walks to the kitchen door.

'No. Stay a while, please, my darling. Please, please stay...'

'I'll come again.' Then he does the off switch, and I'm left alone.

Slumping onto a kitchen chair, I find myself smiling through my tears. Sebastian has given his blessing, and told us we will adopt a little girl. Maybe he could hear my thoughts and came to make me feel better. My heart is bursting with joy and sadness at the same time, and for a good while I can't do anything but stare into space, my thoughts in free fall. Gradually I calm myself with deep breaths, and thoughts of what the future might hold. Charlie will be so thrilled that his boy had such a wonderful message for him. I cross my fingers and wish with everything I have, that he will think bringing another child into our lives is the right thing to do. Because now our boy has visited, I know without a shadow of any doubt, that it *is* absolutely the right thing to do.

***

'You seem quiet tonight, Nance?' Charlie pushes his plate to one side and stretches his arms above his head with one of his jaw-cracking yawns. 'Sorry, knackered.'

'Not surprised. You never stop.'

'Hmm. Our American holiday seems like years ago instead of months, doesn't it?'

'Yeah. Normal life is resumed.' I smile at him across the table, and wonder how to broach the elephant in the room. Though it's only my elephant at the moment, because Charlie doesn't know there even is one.

'So, why are you so quiet?' He takes a sip of wine and waits.

Come on Nancy. Just get it out there. My heart hammers in my chest, and all of a sudden, I can't speak. What if he says adoption is a stupid idea? What if he's upset? What if he thinks it's because I'm upset that I've hit the menopause, and not thinking straight? Because I'll have to tell him about the menopause, won't I? Oh god, this is awful. I take a gulp of wine and it goes down the wrong way, and I end up coughing and spluttering into a napkin. Charlie asks if I'm okay, and I'm tempted to say no. Not at all. But once I've got my breath back, I say,

'Charlie. I have something to share with you. Something serious, but I'm not sure how you'll react. That's why I've been so quiet.'

His brows knit together and he does the trademark fist-

222

scrubbing of his hair. 'Right. Well, I wasn't expecting that. Let's go into the living room and get comfy.'

Once we are side by side on the sofa, coffee at hand, a blanket over our legs and our fingers entwined I say, 'Okay. Just listen while I tell you everything, and then tell me your initial thoughts. And please be honest – totally honest. This is far too serious a situation for anything less.'

Charlie turns to me, his mouth a thin line, his eyes full of concern. 'Shit, you're really worrying me now. You're not leaving me, are you? Or you're ill?'

I laugh and kiss his lips. 'No, love. No, nothing like that.'

Over the next while I tell him everything. All about my talk with Penny, which includes the menopause of course, the adoption, and lastly, the visit from our boy in which I pass on the message that Sebastian loves his daddy.

Charlie's eyes fill with tears and he smiles as they brim over and roll down his cheeks. Mine copy his, and for a while we just sit there, hand in hand, unable to speak.

'Oh, Nance. I wish I could see him, too.'

'I know, love. But take comfort from his words and that he's close by.' I shake my head in wonder and smile. 'It's so wonderful having his blessing...and just think, a girl, Charlie. A little girl.' My throat thickens and I take a sip of coffee.

He presses his lips together and blows gently down his nose. 'I must admit this has all come as a hell of a shock. I feel like I'm in a bloody dream or something.'

Clasping his hand I ask, 'Not a nightmare, I hope?'

'No. Not at all. But there are lots of things to

consider…years ago, when we talked about adopting, we both agreed it wouldn't work. You more than me, so why now?'

You more than me? What's that supposed to mean? 'Not sure I understand. You mean you wanted to adopt, but I didn't?'

'No. I don't mean that. I was very unsure too. But I knew that you'd be the one doing the lion's share of looking after the child, as my job is pretty full on. There was no way I could chuck it in and stay at home, as it brings in the most money.'

'And you'd go round the bend, 'cos you love your job, even though it nearly kills you sometimes.' I kiss the tip of his nose. 'Don't forget that bit.'

'Okay, true. So, what's changed? You love your new work too, much more than you did working in the café, so I'd have thought adoption wouldn't really figure in your plans.'

I shrug and consider this. 'I don't really know. I've been surrounded with babies lately and felt happy for Tilly and…' I remember I haven't told him about Abi as it's confidential. '…them, but kind of resentful…the fact that we lost Sebastian and now I'm going through…' The word 'menopause' swells in my throat and refuses to fit onto my tongue. 'Well, all the changes, I know I will never have the chance to become a mum again.' My breath hitches in the last words and I gulp more coffee. 'Then Penny came up with adoption and it felt right…weird at first, but then, it made sense, you know?'

'I guess.' Charlie stares into the fire, obviously miles

away. Then he turns to me. 'You'd be okay with doing the lion's, or should I say, the lionesses share of child care?'

His hazel eyes are flickering in the firelight, and I think I detect enthusiasm for this wonderful, exhilarating and crazy idea breaking through. 'Of course.'

'You'd have to cut back on the cases you took on, right?'

'Yeah. But maybe I could get Mel to come on board with anything I couldn't handle for a short while?' This was the first time such an idea has come to me, and I'm as surprised as Charlie is.

'You've talked to her about it?'

'Not as such...but something will work out, love. This feels right, you know? A child in our lives.' I smile and he pulls me to him, kisses the top of my head.

'Yeah,' he says into my hair. 'Yeah, it does feel right.'

I pull back, look up into his eyes. 'Really?'

He nods. 'Really.'

Tears and laughter come at the same time. 'My God. We're really doing this?'

'Looks like it.'

'Charlie Cornish, have I ever told you how unbelievably wonderful you are?'

'Yeah, but you can tell me again if you like. It never gets old.'

I tell him, and then we talk about what we should do next to set the ball rolling with the adoption process. But most of the time, I metaphorically pinch myself to make sure I'm not actually in the middle of some fabulous dream.

Chapter Twenty

Two weeks later, we are much more used to the idea of a new child coming into our lives. We have researched the adoption process, and have a meeting set up at a St Austell adoption agency, with a case-worker called Kirsty. We've already had a chat to her on the phone and she sounds really lovely and positive about the whole thing. Can't wait to see her next week. Charlie and I are really positive about the whole thing too, and talk about it incessantly. I have been under caution from my husband a few times though, as I do tend to talk about our future adoptive child as being a baby girl. He reminds me that we might not be able to adopt a baby, as they aren't as plentiful as older children, and it could just as likely be a boy. I pointed out that Sebastian told us it would be a girl, so it would be, but had to concede on the baby issue. Having said that, I feel in my gut we will have a baby girl. My gut has been known to be correct on more than a few occasions.

My mum is completely over the moon about the idea. She's almost as bad as I am when it comes to looking ahead, and planning what we'll all do together in the future. I have to tell her to hold her horses, as it might be a bit of a wait before anything happens, but she flaps this away and says it might be sooner than we all think. We also had a little chat about the menopause and she said her periods dwindled to nothing too, very quickly, and she clapped weight on, which fit with my symptoms.

I might give Mum a call in a mo, and tell her about our appointment with Kirsty, but I have a new job on the horizon too. I had a call a few days ago from Grace, a lady whose eighteen-year-old daughter disappeared three years ago. Megan had fallen in with the wrong crowd, dropped out of university and became addicted to booze and drugs. Despite police efforts, Megan wasn't found, dead or alive, and Grace wants my help to track her down. She lives in Newquay, but was visiting a relative here in Padstow and saw my flyer in the local garage. She was so excited that there might be another avenue to explore at last. I hope I don't let her down. I was busy sorting out adoption stuff at the time, and said I'd ring her back. So maybe I should arrange a time to meet her, instead of phoning Mum.

As I pick up my phone, it rings. 'Mum, just thinking about you.'

'You must be psychic, because I was just thinking about you, too.' She chuckles. 'See what I did there?'

'Have you been talking to Mel? That's exactly what she says when I answer the phone.'

'But she is psychic, and so are you?'

I roll my eyes. 'Yes, Mum. That's the joke.' Sometimes, Mum can be slow on the uptake.

'Oh yeah. Right. Anyway, I was wondering if I would be jumping the gun if I got a knitting pattern, and made some baby clothes for my granddaughter. There was some lovely vintage ones on ebay.'

'Er yes, Mum. You definitely *are* jumping the gun! And since when did you knit?'

'I've always knitted…okay, maybe not since I was a teenager. But I just got the urge with all our talk about babies.'

Suddenly Cecil's jolly face pops into my mind, and I roll my eyes again. 'Doh! You jogged my memory. I promised Cecil a few weeks back that I'd go and see his sister Yvonne about some knitting patterns she'd lost, and I completely forgot about it with all the adoption stuff going on. Damn. I must sort that before I do anything else.'

We end the call, and just as I'm about to call Yvonne, the phone rings. Blimey. I'm in demand today. 'Hi Penny.'

'Hi, Nancy. Just a quick call to let you know I've booked an appointment for you tomorrow morning, as there was a cancellation. It's with Doctor Hennessy, she's lovely. Think you've seen her before?'

I'd stopped listening after, "an appointment tomorrow morning." 'Eh? An appointment for what?'

'A general check-up... we talked about it, remember?'

Penny's tone is suggesting I've lost my marbles. 'Yeah, but that was ages ago. I didn't think you were going to go ahead and make an appointment.'

'Oh…but I thought we'd agreed it would be a good idea.'

I can tell Penny is wearing her disappointed verging on disgruntled expression, and I suppose I can see why. I had agreed after all, and she is just being a good friend and looking out for me. 'Yeah. Yeah, we did, sorry. I wasn't expecting it, I guess. What time tomorrow?'

'Half nine.'

Well, I suppose it will be over and done early, so I can get on with my day. I need to sort out Yvonne and Grace's daughter, for goodness' sake. 'Perfect. Thanks, Penny.'

'You okay? Everything going ahead still with the adoption plans?'

'Yes, we have an appointment to see a case-worker next week. Exciting, but a bit scary too.'

'Must be. But it will all be wonderful. Okay, see you tomorrow. Take care.'

After calling Yvonne, I take a moment to focus and calm myself. I've got into a right old state this morning, because everything seems to be coming at me at once and I'm already so tired. I had indigestion last night and felt faintly nauseous, so didn't sleep much. Then of course there's the whole adoption process, constantly whirling around my brain. Once I have hopefully sorted the next two cases, I might give myself a little break. It's been pretty full on here since we got back from our holiday, to say the least. The Leanne murder case, Mum at death's door, Abi's worries about becoming a parent, Ella's impromptu birth in the woods, Joe's drinking problem, Debbie with Mike's creels, matchmaking Alison and Chris and goodness knows what else. Oh yes, the menopause, let's not forget that. There's also the chat I need to have with Mel about possibly helping out now and then with Nancy Cornish PI, once we have our little bundle of joy. In my mind's eye I see Charlie's frowny face. 'Okay, Charlie, maybe she will be a bigger bundle. Who knows?'

***

Yvonne lives on a big hill in a bungalow overlooking the Atlantic, and I pull up outside and switch off the engine. What a view. Today the waves are petrol blue and charcoal, topped with galloping white horses. A few seagulls try their best in the buffeting wind, but most, defeated, seek the shelter of the dark cliffs bookending the beach. My little car is struggling too, making me feel a bit like the last sardine rattling about in a can. I'm confident we won't get blown off the hill, though. At least I hope I am. A fleeting thought of December next week and Christmas circles my head, but I ditch it. There's no way I can start thinking about Christmas right now, not on top of everything else. Right. Get your arse moving, Nance.

Once out of my car, the offshore wind has me in its Arctic grip, so I zip up my fur lined parka, and pull my cherry red knitted beanie hat firmly down on my head. Battling up the path through the neat and ordered garden, I see a face at the window, a female version of Cecil. Plump, pink cheeks, moss-green eyes and a mass of shoulder length-grey curls. Not that Cecil's hair is shoulder-length of course. Yvonne flings open the front door. 'Nancy, I presume?' I nod. 'Come on in quick before the door flies off into the ocean, maid!'

As I step inside, the homely smells of beeswax, lilac and baking waft into my nostrils, and my pinched cheeks are kissed by a heavenly warmth. 'Oh, it's lovely and toasty in here, Yvonne,' I say, taking my floral Doc Martens off.

230

'I turned the radiators up for you. I know how cold it gets in this 'seagulls nest on the hill' as my husband Dave calls it.' She laughs and I'm reminded of Cecil again. 'Here, let me take your coat. You go through to the living room and make yourself comfy by the fire. Third on the right, lovely. I'll stick the kettle on.'

The living room is oblong, unfussy, cream walled and furnished with streamlined red leather couches and square armchairs, positioned on a sandy-coloured plush carpet. The huge picture window has a view of the Atlantic just like the one outside, but much warmer. I note the seagulls have given up, and the wind's contenting itself with hauling a few bedraggled clouds from the scene. The winter blue of the sky is so pure and clear it makes my heart ache. It's the kind of blue I remember from my childhood, racing my dad along the beach, out of breath with running and laughter. Carefree, windswept days I thought would never end. *Dad. I miss you so much.* I remember that he doted on Sebastian in the short time he knew him, and he would have loved to see his granddaughter.

'Here we are,' Yvonne says, as she enters the room with a tea-tray. 'I have tea, and chocolate and cream cupcakes, specially made this morning.'

I quickly dash away tears with the back of my hand and paint a smile on. 'Wow, those look delicious, Yvonne. I won't be able to do my jeans up soon.'

Yvonne nods at my tummy. 'A little bump like that's nothing to worry about. Look at mine.' She sets the tray down on the pine coffee table and prods her green woolly jumper stretched to capacity over her ample girth. She brushes a hand over the curve of her hip under blue jeans, laughing. 'Nothing wrong with a bit of meat on a woman I always say. Life's too short for diets.'

'Totally agree.' I laugh and sink down into a square armchair, as she sits to the side, on the couch.

'Help yourself to milk and sugar. Cupcake too, goes without saying.' Yvonne pours tea into two floral cups and grabs a cupcake. I do her bidding, then she says through a full mouth, 'Cecil speaks very highly of you, Nancy. He told me the tale of how you helped find the missing ingredient in his special sausages. Heck of a gift you have there, maid.'

I note the respectful tone in her voice, and think it makes a change to have a receptive client for once, after Debbie and Tilly. Though they both think otherwise now, of course. 'Thank you, Yvonne.' I take a small bite of the delicious cupcake and say from the corner of my mouth. 'Okay, tell me about the missing knitting patterns of your gran's.'

'Right. Well, they were in the shed in a big plastic box with a lid on. On the top of that, was a pile of old newspapers and magazines that we use for Nelly.' She stops and takes a drink of tea.

'Nelly?'

'Yes, our rabbit. She lives outside next to the shed in a hutch, and we use the newspaper to line the bottom.' Yvonne looks over her shoulder and lowers her voice. 'Dave reckons he didn't get rid of them by mistake, but I think he did. He took some stuff from the shed, bits and bobs you know, for recycling a few weeks back. I told him to take some newspapers too, as we had far too many, and I think he must have taken the patterns with the bundle he shoved in the boot of the car. The local scout hut takes it all, the lads sort through and recycle what they can.'

I'm wondering where Dave is as she continues to glance behind her. 'I see. Is Dave at home then?'

'Yes, he's in the dining room bird watching. He fancies himself as one of them bloggers. Does a piece once a week on his computer about which birds visit and stuff. Daft, if you ask me. Only he wouldn't be very happy if he caught me telling you that he got rid of my gran's patterns by mistake. Swears to hell and back that I must have dumped them with the rubbish.'

'That's because I know it wasn't me, my dear.' A man, presumably Dave, appears at the door wearing a stormy expression. He's dressed in brown cords and a woolly maroon sweater. A few wisps of hair have been carefully combed over a suntanned scalp, and piercing blue eyes swimming in annoyance look askance at his wife. Removing a pair of binoculars from around his neck, he comes into the room and offers me his hand. 'Pleased to meet you, Nancy. I'm Dave.' A smile transforms his face to gentle breeze, with a chance of sunshine.

'Well, I know it wasn't me.' Yvonne hitches her folded arms under her bosom and glares at Dave.

'And I know it wasn't me.' He glowers at her.

'Okay. Shall we work together on this? Firstly, let's have a chat about what we remember about where we saw these patterns last.'

Dave sits down next to his wife and they look at me

233

like expectant puppies. 'We both last saw them in the plastic box,' Yvonne says. 'Right, Dave?'

Dave nods, but I detect a flush creeping up from under the neck of his sweater. 'Yep.' His eyes dart to the ocean and back to the cupcakes. He's hiding something. Dave picks up a cake and takes a big bite, probably so he doesn't have to say more.

To lighten the atmosphere I ask, 'Did you knit both your jumpers, Yvonne?'

'I did,' she says, pride in her face.

'Stunning. And how lovely that you're expecting a new arrival soon. I bet it will be the best dressed baby in Cornwall.'

Dave puts his arm around his wife and gives her a squeeze. 'It definitely will. We can't wait, can we, love?'

'Nope.'

I smile at them, they're still obviously in love, despite their little argument over the lost patterns. 'When you took the stuff to the scout hut, Dave, did you do anything different. Drop something, or anything like that?' I'm clutching at straws here, but I can't think of how he lost them.

Dave shakes his head and then heaves a sigh. 'Look, I'd better come clean. The time before when I went to the scout hut, I took a handful of patterns by mistake. The lid was off the box slightly, and I got stuff a bit mixed up.' Yvonne looks like she's about to do murder until Dave holds a hand up. 'Hold your horses. I noticed them on the floor at the scout hut before I left, and grabbed them. But there was a helper there at the hut, a woman about our age, Vonny, and

234

she said how lovely the patterns were and could she have them? I said it would be more than my life's worth to let her have them and she laughed. We chatted a bit more, and then I went on my way.' Dave looks at the floor and sighs.

'What else? Yvonne says.

'Thing is. When it was time to take the stuff for the shed, for recycling day, I was busy with the birds and the blog…so I called the scout leader, Bob, asked if someone could collect them. Bob's a good bloke and told me to call anytime if I wanted a collection. He said it would give the lads more to do. Bob turned up with a few scouts when you were at our Bella's, Von. I told them where the stuff was…just didn't go to the shed with them.'

'Oh, for God's sake! Why didn't you say anything before?'

'Because you would have gone nuts, Vonny.'

Yvonne glares at him and sticks her chin out. 'I wouldn't! Nancy must think I'm a right old battle-axe the way you tell it.'

I jump in before world-war three starts. 'No, of course not. I know those patterns are very precious to you. Okay, lets get to business. Do you have any of them left, at all?'

Yvonne brightens. 'Oh yes. I have lots in the spare bedroom. It was just the baby ones we kept in the shed, as we thought we'd never need them after our Bella showed no sign of settling down until last year.'

'Great. Can you get one or two, please? I will try and make a connection with them.'

Yvonne's eyes grow round. 'Oooh, how exciting, Can I stay and watch?'

'Um, it would be best if I was alone, if you don't mind. I find I can concentrate better.'

'Right.' Yvonne's enthusiasm evaporates which is a shame, but I just know she'd be one of those interrupting onlookers. 'I understand.' She goes off to get them, while Dave and I chat about my gift and his love of bird watching for a few moments. He seems like a lovely bloke and I hope we I can trace the patterns and get this feisty couple back to normal again.

Once Yvonne has handed me the patterns, she and Dave go into the kitchen and close the door behind them. I make myself comfortable, stare out at the turbulent ocean and try to clear my mind. The patterns I have look to be from the 1960s and show a woman with a copper beehive, pale complexion and heavily made-up eyes. She's modelling a knitted pink dress with a white hoop around the waist and matching collar. The other is of a middle-aged man smoking a pipe, he's wearing a trilby and a green and brown striped jumper with a yellow cable running vertically from bottom to top. Hideous to me, but I expect lots of people would have knitted it back in the day.

My musings are abruptly halted by an old lady with a look of Cecil and Yvonne, walking through the picture window towards me. Her silver-grey hair is cropped close to her head and she has a merry twinkle in her light-blue eyes. 'She has them. The patterns,' she says in a strong Cornish burr.

Puzzled I ask, 'Who has them?'

The woman who I gather must be Yvonne's gran, points to the wall, and on it appears a 'rolling film' of an attractive older woman with blonde curly hair, and she's sorting through a variety of items inside a large wooden building. After a few moments, she picks up a bundle of newspapers and smiles, because underneath, there're a stack of knitting patterns for baby clothes. I imagine this woman is the one Dave hadn't mentioned to Yvonne, and maybe the fact that she's so attractive added to that, and the wooden building must obviously be the scout hut. The woman takes the patterns to an offshoot kitchen and puts them inside a big brown zip up handbag. Then the film disappears and so does Yvonne's gran. Short and sweet. Suddenly Mum's words from this morning come to me about vintage knitting patterns on eBay...I wonder. I put the patterns on the coffee table and call Yvonne and Dave back into the room.

'You did. You saw my gran!' Yvonne exclaims, after I described the old lady who I connected with. 'Oh, I wish I could have too,' she says, clasping her hands together and sighing.

'How could you, love? You're not psychic, are you?' Dave puts his arm around her and gives her a squeeze.

I tell them about the woman I saw, and Dave says she sounded very much like the woman he chatted to about the patterns. Yvonne gives him side-eyes but says nothing. Then I open my phone and say, 'Funnily enough, I was chatting to my mum this morning, and she said that they have some nice vintage patterns on eBay. I was just wondering if the two things fit together. It's not something Mum normally talks about, and I have a feeling in my gut about all this...hang on.' I pull up patterns for sale and show a selection to Yvonne. 'Are any of these yours?'

Yvonne squints at my phone. 'Yes! Yes, they are. Bloody thief!' She grabs Dave's arm. 'Let's go and find this woman now and demand that she hands them back, or we'll go to the police.'

Dave looks aghast. 'The police? Let's not go over the top, Von.'

Yvonne gives him a look ferocious enough to fell a bull elephant, so I quickly interject. 'There might be a simple explanation. Maybe keep your powder dry until you hear her explanation. Do you know where to find her, Dave?'

Dave's cheeks flush the colour of my cherry red hat. 'Um…I seem to remember she works at the library.'

'Hmm. I bet you do. Right. Get your coat on!' Yvonne jabs a finger at Dave, as she hurries past to the hallway. I follow on, hoping that it's not all going to end in a bloodbath.

'Okay, Yvonne. Well, at least you know where your precious patterns are, hey? It will hopefully be all sorted soon.'

Yvonne wraps me in a bear hug. 'Thank you. Thank you so much, Nancy.' She holds me at arm's length, her eyes glistening. 'My little grandchild will look wonderful in the patterns handed down through the generations. I can't tell you what that means.'

'It's my pleasure.' I open the front door and step out into the wind. 'Let me know what happens!' I call over my shoulder.

As I get into my car, Yvonne and Dave bustle out, still arguing, and above the wind through the trees, I can hear

Dave shouting, 'For goodness' sake, calm yourself, woman. Don't have a fit, or you'll see your damned grandmother quicker than you'd like!'

Hiding a smile, I wave and drive off. Let's hope all's well that ends well. If not, I pity the glamourous librarian, once she's come up against Cecil's sister.

Chapter Twenty-One

Back at Seal Cottage, I take my coat off and relish the warm hug I get as I walk into the kitchen. I left the heating on when I went to see Yvonne, as there was a chill through the house this morning, but I forgot to turn it off. Charlie would be moaning if he knew, as the fuel bill wasn't pretty last month, but needs must. My stomach growls its needs at me too, and I sigh. *You do nothing but eat lately, Nancy Cornish.* The cupcake I had at Yvonne's, though lovely, had a bit of a sickly aftertaste and right now I'm craving a nice cheese and piccalilli sandwich for lunch. The big question is – do I have any piccalilli? The cupboards say no, and can I really be arsed to go out into the biting winter wind just to get some? Scrappy glares at me from the windowsill and that settles it. He needs some more food, so I'll have to pop out anyway.

Deciding the garage is the nearest stop, I don't bother taking the car and hurry down the lane and round the corner to the old fashioned one-stop-shop come filling station. Despite being small in stature, the garage really does have most things you'd ever need. Penny always refers to it as the Biggly Boggly shop, because Ronan, one of her children called it that when he was young. He'd got a rubber finger puppet from the garage which wiggled around, and he called it Biggly Boggly. Ronan had called the garage the Biggly Boggly place ever since. As usual I thought of Sebastian and what little idiosyncrasies he might have developed, and then not as usual, I thought ahead to the future child we would adopt, and my spirits rose.

Cally's behind the counter, and gives me a wave as I wander in. We've known each other since school and she's worked here since leaving. She's not changed since schooldays. Nothing ever got to her then, and she was always cheerful and optimistic, perfect for a job like this. Nobody wants to see a sourpuss behind the counter. 'Hi, Cally, I'm on a piccalilli hunt,' I say, with a smile.

'Second row, third shelf down.'

Odd. She sounds a bit terse, very unlike Cally. 'Cheers.' I find the piccalilli and a packet of cheese and onion crisps to go with the sandwich, and somehow a fruit and nut chocolate bar finds its way into the basket with the cat food. At the counter, I take the items out and shake a carrier bag from my pocket. 'Just those, Cally, thanks. How are things?'

Cally sighs and flicks her long brown plait over her shoulder, her russet eyes sliding away from mine as she rings up the groceries. 'Ah, you know,' she manages, in a flat monotone.

I can't help noticing dark circles under her eyes and her normally plump rosy cheeks are pale and drawn. 'Hmm. You don't seem yourself, love.'

'Myself? I do wonder what that is these days, Nance.' Cally blinks back tears and says, 'That will be £11. 42

241

please.'

Unsure what to say next, I pay for the goods and stick them in the carrier. When I look up, I notice Cally's staring trancelike through the window, a single tear trickling down her cheek. Oh god, I can't leave her like this. Glancing over my shoulder, I note we're alone in the shop and there seems to be nobody filling up with petrol on the forecourt. 'Why don't you put the closed sign up a mo, and we can have a chat.'

'I'm fine, thanks.'

'You don't seem it.'

'People aren't always what they seem, I've found.' Cally folds her arms and looks me in the eye. 'You, for instance, are a psychic.' She nods at some of my flyers at the end of the counter. 'When we were at school you were no such thing – well, not so we noticed.' A brief smile. 'Have you solved the problem of the missing girl for that Grace woman who came in here the other day? Said she was gonna call you.'

Glad to have a change of subject I shake my head. 'Not yet. I'm going to see her tomorrow.' Then I remember I haven't arranged it, and make a mental note to do that pronto after my cheese and piccalilli sandwich.

'Hmm. Hope you find her.'

'Yes. Are you sure you're okay, Cally?'

She flicks her plait again and presses her lips together. 'No. Not really.' Her voice is barely a whisper. 'My Ben's not what he seems. I thought he was a doting husband and father of three, hardworking and loyal. But turns out he's playing away.'

To say I'm shocked, is an understatement. Cally and Ben have been together since they were in Year 10. They were inseparable then, and seemed one of the happiest couples in Padstow. 'Oh no. Who's he having the affair with, do you know?'

'Yes. Well, I have my suspicions. It's Laura, a friend of mine, runs the florists in town.'

I know who she means, though I don't know her that well. I'm almost certain she's happily married, though. 'When you say you have your suspicions...?'

Cally sighs and throws her hands up. 'Well, I can't swear to it a hundred percent, but when Ben tells me he's going to have a pint and play darts with the boys, on a Tuesday night, he goes to her shop instead. What the hell is he doing there after hours, eh? I saw him go in...'cos I followed him last Tuesday. His mate Arnie let it slip to me when he came in here recently, that he'd not seen Ben for a few weeks. Ha! That was a bloody surprise to me, I can tell you.'

The shop door opens and a man comes in to pay for petrol, so I stand to one side. I can tell Cally's only just holding it together and grab her hand when the man's gone. 'Hey, let's think about this. Ben would be the last person to have an affair if you ask me. Have you mentioned anything to him?'

Cally's eyes swim and brim over.' No! Because if I do that...and he says...' Her breath hitches. 'And he says it's all true, then it will be horribly real. I...I couldn't bear it, you see. Losing him.' Her bottom lip trembles and then she slumps back against the wall sobbing.

'Hey, hey.' I reach my hand out to her but she ignores it. 'Look, love. Let me help. I'll try and find out what's going on. There could be a simple…'

Cally puts her hand up. 'No. Like I said, I don't want to know. If it's true then…'

'But it could be false. You're so unhappy, and you might not need to be.'

She blows her nose and blinks owlishly at me. 'Will you use your psychic thingy?'

'I might. But I might not have to, leave it with me. Tell me, what time does he normally leave the house when he goes there?'

'About twenty-past-seven. It's only a ten-minute walk to the…' she does quotation marks in the air. '…pub.'

'Okeydokey, speak soon.' I get a brief smile and a nod and I hurry out, wondering what the hell I've just let myself in for. Don't I have enough on my plate right now? An annoying little voice whispers in my ear – *It's Tuesday, today, Nance.*

***

In the summerhouse, or Nancy PI's office I should say, I relax into my comfy green sofa and put my feet up on the matching footstool. The cheddar cheese and piccalilli sandwich on soft granary bread went down a treat, as did the crisps. Now with a cappuccino by my side and a bar of fruit and nut in my pocket, I'm looking forward to a quiet afternoon doing nothing at all. It's about time. Then tonight I'll wait for Ben outside Laura's shop and ambush him as he goes in. Or wait until he comes out, I've not decided.

There will be no need for any connections, as it's a straightforward sleuthing job. I know where Cally's husband disappears to on a Tuesday, the only thing I don't know, is the why. Charlie will be impressed with me going in giftless.

I unwrap the chocolate bar and snap off a row, savouring a square slowly on my tongue as I think about the upcoming case. Ben is innocent. I can feel it in my bones...I don't need a connection to tell me that. I remember how outgoing and chatty he's always been – a perfect match for Cally. I hope he's as forthcoming when I leap out of the side-street in front of him, doing my caped crusader act tonight. I chuckle at the image I've created, complete with my sidekick Scrappy, dressed like the intrepid Robin. Closing my eyes, I allow my thoughts to drift, and soon I feel myself nodding off. Not so fast, madam. You still have stuff to sort.

I finish my coffee and half the chocolate bar, then pull up Graces' number on my phone. She answers on the first ring, and is thrilled that I'm free to see her tomorrow. We agree to meet for coffee at the Cherry Trees at 11am. It's only thirty-minutes or so from Newquay, forty tops, if the traffic is iffy. This time of year, Grace should have no problem. Now for that little nap. I pull the old red and yellow checked blanket we keep on the back of the sofa over my legs, and tuck it round my chest. Then I put a squidgy pillow under my head and sigh. This is the life. And when we get the little one, moments like this will be few and far between, so I'd better take them while I can.

Moments later, I'm woken with a start, as my mobile

does a little vibration dance on the coffee table. Damn. Who's this now? Yvonne's strident, excited tone quickly drives any vestige of sleep from my head. 'Guess what, Nancy? I have them! Yay!!'

'Have them?'

'Yes. My patterns, thanks to you and Gran of course.'

I put a hand over my mouth and stifle a yawn. 'Oh, that's great. What happened?'

'We tracked down Madame Librarian and she was a bit surprised to see us, I can tell you. Dave explained what had happened, as I didn't trust myself to be civil, and she said she thought he'd changed his mind about donating them. Bob had told her that he and the boys had collected them from our house, and she assumed that Dave had sent them.' Yvonne clears her throat and adds somewhat grudgingly, 'Well, she would, I suppose.'

'Yes, makes perfect sense to me.'

'Hmm. Anyway, she stuck them on eBay, but luckily, she hadn't sold any so far, but had a bit of interest online this morning. She promised to take them off and bring the patterns round to ours in her lunch break, which she did!' A shriek of joy lacerates my brain and I hold the phone away from my ear slightly. 'I am so thrilled, Nancy. Thank you. I will pop some money over to you right now.'

Dear Lord, no. 'Don't be silly! There's no need to rush, Yvonne. I'm just off out shopping. Anytime will be fine.' I cross my fingers and hope not to be struck down.

'Okay. Well, I will be round soon and we can have a cuppa and a catch up.'

'Yes, lovely,' I say, faintly. Then I release a huge sigh

once we've ended the call and pull the blanket over my head.

***

'I don't know, Nance. Do you think this is a good idea, surprising Ben like that? I mean, you might put his back up.' Charlie puts the last morsel of food in his mouth and pushes his plate away.

'This is Ben we're talking about. The Ben we've known since school. Is he likely to chuck a wobbly and give me a right hook?'

Charlie rolls his eyes. 'I doubt it. But I'm wondering if he will thank you sticking your nose in like that. Cally didn't sound too sure she wanted the truth either, so why are you doing it?'

Yes, Nancy, why? 'Look I have my doubts, but I can't bear to see Cally like that. Her sunny personality is totally crushed, and I don't know how long she can go on living like that.'

Charlie takes a sip of beer and holds my gaze. 'And what happens if Ben is playing away? What then? Her sunny personality isn't going to come back, is it?'

I shrug. 'He isn't. I have—'

'A gut feeling? Funny, that.'

'My gut feelings are rarely wrong.'

He nods and takes our plates to the dish washer. 'Yeah, I'll give you that.' Then he turns and folds his arms. 'Shall I come with you?'

'No. I will be absolutely fine. If you come, he might think he's going to be arrested!' I laugh and Charlie's lips

247

quirk at the corners. 'It's just a spot of sleuthing, then I'll be back for one of your luxurious hot chocolates.'

'The squirty cream ones?'

'Yes please.' I go over and give him a hug. 'Back soon.'

Laura's Blooms is in still in darkness as I peep around the corner of the side street, and pull my black scarf higher up my neck. The windows of the shop stare blindly back at me, and I wonder if Ben is actually going to the pub this evening, rather than a secret rendezvous with Laura. It would be just my luck. It's seven-forty-five and my hands are freezing, because I forgot my gloves, and my feet are numb, despite my fur-lined boots. My breath leaves a white plume in the black night air, and I'm reminded again that it's December on Monday...I really must start thinking about Christmas, whether I like it or not. Penny told me last week that she's done all her Christmas shopping already. Nothing like being organised. And I am nothing like being organised.

A faint whistling pricks up my ears, and I peep around the corner again. A dark figure is walking down the narrow little hill towards the shop and it looks a lot like Ben. He's whistling a merry tune and striding out, his boots making a clatter on the cobbles. Not a man who's trying to be furtive, then. He's wearing jeans, red puffer jacket and a black beanie pulled over his sandy-blond hair. He stops outside *Laura's Blooms* and lift his fist to knock, then his phone rings and he answers it. I strain my ears, but there's no need, as I can hear quite clearly in the silent street. 'Yes, love. I'm just going into the pub now. No, not a late one. Be back about ten, or maybe before. No, I won't forget to put the bins out when I'm back. Love you.'

Bloody liar. He puts his phone away, but before he has chance to try a knock again, I hurry across the street towards him and wave as he turns round. 'Hi, Ben, how are you?' I give him my best cheesy grin.

He frowns slightly, and I pull my hood back so he can see my face properly. He gives me a stretchy smile. A smile a kid might wear, when it's caught with its fingers in the cookie jar. 'Oh, Nancy. Hello. Not seen you for a while.'

'I know. Must be at least a year or so.'

'Must be.' Ben glances at the shop window and down the street towards the harbour and looks a bit shifty.

I rock back and forth on the balls of my feet and incline my head towards the florist's. 'You going in there?' I pull a daft face. 'Cos I think you'll find it's closed.'

'Ha…yeah, I know. Just going to see Laura.' I raise my brows and give a slow nod. He shuffles his feet and sticks his hands into the pockets of his puffer jacket. 'She er… well I go and see her most Tuesdays.'

'Nice. Didn't realise this place had living accommodation.'

'Oh, no…it er has a little work room at the back and a kitchen bit…No, Laura lives just outside town.'

'I thought so. With her husband, Paul?'

He presses his lips together and nods. Clearing his throat he says, 'Right, well best be off as I'm late already.'

Ben turns to knock and I say, 'Okay. Nice to see you.

249

I'll mention to Cally that I

bumped into you when I'm next in the garage. I was only chatting to her today, funnily enough, and…'

Ben's raised forefinger stops me. 'No. Don't tell her that, Nancy…she might get hold of the wrong end of the stick.' He blows into his hands and rubs them together. The worse attempt at nonchalance I've ever seen.

I put my head on one side and narrow my eyes. 'Which end is that, then?'

Ben sends a white plume of breath into the night sky and looks at me. 'Look, Nancy. I need you to keep this a secret, but I'm working on a surprise for Cally.' He twists his mouth and looks up to the heavens. 'Well, a surprise for us all really. You see I've only a month to work in my old job and then I'm taking redundancy and starting something new. Something I've wanted to do for ages.'

I frown. 'You work in finance or something, don't you?'

'Yeah, loans and stuff. I hate it – selling high interest loans to people who are desperate and have no choice.' Ben's eyes light up. 'Thing is, my mum was a florist, and I used to help her sometimes in the shop when I was a kid. I loved it…and well, Laura's helping me in her workroom with the arranging, and everything you need to know to start up professionally in the business. I'll do it online for a while first, and see how it goes.'

'Wow, that's great. I can see how passionate you are about it.'

'I am. Flowers are so beautiful and say so many things that the heart can't find words for. People need them at lots of different times of their lives. Times of sadness, times of joy, and times of hope. This is my time of hope.'

Ben's big grin is genuine now and I grin back. But I'm puzzled. 'So why keep it a secret from Cally?'

'Cos she is a worrier. If I told her what I was doing, she'd worry about money coming in, and if it would work and everything. I want it to be a fait accompli when I present it to her complete with a big bow.' He laughs. 'Literally. I want to have a few flower sales under my belt and the website up and running first.'

I'd known already that Ben wasn't cheating, but this is the best news. Relief rushes through my body faster than the Camel Estuary at high tide, and I hug him. 'That is such a lovely thing for you to do, Ben. I just know it will all work out for you.'

'Is that your psychic power talking?' His blue eyes hold a merry twinkle.

'No. My gut, and it's rarely wrong.' I take a step back. 'Bye, Ben, and do let me know how it goes.'

'I will, Nancy. Night!'

My feet have wings as I hurry back through the narrow dimly lit streets to Seagull Cottage. So wonderful that I didn't have to mention Cally's suspicions at all, and that she can be happy once more when I tell her about meeting Ben. I won't be able to tell her what I know, of course. As it's a secret. But I will certainly be able to tell her that her future is bright, and that her husband is exactly what he seems. A decent, loving, loyal man. Just like my Charlie. Thinking of whom. I fire off a quick text to tell him to get the luxurious hot chocolate on the go. I don't need to be psychic to predict that squirty cream, a roaring fire and a big hug from a dark and handsome man, are in my immediate future.

Chapter Twenty-Two

Scrappy's rough tongue licking my face provides a rude awakening the next morning. A shaft of golden sunlight pokes an accusing finger through a crack in the curtains, and a glance at the bedside clock tells me it's 9.05 am. I sit bolt upright and Scrappy flies off the bed. How the hell have I managed to sleep until this time! The doctor's appointment is in twenty-five minutes and I have to have breakfast and shower. Damn it! I'll have to skip breakfast. Why the hell didn't Charlie wake me? A cold cup of tea on the nightstand tells me he did. I vaguely remember telling him I was awake, and kissing him goodbye. I sigh and get out of bed. Must be more knackered than I thought.

I perform the quickest shower in history, brush my teeth, feed Scrappy, and am out of the door in ten-minutes flat. When I fly into the surgery almost seven minutes late, Penny looks over her reading glasses at me with a deep frown, which gives her a school teacher vibe. 'Ah, Mrs Cornish. Please take a seat in the waiting room.' She doesn't crack a smile, and she nearly has me, until she hisses from the corner of her mouth. 'Get your arse in there, woman!' She winks and I pull my tongue out at her as I hurry through the swing doors.

I'm back home in forty minutes after a thorough health check. Blood pressure, urine and blood tests, weight, and numerous questions about diet and lifestyle. Dr Hennessy was a lovely woman, caring, yet very professional. We discussed the possibly of HRT amongst other things, and she gave me a leaflet with lots of relevant websites relating to the menopause. The results would be in the surgery in a couple of days, and someone would ring me. Now for breakfast. I'm starving. My brain suggests scrambled eggs on toast and I accept.

After breakfast, I catch a glimpse of my reflection in the hall mirror and cringe. I went to the surgery looking like this? Why didn't Penny tell me? My top is on back to front, and my hair is stuck up at one side, like someone has used me as a floor mop. Maybe Penny kept quiet, because she thought I'd rush to the loo to sort myself out if she'd said anything, and I was late already. Right, get changed and smarten up your act before you meet Grace at eleven o'clock. Which is, I glance at my phone, in twelve-minutes. Marvellous. I heave a sigh and stomp upstairs. I'll be glad when this last case is done; I need a break.

***

Grace Flynn is sitting at a window table, biting the edge of a thumbnail. It has to be Grace because she's the only woman in there around my age, and she's alone. She's slim, wearing a black and white hooped jumper, paired with red jeans and has a mop of dark blonde hair pulled into a messy ponytail. Her angular face looks unused to smiling, but then I suppose it would, having lost a daughter, and her large grey eyes keep darting nervously to the window and back to her thumbnail. She's looking through the window again as I walk up to her table and she gives a start when I say, 'Hi, are you Grace?'

Her eyes scan my face and her cheeks flush. 'Yes, sorry - you made me jump. Nancy?' she stands and offers me her hand.

I nod as I shake it. 'Yes, great to meet you.' We sit down. 'Have you ordered?'

'No. I thought I'd wait for you. What's good here?'

'Everything,' I say with a chuckle, just as the waitress appears. We order carrot cake and cappuccinos. 'Okay, Grace. Tell me about what happened with Megan.'

Grace sighs and plays with the edge of a napkin, her eyes drifting to the window and back to my face, like the gentle swell on the harbour. 'Like I said when we first spoke, Megan, my lovely daughter, disappeared three years ago when she was eighteen. She'd always been a homebody, only had a few friends really through school, and didn't seem to have much confidence, even though she was very bright and had a great sense of humour. We, her dad Pete and I, always wanted her to do well, and we knew that any career path she picked, she'd fly along, because she was so bright.' Grace stops and gives me a little smile which lights up her face. 'Not that she gets it from me and Pete. We're Joe average.' Her eyes suddenly fill and she looks at the napkin. 'We miss her so much, Nancy. It's been three years.'

My heart squeezes and I pat her hand. 'Must be a nightmare for you, not knowing where she is.'

'Yeah. Or even if she's still...' She clears her throat and dabs her eyes on the back of her hand. '...if she's still alive...but somehow...' Her grey eyes shine like silver behind a film of tears. 'But somehow in here,' she thumps her chest. 'I know she's still with us, somewhere.'

Just then, the cake and coffee arrive and she takes a grateful sip of hers. 'A mother's intuition is rarely wrong. I suppose it's the not knowing that's the killer,' I say.'

Grace nods in agreement. 'It really is. Do you have children, Nancy?'

I've just taken a big bite of cake, and am glad of it, because an unexpected rush of emotion clogs my throat. I hold up a finger while I swallow the cake and think about how to answer her, without making her feel bad for asking. After a gulp of coffee I say, 'I did have a son. He died when he was three-months old, eighteen-years ago.' Her face is a mask of concern and I can tell she's struggling for a reply, so I rush on. 'But funnily enough, we're going in for adoption very soon. Charlie and I are so excited.'

'Oh, that's wonderful.' Grace smiles and briefly touches my hand. 'But I'm so sorry about your little boy.'

'Thank you.' I brush a few crumbs from my top and decide to quickly push on. 'Now, can you tell me what happened next with Megan?'

'Yeah. Megan went to university to study law. Me and her dad were so proud as you can imagine...' Grace stares past me, lost in thought for a moment. 'Thing is, she fell in with the wrong crowd. Apparently, friends of friends at uni.' A little shrug. 'I think it was because she'd led a quiet life up until leaving home, she went a bit crazy. Meg was more outgoing and confident than we'd ever seen her, which could have been down to the drugs and booze she got into. She had lots of new friends too, which was a departure for her, as I said, she'd not had much of a social life before then. Trouble was, they were the wrong type of friends, sadly.'

I give her a sympathetic smile. 'You say she became an addict?'

'Yes. We discovered she'd dropped out of uni from a girl she was friendly with who lived down the road from us. She'd heard it from another friend and was worried about Meg, so told us. We had no idea, as Meg would keep in touch pretty regular, but not talk much about her studies. According to this girl, she'd dropped out a few months back and was living in some kind of squat with some crack addicts.' Grace's voice breaks and she drains her coffee cup. 'God, it still kills me to imagine it.'

Poor Grace. 'Yeah, it must do. Did you find out where this squat was?'

She heaves a huge sigh. 'Yeah. We tracked her down in Cardiff where she was at uni. It was a hovel in a backstreet...turns my stomach to think of it. She was in a complete and utter mess. I hardly recognised her. Hair long and greasy, sores on her face, fingernails black...my baby...' Grace closes her eyes and takes a moment. 'Anyway, we tried to get her to come home, but she said no and told us to leave. She wouldn't discuss anything with us – was barely rational. Her dad tried to physically carry her to the car, but she clawed his face and spat at him. Said we should just fuck off back to Cornwall and leave her to get on with her life. Grace shook her head, bewildered. 'We left her to cool off for a while and went to the police for help. They said there wasn't much they could do, and gave us some numbers for social services, drug rehab and the like. When we went back to the squat in a few hours she'd gone.'

Jeez. What a bloody nightmare. 'Oh, hell, Grace. I'm so sorry.'

Grace hunches over the table, her head in her hands. 'Pete blames himself. Said he should have just picked her up again after she'd fought him and shoved her in the car. I said she would have only fought us again and jumped out. If she was determined to go, there would have been nothing we could have done to stop her, except tie her up and keep her locked away. It was bloody hopeless.'

'Hmm. I tend to agree with you. Megan wouldn't have listened if she was in that mindset. So no one heard from her after that?' Grace shook her head. 'Not even the girl that had told you she'd dropped out?'

'No. It was if she'd just disappeared off the face of the planet.' Grace pushed her half-eaten cake to one side on her plate and folded her arms. 'I expect it's a tough ask wanting you to try and find her now, but we have to do everything we can. The police drew a blank, so did the missing person posters, radio and internet pleas, you name it. You're our last hope, Nancy.' Then she noted my look of disquiet and tempered her words with a chuckle, 'No pressure.'

I laugh too, to relieve the tension. I finish my coffee and say, 'I'll certainly try my best to make a connection. What have you brought me of Megan's?'

Grace picks up a large black leather handbag from the chair next to her, and digs around inside it. 'Here's a photo we had taken the last Christmas before she went missing.'

I'm looking at a heart shaped face, framed by blonde whisps of hair which have come loose from an updo, her big blue eyes look from under dark lashes at the camera, and her generous mouth is twisted to the side, in what I feel is a self-conscious smile. 'She's very pretty.'

'Yeah. She never realised it though. Always complained that she was nerdy looking compared to her friends.' Grace digs into the bag again. 'And here's her old sleeping companion, Rob the dog. Megan couldn't sleep without him.' She's overcome with emotion and can't look at me as she hands it over.

I take the floppy, threadbare and obviously much-loved black and brown fluffy toy dog, and look into its button black eyes. 'Hello, Rob. You gonna help me find your mistress, eh?'

A sob from Grace has me kicking myself. Idiot. This isn't helping her one bit. 'Okay, love. Cheer up. I'll get onto this right now.' I shove the photo and dog into my bag. 'I can't work here in the café, obviously. I'll take Rob home and call you after I've tried to make the connection. Hopefully today, maybe tomorrow, or the next day, depending on how hard or easy it proves to be.'

We both stand up and Grace gives me a quick hug. 'Thanks Nancy. I'm sorry to put so much pressure on you. All I can ask is that you do your best. And if my Meg remains missing. At least Pete and I can say we tried everything.'

Once back home, I decide I will try the connection with the photo and Rob the dog before I do anything else. Grace's story and the emotion of its telling is fresh in my mind, and I want to strike while the iron is hot. My summerhouse office has often been the ideal place to try and solve my cases, and it's to there that I hurry now, with Megan's photo and Rob in one hand, and a mug of tea in the other. The chill winter afternoon is accompanied by a playful salt-wind that pushes me down the garden path, and I rush through the office door and turn the heaters on full blast. The image of Christmas pops into my head again, and a nagging voice whispers in my ears, so I say bah humbug to it, and flop down on the comfy sofa, pulling my blanket over my knees and chest.

The playful wind becomes more boisterous as I sip my coffee and watch the trees bend under its force. The taller trees, as if in anger, rattle their spindly branches at the purple and grey clouds as they stream past in tatters, and a couple of crows try valiantly, but in vain, to make headway in the direction of the coast. I'm soon feeling warmer, and think how lucky I am to be doing what I love, looking out at a winter scene, wrapped in a blanket. I yawn and my eyelids grow heavy...would it be a bad idea to have a little nap? My sensible head tells me it would, and I should get on with finding Megan. *Okay, let's get connecting. This is the last case for a bit, Nancy. Then you can slob about for a while.*

Rob the dog looks at me from the coffee table, and I look back. 'Right, matey.' I grab him and hold him between my two hands on my lap. 'Let's find your mistress.' I take a long look at the photo of Megan propped up on the cushion next to me, close my eyes, take some deep breaths and picture her in my mind. Nothing happens for ages and I'm worried I'm in danger of falling asleep again. Then at last, heat floods through my hands, and I grip Rob tight, as a surge of energy flows through each finger and along my hands and arms.

Moving images flood my mind so fast I can barely follow them. A small blonde-haired girl of about three-years-old, rips Christmas paper from a parcel to reveal a brand-new Rob. Her big blue eyes grow round and she squeals and hugs him to her chest. Megan. Next is Megan in her early teens, crying into her pillow with Rob tucked under her chin. My heart goes out to her. I sense she's sad because she doesn't fit in with kids at school. Megan in her late teens, getting drunk at a party, a pimply youth all over her, she doesn't want his attention but she's numb inside. Megan in a dark room, damp running down the walls, hair a bird's nest, scabs on her face, her eyes wild and staring – must be in the squat Grace told me about.

I shudder and take a breath as my view retracts. It's like I'm looking down the wrong end of a telescope. There's a building I recognise...but where is it? It's a grand gothic affair, with pointy turrets and a wide clock tower centred between them. Yes, I remember! It's Bristol Temple Meads Station. My parent's and I used to get off the train there when we visited my auntie Kath years ago. I swallow as the scene rushes on, and the view widens to reveal what looks like a soup kitchen, or homeless shelter near the station.

Lots of unkempt, ragged people are shuffling along, queuing for food. Bugger, does this mean Megan is homeless? Poor kid. But then again, if she's there, she's not dead. This is good news!

My view is pulled in sharp focus to one of the people serving the food, and my heart leaps. Even better news! It's Megan. She looks well, clean and healthy. She's smiling, and joking with a man at the head of the queue as she hands him a plate. This is brilliant! Eager for more, I'm disappointed to have the scene plunged into darkness. My eyes snap open and I'm looking at Rob again. 'Well, well, well, Rob. Looks like we found your mistress.' Rob doesn't reply, but I think his eyes seem a bit more twinkly than they did before.

In the kitchen again I look for my mobile phone. Just for a change I can't find it…ah yes, it's in my coat pocket hanging up in the hallway Of course it is. I ring Grace.

'Nancy? Don't tell me you've found something already?'

Grace's voice trembles, and I can tell she's expecting the worse. Joy floods through me as I anticipate her reaction to my news. 'I have found something, Grace. It's good news! I saw Megan alive, well and living in Bristol!'

Grace's shriek almost deafens me. 'Oh my God! Really? Tell me all about it!'

I tell her, and we chat for a while discussing the whys and wherefores and logical next steps. Grace decides she won't contact the homeless shelters near the station, just in case Megan doesn't want to be found and takes off again. But she and Pete plan to go up to Bristol tomorrow and hope their daughter will see them. 'My fingers are firmly crossed this end, Grace. So thrilled for you.'

Grace blows her nose for the umpteenth time and gulps down a sob. 'I can't tell you how relieved I am that she's alive. Even If she doesn't want anything to do with us, at least we know where she is. Just wait until I phone and tell Pete! He will be in bits.'

'He will. And please let me know what happens as soon as you can.'

'Of course.' I wait for more tears to subside. 'I can't tell you how much this means to us. There are no words to tell you how grateful I am, Nancy.'

'No words necessary. Just say hello from me to that girl of yours, and tell her Rob sends his love.'

After I ring off, I hold Rob tightly to my chest. I'm totally drained, and overcome with emotion. A child has been found, and soon to be reunited with her parents, hopefully. I sigh and close my eyes. Soon me and Charlie will have found our own child, with any luck.

Chapter Twenty-Three

It's Friday and I'm sitting in the kitchen, having just finished breakfast. I slobbed about all day yesterday, doing nothing but reading, watching TV and staring out of windows. This did me the power of good, and I think I should do more of that kind of thing, before we have another little person running around the place. Scrappy jumps on my lap and does a huge yawn. 'I wasn't thinking of you, my boy.' I stroke his head and cup his face between my hands. He holds my gaze for a few seconds and then twists his head to one side. 'Yes, I know you're a little person too, but we'll have another one before very long. You'll need to do more to help with chores. Maybe lend a hand with the dishes now and then?' He jumps down and wanders off. Charming.

Okay, so today I could either slob about a bit more, or maybe write up my case notes in my journal. I've not caught up since I solved Debbie's, and I need to do it while it's all still fresh in my mind. My note pad and pen sit opposite on the table, so I pull them towards me. I'll just jot down who I need to write notes for, and do it properly in the journal later on. So... there's Debbie, Yvonne, and Grace, though hers isn't resolved yet. I need to hear back from her before I write anything. I underline their names, then tap my pen against my bottom lip...and someone else. Who was it? Oh yeah, Cally! I almost forgot. Damn it. Worse, I actually forgot to tell her that I'd talked to Ben and everything was okay! It's because I've been up to my eyes with the menopause and general health tests, racing from one case to the other and feeling totally knackered. Is there any wonder?

As I wander to the living room from the kitchen, I watch a few red and sparrow-brown leaves drift by the patio doors. Then the sun bursts dramatically through the clouds, illuminating the garden with her stark winter rays. Suddenly I want to be outside. No, I *need* to be. That's decided my day, then. I'll pop to the Biggly Boggly shop speak to Cally, then I'll go for a stomp along the coast path. It's ages since I've felt sand between my toes and heard the roar of the ocean in my ears. I want to take great gulps of salt air, throw my arms wide, and feel my soul lift with each crash of the waves. The case-notes can wait.

Cally looks at me with trepidation as I walk into the shop. She's just served a customer and the guy's chatting to her about the weather, but she's more or less blanking him, because she's obviously apprehensive about what I have to say. He takes his change, huffs and leaves. As I approach the counter, she does the nervous plait flicking thing, and her russet eyes flit to mine and away like restless birds. 'All right, then?' she says, and folds her arms.

'More than all right, love. Great news, in fact. I saw your Ben on Tuesday evening and we had a little chat. I would have told you about it sooner, but my life is a bit mad right now, and to be honest, it went right out of my head. So, I'm sorry for that.'

She takes a step forward, a glimmer of hope shining behind those restless birds. 'Oh, don't worry. Great news, you say?'

'Yeah.' I smile, then twist my mouth to one side. 'Thing is, I can't tell you what I found out because it's a surprise for you. But I can tell you that he's definitely *not* having an affair with Laura from the florists.'

Cally's whole face lights up as she blinks back tears. 'He's not? You sure?'

'Positive. And I'm sure what he's doing will make a big difference to you all. It's something that will make him happy, you too.' I grin and hold my hands up. 'But I can't say more. Has that put your mind at rest?'

Cally grasps my hand across the counter. 'Oh, it has.' She sniffs and wipes her eyes on the back of her sleeve. 'I can't tell you how much. My Ben isn't playing away and about to leave me. I can hardly believe it, after all this time of thinking the worst.'

'Believe it. And now you can get back to being your old bubbly self, hey?'

'Yes.' She shakes her head and squeezes my hand again. 'Thanks a million, Nancy. You're a godsend.'

'You're most welcome. And let me know how it all turns out, yeah?'

I will. You'll be the first to know.'

∗∗∗

Returning Cally's happiness has left me with a warm fuzzy feeling in my chest, and after I leave the shop, I practically fly down the streets with a big smile on my face. Within twenty-minutes, I'm clear of the town and harbour and up on the tops, as my mum calls the headland past St George's Cove. I'm tempted to go down to the beach there, but though the estuary is lovely, I yearn for the Atlantic. So, girding my loins, I turn back and do the extra miles to Trevone. The sun has been kind since it pounced out of the clouds earlier, staying around in a fairly cloudless sky, trying to add warmth to the late November day. It's not succeeded much though, and I'm glad I stuffed my hat in my pocket at the last minute before leaving the house.

At last, a bit bedraggled and windswept, I approach the stunning blue and gold vista of Trevone Bay. I pause on the high green headland, and think back, as I often do, to when I used my gift to track down Mum's partner Rory at the round hole, the eighty-foot collapsed sea-cave just a little way to my left. Rory was extremely lucky that he hadn't fallen all the way, and was rescued by the coastguards. Lucky for Mum too, as she's so happy now. We will never really know what exactly Rory had intended, that night when his spirits were at their lowest, because he says he can't quite remember. In the end, it really doesn't matter. I'm so pleased that the old school sweethearts found each other again.

A seagull yells as it swoops low over my head, and as my eyes follow its path across the patchy blue and grey sky, a vibrant memory of my dad brings me up short. We're walking together on this very path, he's smiling at me, the wind's in his hair, and his twinkling eyes reflect the colour of the sea. As the memory fades, I turn my face to the wind, let it take my tears, and suck in a gulp of sea air to steady my emotions. Dad. How I wish you were still with us. Why he's only visited me once since he passed, I don't know. There are many mysteries about my gift that I can't fathom. But I'm thankful he came with a message to help Mum, and one day, I know I'll see him again.

On the edge of the land, I stare out across the blue and spread my arms wide. Inhaling a deep breath, I close my eyes and feel my spirit, light as thistledown, float up to join the clouds. I'm so thankful for my life, my gift, and the loves in my life...

'Oi, don't jump off the edge, woman!'

I spin round to see one of those loves bounding over to me, the sun turning her windswept bob into a messy golden halo, her cheeks ruddy apples, bunched over a huge grin. 'Mum! I was just thinking about you.' *And Dad*, I add to myself. She'd only get upset if I shared the memory.

'I should think so,' she says, pulling me towards her and enveloping me in a tight-hug. 'I'm *very* important, after all.' She chuckles and pulls a silly face.

'You are indeed. What a coincidence that we both picked today to come out here. I haven't been this way for ages. Well, since some daft woman got herself kicked unconscious by some cows.'

Mum steps back and shakes her head. 'No idea who that was.' Then she laughs. 'Me neither. I just couldn't stand being inside the four walls any longer. Had to get out to feel the wind on my face - smell that big ocean over there.'

'Exactly the same!' I laugh.

We both turn to face the water, and stand quietly, watching the white horses race each other ashore. It's a lovely moment, until Mum says, 'December in two days. You prepared for Christmas?'

'Oh Mum! Ruin the moment, why don't you.' I huff and fold my arms.

'No point in burying your head in the sand.' She smirks and points to the golden strip of beach down the slope. 'Speaking of which, want to go for a paddle?'

I give her my best incredulous look. 'Paddle. In the dying days of November?'

'Of course. Carpe diem, young lady. There will be times in the future, when neither of us will be able to shuffle our old bones down here. Those times are a lot closer for me than for you, so let's get paddling.'

Before I can respond, she sets off at a lick down the slope and jumps onto the beach with a whoop. The old bones comment makes my eyes sting, and I sniff as I think of the day when she, like Dad, will be gone. Not yet though, thank God. I blink back tears and smile at her hopping about on one foot, while trying to pull a sock off the other. Mum. Don't ever change.

'Hell's bells, it's cold!' I hang onto Mum's arm, as another surge of ice water bashes into my knees and soaks the edge of my rolled-up jeans.

'Nah. Just wait until we do this in February, then you can complain!'

269

'Er, you'll be doing it on your own, Ma.' I let go of her arm and take a few hurried steps backwards, as another barrage of waves prepares an onslaught.

'Hm. We'll see. Anyway, I was thinking Charlie might like a jumper for Christmas. I've already started a greeny-blue Aran one, and thought it would look lovely on him.'

'Ignoring her mention of the 'C' word, I say, 'That sounds lovely. I had no idea you'd started knitting, already.'

'Yep. I've made a little outfit for my new grandchild. A lemon cardie with white piping. It has two little pockets too – so cute.' Mum looks at me, with sparkly eyes and a smile as wide as the beach.

'But we've no idea how old the child will be, Mum. What size did you make?'

'Well, I thought I'd make three in total, all different ages. One of them should fit.'

I shake my head. She's incorrigible. 'Thanks, Mum.'

'And what would *you* like for Christmas?'

Slipping my arm through hers, I lead us out of the water and up the beach. 'I haven't a clue. Maybe a present that makes sure Christmas is all organised, the presents are bought and wrapped, the decs are up, and I don't have to start thinking about any of it?' I give her a hopeful glance.

'Well, not sure I could do all of that. But you and Charlie could come to ours on the day? That will be the Christmas dinner bit solved at least. It's our turn, I think.'

I give her a smile. 'So it is. I'd forgotten that.' This cheers me up no end. I love cooking, but the way I'm feeling at the moment, I'd rather just arrive at Mum and

Rory's on the day without having to lift a cooking finger. 'So what present would my favourite mum like?'

Mum sits on a rock and looks up at me, head on one side. 'Present? I think I've had mine this year and for a good while to come. My best present is life. It was touch and go after the cow field nightmare, and thank god I didn't snuff it.'

Emotion rises in my chest and forms a knot in my throat. Little does she know I'd been thinking along those lines, when I was watching her hopping around on the beach before. I sit down next to her and clasp her hand in mine. 'I'm so grateful you didn't snuff it too.' I give her a cheeky smile. 'I mean, who would I get to cook Christmas dinner and make three different sizes of baby clothes - just in case - if you had?'

Mum leans a shoulder into mine. 'Who indeed?'

We sit quietly for a few minutes, watching the white topped navy waves racing to the shoreline, then withdrawing through the shiny black and brown pebbles with a hiss. 'I reckon it's going out,' I say, absently.

'What?'

'The tide.'

'Hmm. I don't know. Seems to me that it can't make its mind up. One minute it's coming in, the next it's going out. Look at that wave there. Crashing in like its life depends on it, then it's hurrying back out again, as if it's scared of the sand.'

I roll my eyes at Mum. She's always had an oddball sense of humour. 'And on that note, shall we walk back? That black cloud on the horizon looks like it means business, and it's a good hour or so to home.'

'Yeah, I suppose we should.' She grabs her gloves from her pocket and dusts her feet free of wet sand. Catching me watching, she says, 'You won't have come prepared for feet dusting, will you?' I shrug and pat my pockets hoping for a tissue but there's none. 'Didn't think so.'

She hands me her gloves and starts to tug her socks on. I smile to myself, as I dust off my feet. It's been one of those unplanned, unexpectedly wonderful afternoons, when nothing remarkable has really happened. But it's meant so much. Not for the first time, I remind myself that we should enjoy the little things, because that's what life is made up of. Little, unremarkable, but wonderful moments that mean everything. Once my trainers are on, I look up into Mum's smiling face, the breeze whipping her hair around her face like strands of honey and say, 'I love you so much, Mum. I know we always say it after we end phone calls, or texts, but 'I love you' can sometimes get lost in all...' I flap my hand struggling for the right words. '... the noise. So I'm saying it now, in the quiet. I love you and I'm so grateful that you're my mum.'

I stand up and glassy-eyed, she pulls me into her arms, whispering into my hair. 'And I'm so grateful to have you as my daughter. I love you, Nance.'

***

Friday night is curry night in the Charlie and Nancy Cornish household. It's the law. Sometimes we have a takeaway, but tonight it's homemade chicken saag made by yours truly. Charlie reckons he'll be home at a reasonable time, so at just before 5.pm, I decide to make a start. That way I can leave it in the oven to 'percolate in the spices' as Charlie says.

The chicken's in the pot with the chopped onions and spices on a low heat, creating the most mouth-watering aromas, and I'm just grabbing a handful of fresh coriander leaves, when my mobile rings faintly from somewhere not too far away, but not in the kitchen. Hmm. Now let's have a guess where *that* might be, Nancy. I wipe my hands and hurry to the hallway. Yup. In my coat pocket, just for a change. Oh? It's the surgery. Must be the results.

'Nancy Cornish? It's Doctor Hennessy here.'

'Hi, Doctor Hennessey, you're ringing about my results I expect.' I hurry back to the kitchen to turn the heat off under the pot.

'Yes. But they aren't what either of us were expecting.'

A cold spike of fear shoots through me and I plop down on a kitchen chair. Shit what if it's something bad. 'Oh…not the menopause then?'

'No. Are you sitting down?'

'Shit - it's cancer, isn't it? How long have I got?' I rake my hand through my hair and lean forward, elbows on knees.

Dr Hennessey laughs. 'Good lord, no. It's nothing like that, but it *is* a life-changing result, Nancy. You could be very shocked. Is anyone there with you…would you like to perhaps pop in and we can discuss it face-to—'

'No. Please just tell me.' I grip the edge of the table and hold my breath.

'You're pregnant, Nancy…about three months.'

Chapter Twenty-Four

This is some surreal dream. Has to be. It's not possible.
Pregnant. Me. Ohmigod, ohmigod, I'm pregnant! These
same thoughts have been racing round my head, doing laps
at Formula One speed since Doctor Hennessey's call.
Nearly an hour has passed. An hour of pacing, thinking,
muttering, thinking, thinking, thinking, and hair raking,
while a million butterflies in my stomach all take off at
once. I need to calm down, process everything the doctor
told me properly.

Sit down.

Have some water.

Have some gin.

No. No that won't be happening for a long time. Shit. I
can't think straight. I'm shaking. My head's about to
explode. I need Charlie.

'Hi, sweetling. I'm home!'

The front door bangs and in walks my husband in the
nick of time. 'Charlie!' I jump up from the table and
launch myself into his arms. 'Thank God you're here,' I
mutter over and over into his coat, which smells like winter
and polo mints.

'Hey, hey.' He holds me at arm's length and peers at

my tear-streaked face. His is a mask of concern. 'What's happened?'

I shake my head and can't get the words out, so he leads me into the living room and we sink down on the sofa, his hand in mine. 'I…I…' Another head shake.

Charlie gives me a steady look, deep concern in his hazel eye. 'Just take your time, love. Do you want some water?'

'No.' I heave a sigh and squeeze both his hands so hard, I notice him wince. Then I take a big breath and say, 'Dr Hennessey called this evening and told me…told me…' Tears pour down my cheeks and I can hardly believe I'm going to say words. 'I'm three months pregnant, Charlie.'

I watch his face drain of colour and his mouth drop open. He shakes his head in bewilderment and scrubs his hair with his fist, like he always does when he's anxious. This, of course, makes it stick up at all angles like the bristles on a bottle brush. If it wasn't such a serious situation I'd laugh out loud. 'Pregnant?' he whispers. I nod. 'But how?'

I consider making a flippant comment about the birds and the bees, but say instead, 'The doctor said getting pregnant again was rare with my condition as we know, but not impossible. She also said because of the uterine scarring that happened last time, it could mean I could miscarry, so they will monitor me very closely. There's my age to consider as well.'

Charlie puts his arm around me and a tear slips down his cheek. 'I can hardly take this in. Will your health be in danger?'

'There's always a risk, but the doc says with careful monitoring, the baby and I should be absolutely fine.'

He's silent for a few moments and throws a hundred-yard stare at the wall. 'But how do you feel about it, love? Because if you think it's too risky, then you know you don't have to go through with—'

I hold up a silencing finger. Until Charlie had almost voiced the alternative, I hadn't known what I really thought about it all, as my brain had been numb with shock on the one hand, and in freefall-panic on the other. But getting the words out in the open, and explaining the possible pitfalls to Charlie, means that clarity at last settles in my head and heart. 'How do I feel? I feel shocked, scared, excited, a bit weird, but overwhelmingly, my feeling is one of happiness. In fact, I'm ecstatic!' I burst into hysterical laughter, and soon Charlie joins me.

'It's been a hell of a shock, Nance. A hell of a shock.' He stops and draws his hand down his face. 'But yeah. Yeah, I'm ecstatic too! A baby after all these years!'

'That's what Gran was on about in her cryptic message, and what Sebastian meant when he said we'd have a sister for him. I thought it related to adoption. I mean, who would have ever thought we'd have our own?'

He kisses me and grins. 'It's mad. Totally surreal. And why now, after all this time?'

'Who knows, Charlie? Ours is not to reason why.'

Charlie stares into my eyes, and takes a deep breath. 'So it will be a girl, then?'

'That's what Sebastian says, so yeah. Yeah, a little girl.' I laugh as I picture an auburn-haired child with green

277

eyes.

Flopping back against the cushions he closes his eyes. 'I'm so happy, Nance. Happy, bewildered, excited…' He hugs a cushion to his chest. 'It's only five minutes ago that we decided on adoption. Now this.' He blows down his nostrils. 'Just had a thought, we'll have to tell the adoption lady we don't need that appointment next week. Hope they find a family for the child we would have adopted.

Bless my husband, always thinking of others. I cuddle up next to him and lay my head on his chest. 'I'm sure they will, love.'

'Yeah. Hope so.' He shifts under me and quickly sits up. 'Hey, we should celebrate! Let's get your mum over here and all our friends for a big baby party!'

I raise my eyebrows. 'Er, I don't think so, sweetheart. I know you want to shout it from the rooftops, so do I. But until I've had a scan and talked to the doctor, we should keep it low key. Yes, I'm three months, but I'll just tell Mum, and that's all for now, okay?'

He presses his lips together and nods. 'Yeah, of course, I wasn't thinking.'

'Not surprised. I mean, it's not everyday that you come home to find you're going to be a dad, is it?'

A cloud passes across his face. 'I wish my mum… and even my dad, the old bastard, would be able to meet their granddaughter. I suppose when you're going to be a dad, it makes you think about your own parents.'

I swallow hard. I wish Charlie could have had a happier childhood and that his parents were still around, but he didn't, and they aren't, and there's nothing I can do. 'I

278

know, love, so do I. But let's look to the future now. Something tells me it's going to be good.

Charlie gathers me in his arms and gives me a long lingering kiss. 'I think you're right, Nance. I love you so much.'

I smile and trace my fingers along the curve of his face. 'You're not so bad yourself, Mr Cornish.'

* * *

A flurry of excited butterflies show up in my stomach the next day, as I put the finishing touches to a freshly baked celebration cake. It's just coffee and walnut with butter icing, but it's Mum's favourite. We invited her and Rory over for lunch, and plan to spring the baby news on them afterwards with the cake. It's not quite the party that Charlie wanted, but it's going to be lovely. They will be here in an hour, just time to make the ham, and egg mayo sandwiches and pop the sausage rolls and quiche in the oven. As I get the butter out of the fridge, my phone rings, and for once it's not in my coat pocket, but on the kitchen table. It's Grace. I cross my fingers and answer it.

'Nancy? You'll never guess what?'

From the excited tone of her voice, I'm guessing it's good news. 'You found Megan?'

'Better than that. She's here with us at home!'

'Wow! That's amazing, what happened?'

Over the next few minutes, she tells me that Megan was found at the homeless shelter and she'd been working there for about six months. Megan had been homeless herself for a while after leaving the squat, but had managed to kick her drug habit, with help from people who worked at the homeless shelter, and had managed to turn her life around. 'Pete and I were so thrilled, Nancy. We went for a coffee and talked everything through, and she said she'd come home with us for a few days.'

'That's wonderful. Did she explain why she ran away from you in Bristol, and not been in contact since?'

'Yeah. Poor love felt ashamed, because we'd had such high hopes for her at uni and everything, and she blew it. She said she felt unworthy of being our daughter after everything we'd done for her. She couldn't look us in the eye.' Grace's voice breaks and she clears her throat.

'Oh, poor love. I'm so glad she's in a better place now.'

'Yes. She explained that she'd refused to let those helping her contact us and gave them a false name. That's why the police couldn't find her. She couldn't apologise enough. We told her whatever had happened before, is all behind her, and we'd could never ever be ashamed of her. She's our daughter and we love her.'

My hand goes to the little round of my stomach. The little paunch that I'd imagined was just over eating and middle-age spread. I find myself smiling. A daughter.

Grace blows her nose. 'I said we were so proud of how she'd turned her life around, and so happy to have found her again, with your help. We've all agreed to take baby steps, but I'm very positive about where it's all going.'

I stroke my bump. Baby steps, indeed. 'That's brilliant. I'm so pleased for you all.'

'You're a wonderful woman, Nancy. Without you, we would never have found Megan. I'll send you some money over soon.'

'No rush. You just enjoy the time with your daughter. You'll have lots to catch up on.'

'We will. I can hardly believe my Meggie's back. I crept into her room this morning before she was awake and just gazed at her sleeping. It's a miracle.' Grace's voice cracks again, and she laughs. 'Gosh, I can't stop blubbing either. Anyway, thanks again, Nancy. I'll be in touch.'

'Thanks, I'd love to know how it all turns out.'

Charlie's putting the kettle on, as Mum and Rory walk through the door. 'Perfect timing, you two. Tea or coffee, Karen?' he asks, as Mum plants a kiss on both of his cheeks.

'Tea for me, thanks, Charlie,' Mum says, shrugging her coat off and Rory takes it to hang in the hallway with his own. I'm glad he looks after her. Quiet understated little acts of love go a long way.

'Tea for me too,' Rory says, coming back in and drawing a chair up to the kitchen table next to Mum. 'It smells lovely in here, Nancy. Been baking?'

I smile and lean my hip against the worktop. 'Might have made sausage rolls, quiche and a cake.'

Mum fluffs her hair and straightens her strawberry-red cardigan. 'Now, you're talking. Our Nance makes the best pastries and cakes, on the planet, don't you, maid?'

'Not sure about that, but I'm not a bad baker.'

'Ooh. I almost forgot!' Mum jabs a finger at me. 'I'm glad you said baker, because it made me think of that old rhyme. You know, the butcher the baker, the—'

'Candlestick maker,' Rory chimes in.

'Yes.' Mum sniffs, obviously disgruntled at being interrupted in full storytelling mode. 'Well, it's the butcher bit that jogged my memory. I was in Cecil's yesterday and there was a woman chatting to Cecil who looked just like him, but with long curly hair. Turns out it was his, sister Yvonne.'

'Ah, the lovely Yvonne,' I say, with a smile.

'Yeah, seemed nice. But boy can she talk. Cecil asked after you, and once she realised I was your mum, she never stopped yakking at me. I couldn't get a word in edgewise.'

I hide a smirk, as I realise that the two women are a bit similar. I'd have loved to be a fly on the wall to see the battle of the chinwaggers.

'Anyway, the upshot is, she gave me an envelope for you. Said she was coming to see you with it, but she asked if I'd give it to you next time I saw you, save her a job.' I send a thanks heavenward. Yvonne would have been here for the duration. 'It's money for that knitting pattern case you solved.' She delves into her bag and hands me the envelope. 'I might have a go at one of those vintage baby patterns she has. Said I could borrow one anytime. I know you might not be adopting a tiny baby, but still.'

Charlie and I share a knowing look. Mum might be borrowing one sooner than she thinks. I open the envelope. 'A hundred pounds, that's nice.'

'Very nice,' Charlie says, coming over with the tea.

I put the plates of sandwiches, crisps, pickles, quiche and sausage rolls on the table and we dig in. Though I don't eat that much, because I'm giddy with excitement at the thought of spilling the beans. 'This feels like a little party,' I say with a sly wink at Charlie. 'You know, with the egg sandwiches, sausage rolls and stuff.'

Rory nods. 'I love lunches like this. And cake to come, can't wait.'

And suddenly neither can I. A few minutes later, I nod at Charlie and whisper. 'Go get the cake, love.'

He smiles and fetches the cake from the pantry and sets it down. 'Here we are. A celebration cake.' We agreed that's what he'd say beforehand. Then I knew Mum would respond with,

'Celebration cake? What are we celebrating?'

Charlie sits back down, takes my hand under the table and we look at Mum and Rory's expectant faces. Charlie turns to me and we do big goofy smiles at each other until Mum looks like she's ready to explode. 'Mum, Rory. You're going to be grandparents!' I blurt, and carefully watch their faces.

Mum and Rory look at each other with identical puzzled expressions, and I have to bite my lip. Mum turns back to me. 'You've got the go ahead with the adoption *already?* But you haven't even had a meeting with the case worker, yet. Thought these things moved at a glacial speed...'

Suddenly I can't speak. Hell, I can hardly see through the tears prickling my eyes. 'I...we...we're not adopting. We're pregnant.' I put my hand over my mouth as I watch Mum's face crumple.

She shakes her head bewildered, then she's crying and laughing at the same time. 'Nancy. Oh. Oh... my baby girl.

Is it really possible?

I go round the table and envelop her in a huge hug. 'That's what they tell me.'

And there we stand, hugging, laughing and crying. Mum's mumbling about miracles and matinee jackets, and generally making little sense, until Charlie says, 'Right, ladies. Let's get this celebration cake cut!'

***

Three weeks later, Charlie and I are cuddled up on the sofa in front of the fire. The Christmas tree is twinkling at us from the corner, and Scrappy is snuggled up on Charlie's lap. Contentment floods through me, and as I gaze through the patio doors, the pale light begins to hide away under the trees as the winter afternoon draws to a close. A cosy evening is just what we need. The scan I had a few weeks back shows everything is as it should be, and our daughter seems to be doing all the right things. Our daughter. I will never tire of thinking and saying those words. Christmas in a few days no longer fills me with trepidation, either. It's perfect. Christmas in our little cottage, with our cat, a tree and a fire. Three of us, soon to be four.

Charlie stokes my hair and whispers in my ear. 'Penny for them.'

'Just thinking how perfect all this is, and how content and happy I am right at this moment.'

He smiles. 'I was thinking exactly the same.'

'You must be—'

'Psychic, yeah.' Charlie looks out of the patio doors and frowns. Then he laughs. 'And to round off the absolute perfectness, it only looks like it's bloody snowing out there!'

'No way!' I sit up and peer into the gloom. Unable to be sure, I jump up and hurry outside, Charlie right behind me. A flurry of snowflakes land on my upturned face and I catch some on my tongue. I turn in a circle, my arms flung wide. 'It is! It's snowing!'

'It is. And we'll be much comfier and warmer watching it fall from the living room, Mrs Cornish.' Charlie laughs and takes me in his arms. I look deep into his eyes and my heart is so full of love, I can only manage a smile. Then, hand in hand, we walk back inside.

Case-Notes Updated

January 12th - Abi and Vicky are all signed up for IUI at a fertility clinic, so with any luck, my little one will have a playmate around the same age. Charlie is over the moon for them, but a bit disgruntled I never mentioned going to see his boss at home. I explained that my cases are confidential, just like his, and he very quickly changed his tune. He said he was proud of my integrity. I had to laugh, maybe he knew not to get on the wrong side of a pregnant woman.

February 1st - Tilly and Ella are doing so well. I saw them in town the other day, and Tilly was thrilled that I was expecting too. She's going to Falmouth uni next year, to do an English degree, part-time. Some lectures can be accesses remotely, so that's ideal. When she has to go in, Ella will be looked after partly by a childminder and partly by Alison. Alison's new book is doing extremely well, and so is her relationship with Chris, apparently. Tilly joked that she has to tell them to get a room on occasion, but she's so happy for them both, as am I.

February 20th – Another young woman on the

university track is Megan. Grace called the other day to say she's off to Exeter uni in September to study law. She is a completely different girl now. She's settled, has a good circle of friends and a boyfriend, who's going to the same university. He was the one who persuaded her to rethink her plans. So, another happy ending, thank goodness!

March 3rd - Debbie and Mike sent me a postcard from the Grand Canyon! They are touring America and have seen some wonderful sights. They're having such fun and closer than they've ever been. Debbie says it's thanks to a weird woman called Nancy, rocking up at her house one day and sticking her nose into her business! That bit made me laugh. She said they would be back soon, because Mike is missing the sea, but they'll be off again somewhere else before too long.

*April 10th – Cally grabbed me yesterday in the Biggly Boggly shop, and announced that Ben had revealed his secret florist venture! His business is doing so well online already, and if it carries on, he might be able to open a little shop in future. Cally says he's so happy doing what he loves and is no longer stressed and miserable. He'd laughed when she'd confessed that she thought he'd been having an affair with Laura, and sent me to investigate. Ben had said I was a sneaky one, and no mistake. I was so delighted to see Cally back to her bubbly, gregarious self. She said that any time I needed flowers, I should come to Ben. He's promised me a lifetime's supply - no charge of course. So now I have free sausages **and** flowers for life,* *whatever next!*

April 15th - Almost forgot, to note it down, because it's not strictly case-note stuff, but– Lucinda gave birth to a baby boy a few months back! He's called Luke, and has big blue eyes and fair hair. Mel is loving her maternity cover, working in West of the Moon, Lucinda and Will's bookshop. She and Anthony are getting married next year, which is something else to look forward to! I need to talk to her about helping out with Nancy Cornish PI when the baby comes, because I'll need all the help I can get to keep my service ticking over. Service sounds better than business, I think, because at its heart is this wonderful community I'm lucky enough to live in. I've met so many wonderful people who have needed me and my gift over the past few years, all keep in touch, all friends.

April 16th – Penny's Joe is having an exhibition of his work in the summer in St Ives. He's part of a local art group and so many have said his work is exceptional. One of his seascapes was on the local news the other day, and even some London galleries have been showing considerable interest in his work. Penny says he's 'chuffed to little mint balls' about it all, as her Yorkshire granny would have said, and for once, because of his brother Terry, he actually believes he's good enough.

As an extra note, Penny is beside herself with joy over my pregnancy. She rings me endlessly, asking after my health and offering to do shopping, or wondering if there's anything I need? She told me the other day that she's laid a few little things aside, for when my daughter is here. I saw her coming out of the baby shop the other day, with god knows how many bags - her few little things looked more like a mountain to me! Add my Mum's contributions to that, and we'll have to move house to accommodate it all.

This year will be one of the most incredible of my life, with our own little gift on the way, next month. I just felt her kicking. So wonderful. She'll be playing for the Lionesses at this rate!

I love being Nancy Cornish PI, and I love my life!

The End

Acknowledgments

A huge thanks as always to all my friends and family. A special thanks goes to the many readers who encouraged (nagged and nagged) me to write a third Nancy Cornish story. I'm so glad they did! And a big shout out to lovely writer friend Linda Huber and Kelly Florentia who read an early copy. They have the best eagle eyes!

Lastly, a big thanks to Amanda of Let's Get Booked, for the formatting and stunning cover!

Printed in Great Britain
by Amazon

20953731R10169